Hell's Belle

Karen Greco

For Mom.

And for Sydney.

CONTENTS

ACKNOWLEDGMENTS

Novel writing is solitary work, until the end, when the process relies very much on the kindness of others.

I owe a huge debt to my editor Rakia Clark, who turned me into a much better writer. And a big thank you to my copy-editor Andy Lefkowitz, who cleaned up my messes! I don't know what I would have done without their knowledge and professionalism. And thank you to my awesome cover artist, Robin Ludwig Design Inc.

I could never have gotten through 75,000 words without the help of my friend and writing buddy Jaene Leonard.

And to my early readers--thank you for sticking through the early versions, and for several of you, for reading it more than once. Ingrid Vincent, Lia Resin, Doug Strassler, David Johnston, Tiffany Douglas, Andrea Freund, Jean Teresi. You were all instrumental in driving my madness to the bitter end, and I am grateful. Best team of beta readers on the planet!

And a huge thank you to my family. My Dad, my husband Anthony and my brilliant daughter Sydney. There is no way I could have done this without your support.

PROLOGUE

I was wearing the wrong damn shoes. Bounding through the pitch-black overgrown empty urban lots, my legs were long past aching and well into screaming territory. I gulped in the crisp fall air and forced myself to sprint harder.

"Do you need me to carry you?" My partner Frankie, the vampire I was trying to keep pace with, shouted over his shoulder. His voice was thick with sarcasm.

I slowed down just enough to yank off my heels, carrying one in each hand. I wasn't expecting to play decoy tonight, and I'd be damned if I was going to lose my shoes in some godforsaken overgrown lot in the middle of Newark, New Jersey. These were custom-designed heels from SteamTropolis in Seattle, after all. These vampires would have to pry them from my cold, dead hands before I let them go.

Newark had a pretty major vampire infestation. The despair and decay that the city had fallen into over the past several decades lured us, and the population was exploding.

Frankie and I had spent the last three weeks here, advising the Mayor on how to eradicate the pests. We are part of a small but efficient top-secret task force of hunters that handle rogue supernaturals for the Defense Department. The program had the highest security clearance. Even the President had no idea we existed, or that the crew Frankie and I assembled to help eradicate their vampire pest problem was flying in to join Newark's finest the next day.

So Mayor Cory Booker, head of a crime-soaked New Jersey city, had one up on the Commander-in-Chief. We only let the mayor in on what we were doing because he walked in on a vampire sucking the life out of one of his staffers in his office in City Hall. Even more shocking, Mayor Booker kicked the vampire's ass before driving a stake through his chest. Not only was he unflappable politically, but Mayor Booker's wild adrenaline surge also made him a first-rate vampire slayer. With that kind of muscle, he deserved to know the truth.

It was our last night in Newark and, to show his thanks, Mayor Booker threw us a bon voyage party at his home. I busted out my best outfit for the occasion: a beautiful strapless number that looked like long silk bandages crisscrossing over each other. The addition of a bustier underneath made my usually small boobs appear more ample. And, of course, finishing the outfit were my fabulously impractical heels.

Since Mayor Booker was the newest threat to the vampires' stronghold, a vampire nest crashed the party. Six very motivated vamps thundered feet first through his front window. Clearly whoever was in charge considered it a suicide mission and sent out his flunkies. Dressed like a cheap imitation of a Hell's Angels biker gang, it was vampire amateur hour at the Booker household. They actually brought human weapons in with them, including a submachine gun. Some waved metal pipes.

An amateur vampire is still a vampire, and still just as deadly. Between the fangs, the pipes and the gun, not to mention the glass shrapnel from the window, the place was a bloody mess. Newark's police chief had a nasty gash on his throat, the vampire missing his jugular by mere centimeters. I was able to stake him with a broken broom handle before he could kill the poor man. Shattered window glass embedded into the arm of the Mayor's press secretary. Vampire Moron started shooting up the place, so blood was flowing freely. The carnage appeared to be a violent political hit gone wrong. It's shockingly easy to hide a supernatural attack.

It was bedlam. Frankie and I distracted the hit squad so the Mayor's security forces could get him out of there. It was a good reminder of why I don't usually get dressed up.

After kicking my heels off, I closed the distance between me and Frankie. I could barely make out his aristocratic profile in the sliver of moonlight peeking through the dark clouds. Frankie still looked impeccable in his fitted black blazer, skinny trousers and dress shoes, which he was running around in just fine.

"You need me to carry *you*, old man?" I huffed, throwing his earlier sarcasm back at him.

Frankie laughed, the rich sound echoed down the alleyway we had turned into. He wasn't the least bit out of breath.

Wait. Echoed? Shit.

I reached out and grasped Frankie's forearm and squeezed. We skidded to a stop, gaping at the brick wall in front of us. My eyes darted around. There was a fire escape about 15 feet above us. Frankie could probably jump it. But there was no way I would make it up there. And Frankie wouldn't be able to jump it with me on his back. Too much weight for a straight-up vertical leap. At over 500 years old, Frankie was one of the strongest vampires I had ever met. But a jump like that was pushing it.

I bent over at the waist, grasped my kneecaps and sucked in air as my mind raced through scenarios for escape. None of them were good. We were going to have to fight our way out of this.

Reluctantly dropping my exquisite shoes on the ground, I reached down the front of my dress and pulled a silver-tipped stake from my bustier.

Frankie's eyes were wide. "Nice tailoring." He nodded appreciatively and peered down my dress. "What else do you have in there?"

I smacked him upside the head. "Focus!"

The five vampires appeared at the mouth of the alleyway.

I crouched low, trying to pick out the weakest link in the dim light. With my mixed blood, I was stronger than a regular human, but I had to be realistic.

"Second from right," Frankie whispered, nostrils flaring. He knew my limits too. "Pretty new dead. Still smells almost human. But watch your back."

I nodded, my eyes now on the man. He looked close to 50, an ill-fitting denim jacket accentuated his middle-aged paunch, his long curls coarse and gray. His brown eyes glowed rabidly, appearing almost yellow. Crap. He was really new dead. I almost preferred going up against someone Frankie's age than a recent turn. They were always unpredictable.

With a howl, the pack of vamps charged us. Frankie stepped in front of me and pushed most of the pack out of my reach, leaving me with my one opponent. The vampire charged me blindly, fangs gnashing out uncontrollably. Passing the stake to my left hand, I brought my right around and backhanded him in the face. It sent him reeling and put a little distance between us. But it also pissed him off.

The vampire football-tackled me, hitting me hard in the stomach. The tight corset worn under my party dress (the one that also stored a small arsenal of stakes) impeded my breathing all night, which saved the wind from being knocked out of me. I skidded on my ass about four feet, his head still pressed in my stomach. I dropped my elbow into the back of his neck and heard a satisfying crack of it breaking. I scrambled out from under his limp body.

Then I turned to the melee beside me. Frankie was cracking two vampire's heads together. A third came up behind him and pushed a knife into his back.

"Frankie!" I charged at the pile of vamps. At the sound of my voice, the knife wielder turned towards me and my eyes focused on the sweet spot: his heart. I tossed my silver-tipped stake into my right hand, and with a primal scream, I pushed it in. The bones in his chest splintered with several loud cracks, then I felt the stake glide into the meat of the heart. He slumped to the ground.

Yanking the knife out of Frankie's back, I shifted to the left when something slammed into the side of my face. I landed on my side, and heard the tell-tale zrrippp of my skirt tearing.

Rubbing my sore cheek, I tried to get up, but the vampire grabbed me by my hips, dragging me backwards. The pavement shredded both my expensive fishnet stockings and the skin on my legs. Sticky, coagulating blood glued the threads from the stockings into my torn skin. The metallic scent of blood hit my nostrils a few seconds later.

Twisting, I kicked out and knocked my attacker in the kneecaps. These asshats were ruining my favorite outfit. The satisfying crunch of his kneecap shattering made me grin. Before I could lash out again, Frankie's hands gripped me under my arms and he pulled me closer to the brick wall, just as the one in the leather vest brought down a pipe aimed at my head. Sparks flew when it hit the pavement.

Frankie's fangs were completely extended and his normally sky-blue eyes were a brilliant cerulean glowing against his porcelain white skin. His overgrown black hair was matted with blood. Frankie was terrifying when he was full-on vampire.

Frankie drew my attention back to the vampires with the point of a finger. Like teen girls at the mall, the horde moved in a clump, their broken and battered limbs pushing and kicking at each other. Their heads were twitched and twisting, noses in the air, picking up the enticing aroma of my Type O Negative.

Headlights turned into the alleyway, and the shock of light made me lose sight of the vampires just feet away from me. I tried to shield my eyes from the bright lights as the SUV shrieked down the alley. It smashed into the vampire cluster, scattering them. A hulking figure popped out of the open sunroof, wooden stakes in both hands. It was Mayor Booker, arriving on the scene like a superhero. I half expected to see a cape flapping behind him.

"Y'all got to get the hell out of my city!" Mayor Booker's resonant voice boomed down the alleyway.

He jumped down to the hood of the SUV. The vampires surrounded his car. With their attention diverted, Frankie and I needed to move. Mayor Booker may be bad-ass, but there was no way he could take on five full bloods.

Frankie pulled three stakes out of his jacket and tossed one to me. Grabbing it one-handed, I reached down into my dress again and took out my last stake. Frankie, moving faster than me, staked a young male vampire through the back, going straight through his heart. I staked my middle-aged vampire in a similar fashion. Two vampires down, three to go, only one stake left in my hand.

The three remaining vampires were now on the hood of the car, facing off with the Mayor. Frankie caught one by the ankles and pulled him down off the car, leaving the Mayor to battle it out with two. Booker swung a right hook, destabilizing the taller one, before bringing the stake in his opposite hand directly into the other vampire's heart. While he shoved the dead vampire off the car, the other reared up and pushed into the Mayor, sending both onto the pavement with a slam.

The tumble smacked the Mayor's head into the ground, and he seemed disoriented as he staggered to his feet. The vampire loomed over him. Grabbing the Mayor by the shoulders, fangs grinding, his eyes had that sheen of crazy that a vampire gets just before a kill. He brought his barely 18-year-old face towards Booker's neck.

I sprinted towards them and launched myself into the air, landing on the vampire's back. Grabbing him around the head, I twisted his neck, breaking it. He slumped to the ground. Good thing he was built more a basketball player than a football hero. I drove my last stake into his heart.

With a grunt, Frankie nailed the final vampire with a stake. "Are you all right, Mr. Mayor?"

"Yes, thank you," Mayor Booker said as he rubbed his shaved head, leaving a streak of blood on his scalp.

The three of us stared at the bloodbath around us.

"You two okay?" Mayor Booker asked, trying to catch his breath.

I yanked mournfully at my tattered skirt. "My outfit is fucked."

Mayor Booker dropped his arm around my shoulders, "That dress was beautiful."

My heart skipped a few beats. This man was smart, hot, and could take on vampires. I could feel a major crush coming on. I glanced at him and smiled shyly.

Frankie gave me a little shove, bringing me back to earth. "Oh God. Stop being such a girl."

I nodded. "Mr. Mayor, Frankie and I will clean up. You shouldn't be here for this."

He began to protest, but Frankie, removing his coat and pulling out a scythe-like knife that was holstered on his side, intervened. "Nina's right, Mayor. They aren't completely dead yet. We have to finish them off. And you really don't need to be party to this."

"How do you kill them, then?" The Mayor was determined to see this through, but it was time for him to get out of here.

"We have to cut off their heads, then remove their hearts and burn them," I said. My matter-of-fact tone made him look momentarily uncomfortable. "Seriously, Sir, if someone saw you decapitating something that looks like a human.... Not good."

"Point taken," he nodded. "Thank you both. For everything."

He shook our hands, climbed into his SUV and was off, leaving Frankie and me to do what we did best: destroy vampires.

CHAPTER 1

He looked like the sort of guy who always found trouble, so I didn't notice that trouble followed him in, ordered a pitcher of Budweiser, and plopped themselves down at a table in the other room.

I caught my reflection in the mirror behind the bar. My shoulder-length dark hair was lying a bit flat on my head. Giving it a quick fluff, I slipped toward the far end of the bar where he was sitting. Readjusting my black t-shirt, I tried my best impression of a sultry walk. I probably looked more like a chicken.

"What can I get you?" I offered. I smiled but not too wide. My slightly fanged canine teeth make me look like a wolf.

He winked. "Raging Bitch," he said, stealing a glance at my boobs. They were popping out of my t-shirt thanks to my awesome, cleavage-boosting bra.

"That's what Babe calls me," I said winking back.

Flirt a bit. Why not.

"I'm Max." He smiled, extending his hand.

"Hi, Max," I said reaching across the bar to shake. "Nina. Nice to formally meet you."

He touched my hand, sending a surge of hormones straight to my lower regions. I swallowed an impulsive giggle, so it came out more like a burp. Mortified, I bent down to dig his beer out of the fridge that sat under the bar.

Above the counter were shelves that went almost to the ceiling holding bottle after bottle of liquor. Babe's was mostly a beer kind of place. Only shots popular with the college kids moved off those shelves. That meant that the usual cheap brands of student-favored tequila, rum and vodka sat on the bottom, easy-to-reach shelves. But on the high shelves were dusty cobalt bottles with no labels, the tinctures inside unknown. Except, of course, to Babe. But those bottles remained in their spots, one inch of gray dust dulling their vibrant blues.

Smack in the middle of all those dusty bottles was a lone Veladoras, one of those tall religious candles found in Spanish grocery stores. The Veladoras was always the same and always lit. The flicker of the yellow flame glowed behind frosted white glass and an obscured picture of a Saint, in this case Our Lady of Guadeloupe. Babe loved her Veladoras, and she installed one in my apartment as well. She checked on it monthly, insisting it stay lit. Good thing I don't have a cat to knock it over.

I cracked open a Raging Bitch micro-brew, poured it into a glass, and placed it in front of Max.

I smiled at him. "So what brings you to Babes?"

"I heard this was where the cool kids hung out," he said, taking a long pull straight from the bottle.

Damn it! I shouldn't have poured. I still had a lot to learn about this whole bartending thing.

"Next one's on me. For pouring." I offered, smiling sheepishly.

"I never turn a free beer down. Thanks! So, when do things heat up around here?" He gave the near-empty bar a once over.

"End of the semester, the kids are studying for finals," I explained. "We'll probably get back to normal toward the weekend. You should come back."

Oh God! Desperate much?

"I think I will," he agreed.

Cocking my head, I shot him a quick smile and collected the cash he dropped on the bar. I swayed to the till, giving my hips a little wiggle as I walked.

Of course I tripped.

I grabbed the first thing I could catch, which happened to be the Bud draft pull. Beer sprayed out all over the place.

"Damn it!" I swore under my breath.

Babe, who was sitting at the other end of the bar with a pile of bills, collapsed in a fit of laughter.

She looked at Max over the rim of her glasses that were propped at the end of her nose. "He's a looker!"

Glaring, I shushed Babe, hoping Max didn't overhear, and pulled on the draught again, this time with a pitcher underneath. I placed the pitcher next to her and lifted the doorway to the bar. I took the pitcher to the small area of tables to the right of the door.

Two women, their heads close together and arms intertwined, sat at a far corner table. Every now and then, they would stop whispering and the blonde one would trace the brunette's lips with her tongue. I saw the brunette slide her hand up the blonde's skirt. I felt like an intruder as I placed the pitcher on the table and waited to collect the five dollars.

I peeked at Max while I waited for the cash. His slightly overgrown golden curls flopped a bit in his face. He reminded me of an aging surfer -- athletic body, skin tinged gold by the sun. Eyes as blue as the ocean, with slight good-natured crinkles around the edges. He must laugh a lot. What would bring Surfer Boy to frigid New England? He wasn't a student; that was certain.

With the fiver in hand, I moved back to the bar and plopped down beside Babe.

Short, feisty and well into middle age, Babe had long black hair streaked through with gray. With her t-shirt, jeans and an overload of Mexican jewelry, Babe looked strikingly out of place in a small New England city. She was a throw back from Haight-Ashbury.

The front door opened with such force that it slammed into the wall. Frigid December wind burst into the room. Babe's paperwork went flying. I scrambled after the papers, shivering.

A skinny guy with long black hair, pale translucent skin and a black overcoat stumbled in behind the bitter night air. He looked around the tiny bar, catching my eyes for a split second. I gave him a slight sneer. I didn't like the looks of him. He gave his hair a toss and joined the two women at the table.

The voices on the television began to cut through the din of people talking in the bar. I looked up at the flat screen. Ami Bertrand, a wealthy philanthropist, was giving an interview. He was angling to be Mayor of Providence, running in a special election to be held next week.

There was something familiar about Bertrand, and not in a good way. He had moved to Providence a few years ago, and his background was shrouded in mystery. But he said the right things publicly, and poured money into various social service and arts charities. He was hugely popular.

Bertrand was a handsome, charismatic guy, in his early 50s, with short-cropped dark hair, graying in the right places, high cheekbones and an athletic physique. He could charm the habit off a nun. And he creeped me out.

Babe was muttering something in Spanish as she rearranged her messed-up paperwork.

Alfonso, our neighborhood drunk, had Max captivated with talk of Providence politics, probably inspired by Bertrand's television appearance. Three college students played a game of dirty word Scrabble.

A commercial for Cirque du Soleil came on the television, reminding me of Frankie, one of my best friends. It had been a few months since I left my home in Nevada to make a new one with my Aunt Babe in Providence. I missed the dry heat of the desert, the Vegas strip, and my friends. Frankie was a huge Cirque du Soleil fan, and they had a new show opening on the Strip on Christmas day. I was sure Frankie would be there. I would have gone with him.

But the rich history of New England was a draw. I was definitely enjoying the seasons, and living so close to the ocean was amazing. I always felt like a visitor in Nevada. Maybe it's just the transient nature of the place. Rhode Island felt like home.

I grabbed a clean glass from behind the bar, and headed over to the two women, and the skinny guy who had seated himself at their table. Two beers had been poured but the booze remained untouched.

"You want an extra glass for the beer, or did you want to order something else?" I asked. I hoped that my question didn't come off as threatening, but they were throwing off a strange vibe that had me on alert.

The skinny man gestured to the glass. As I placed it on the table, he grabbed my wrist and held onto me, his hand burning into my flesh.

I tried to yank my arm away, but he held fast. I'm strong; very strong, in fact. But his grip was ironclad.

"Let go," I said low and hard.

He snarled back, showing me fangs. "I know what you are, Nina Martinez."

Oh shit.

My heart pounded. My canine teeth shifted and elongated, the adrenaline masking the pain as they tore through my gums. I flashed my fangs.

"Who sent you?" I hissed looking straight into his black eyes, daring him.

He simply grinned.

I kicked at the table. The table, the pitcher, the pub glasses, even the two women went airborne. The man held tightly to my wrist. He pulled an old, rusted dagger out from under his coat with his other hand.

I twisted my body and threw him over my back. He was still hanging on. We both sailed several feet in the air together. I landed hard in a puddle of booze, my assailant beside me, still with the death grip. But he had lost hold of the dagger in the struggle. I could see it just a few feet away from him on the floor. Cold beer seeped through my jeans as I scooted towards it.

"Don't FUCKING MOVE," a deep voice bellowed.

Max moved from the end of the bar, a gun in one hand and a badge in the other.

Dropping my wrist, the stranger, with a sadistic smile on his lips, moved towards Max.

With his attention on Max, I pounced. In one swift move, I dove at his knees and sent him tumbling to the ground. Before I could scramble to my feet, he snatched the dagger. He grabbed a fist full of my hair and pulled my head back, exposing my neck.

The gun cocked and Max growled, "Let her go."

The dark-haired man flashed a grin. He whispered into my ear, "Ego tineo tu specialis."

I recoiled. "Who are you?"

"Marcello." And with that, he drew the blade across my neck before rolling away. My hands flew to the gushing wound, blood hitting the worn wooden floor in spurts.

Max dropped to the floor beside me, and I cowered with my back to him, trying to hide the wound that was already starting to heal.

Marcello leapt through the front window, glass shattering, his companions following behind. The burst of frigid air sobered everyone left in the bar.

CHAPTER 2

By the time the cops showed up, my hair was crunchy and had that yeasty, dry beer smell. I sat at the far end of the bar, far away from the huge hole in the wall that used to be a window. I rubbed at my head trying to get the crunch out, while applying pressure to the gash on my neck.

My heart was still racing, even an hour after the attack. The adrenaline surging through my system was giving me the shakes.

The police milled around taking statements. Max raised his eyebrows at me when I gave my recollection of events. Just a neighborhood junkie trying to rob the place. It wasn't inconceivable.

Babe's on the Sunnyside sits on the cusp of gentrification on Providence's east side. Brown University was buying up property to the south, but Babe's was just north of that line. It was an interesting mix of college students living in slumlord apartments along with Portuguese and Spanish old-timers. While the neighborhood was certainly rough around the edges, it wasn't gang-banger territory. But there was still crime, and a robbery at gunpoint was not out of the norm.

Babe was furious. Her place may be a dive bar, but crime simply didn't happen here. Babe's was an oasis. Lulls in conversation with the cops were punctuated by her colorful curses in Spanish.

Babe broke away from the police and stalked over, rolling her eyes. "Estupido." Then she sighed and looked me over. "Are you okay, Nina?"

I nodded. An EMT pushed his way through the crowd of cops, zeroing in on me. I slid off the bar stool and used my short stature to my advantage. I didn't need an EMT probing me right then.

"This was not random," I whispered into Babe's ear as I skulked behind her. I kept my voice low. "He knows what I am."

Babe turned to face me with a look of fear that betrayed her calmness. "Does he know WHO you are?" Handing me a clean bar rag, Babe tried to shelter me from the incoming paramedic.

I nodded and peeked past Babe's head to see Max at the other end of the room, giving his statement to the cops. I would totally take another gash on the neck to hear what he was saying. How obvious was it that whatever happened in here wasn't exactly normal?

"I'll call Lochlan," Babe said as she moved toward the phone.

I grabbed her arm to keep her in place, but it was too late. The paramedic was right beside her.

"I need to take a look at your wound, ma'am," he said politely.

"This little scratch?" I held my breath as I pulled the rag off. I didn't dare exhale until I saw that the gash had healed enough to indeed qualify as just a little more than a scratch.

The poor EMT stared at the blood-soaked rag on the bar and then his eyes moved back to my neck, then back to the rag. His mouth gaped open in shock.

"I'm a bleeder." I shrugged, doing my best to look embarrassed.

"You need to go to the ER, get a tetanus shot and get checked for a concussion," he said, not sounding completely convinced of his own words.

"Oh, I am perfectly fine, thank you," I said. The pent-up adrenaline was making me punchy. My fangs still hadn't retracted all the way. I really didn't want a close examination.

"Ma'am, please." This paramedic was relentless.

I turned my back on him and pretended to watch the television that was still humming above the bar. I took steady deep breaths, trying to calm my nerves.

My dad was a vampire. He was a very old and powerful vampire. Rumor was, he was one of the first in the line of vampires. My mom was human. And while I am very much alive, I have vampire traits -- traits that can be quite useful. I heal quickly, I'm crazy strong, really fast, and, my personal favorite, I look younger than my age. So even though I am in my early 30s, I still get carded at bars.

But there are drawbacks, too. I am sensitive to sunlight. I have a temper and fangs that require a lot of restraint to keep in my gums. And I know it's gross, but sometimes I crave human blood. If I drink it, though, Lochlan O'Malley and the members of my team will stake me.

Someone lightly touched my back. I whipped around, with one finger pointing outward, ready to tell Mr. EMT to piss off. But it was Max. He definitely saved my ass. Marcello was ready to pull me out of the bar to who knows where. I really needed to calm down.

Max looked curiously at the dramatically healed knife wound on my neck, dipping his head close to my face. "So I guess that looked worse than it was."

I inhaled. He even smelled like the ocean. Slightly salty. Definitely sexy. This was absolutely helping my disposition.

"Yeah." I smiled. "I'm okay, thanks."

"I can see that," Max drawled. "But how about you listen to the paramedic and go to the ER?"

"Thank you, Agent Deveroux!" the EMT called out over my head.

"No, thanks," I said, digging in my heels and gripping the bar. Now I felt bamboozled.

"Should I make this an order?" Max sounded firm.

Alfonso whooped, "Oh no he didn't!" and pushed Mr. EMT out of his line of site so that he could better see what would happen next. Babe, who was pouring Alfonso a shot of tequila, looked at Max with a mix of shock and curiosity.

My blood boiled and I could feel my teeth shifting again. I took a breath to calm down. A roomful of cops and first responders wasn't the place to vamp out.

"How about this? I'll take you myself." Max snatched me around the waist and tossed me over his shoulder like a sack of potatoes.

"Put me down!" I shouted, while the entire bar turned to watch the show.

First I heard snickering. Then Mr. EMT howled with laughter. His howl was so guttural, for a second, I considered the possibility that he was a werewolf.

"Are you kidding me?" I pushed on his shoulders, trying to get down. It was an awkward position. I kicked my legs like mad, not caring that it looked ridiculous.

"Nope, I am not kidding," Max said stubbornly. "We can either walk out of here like normal people and I will drive you to the ER. Or I'll carry you out of here just like this. How do you want to play it?"

After one last kick, I stopped struggling. "Fine, I'll go."

"You will?" He didn't trust me.

"Yes. And I'll walk."

He placed me gently back down.

"Thank you."

His first instinct was right. I turned away and hauled a brutal right hook at him that connected with his jaw. He staggered back and then fell to the floor.

"I could have knocked your ass out if I wanted to," I sassed, reaching behind the bar to grab my leather jacket. The room erupted into whoops of laughter.

"But you didn't," he pointed out. "It must be love."

The hint of sarcasm made the squirm. The cops really busted a gut over that one.

"Just take me to the damn hospital," I grumbled. I bet I could lose him before we got to his car.

Max rubbed his jaw and grinned. I held out my hand and helped pull him to his feet. Then he turned me around, put his hand on my back, and edged me towards the door. My body temperature rose at his touch. The entire bar stared as we walked out together.

I was too hot to notice the blast of cold December air as we stepped out.

CHAPTER 3

"So do you always require police protection, or was tonight just for my benefit?" Max teased me as we stepped into the frigid night.

I inhaled the cold air, taking it deep into my lungs. "It's never that exciting at Babe's. Tonight was definitely weird."

"Well you proved you can hold your own in a bar fight," Max said, rubbing at his jaw.

"Yeah, but drunks and junkies are easy to bounce." I tried to sound casual but I was sure he could hear my racing heart.

"What did he say to you back there? It didn't sound English." Max looked at me, curiosity mixed with uncertainty, like he wasn't sure I was telling the truth. Which, you know, I wasn't.

I shrugged. "Pig Latin?" God, I was not up for this conversation.

I stopped short and stared into the shadows across the street. Marcello was there. I could sense him, even though I couldn't see him.

"You see something?" Max gripped my arm and followed my gaze.

"Nothing. Nothing at all. Just a little spooked," I said giving Max my best brilliant smile.

I made my way down the hill that Babe's was perched on, with Max close behind me. The sound of loud music came from a bar that was tucked down a side street.

"Funny, of all the bars for a junkie to hit..." Max stared at the other bar, clearly a better mark for a robbery, with its location off the main drag.

"Drugs make 'em stupid," I said with a shrug. "So what's an FBI guy doing at a dive bar anyway?" I hoped to divert the conversation.

"Trying to take a break from crime scenes," he quipped.

"Clearly you weren't very successful at that," I retorted.

"Very observant," he countered.

I knew Marcello was lurking behind us. We had to get out of there, and my ride was right in front of us.

I laid a smile on him and unstrapped the helmet from the bike. "Put this on." I shoved it into his hands.

Max's jaw dropped at my custom Triumph. It took my best friend and partner Frankie months of intricate fabrication to get this bike into fighting shape. The 2007 Bonneville base was stripped bare of non-essential hardware, keeping it light. With its low-to-ground profile and black-on-black paint job, it was stealth. Now it was one sick ride.

"I bet I can beat your FBI-issued Suburban in a street drag," I said with a grin. I mounted the bike, turning the key in the ignition. The engine purred. "Get on."

"You're joking, right?" He crossed his arms across his chest and gave me a withering look.

"I don't joke about my Triumph." I patted the rear seat.

"You landed on your head back there." He said it slowly, like he was talking to a child. "I really don't think you should be driving a motorcycle."

"Where's your sense of adventure," I grumbled, but I knew he was right. I felt a little woozy. But that might have been hunger, not the blow to the head. My metabolism spikes when I get vamped up.

With Marcello lurking, I didn't want a drawn-out pissing contest over who drove, and I had no idea where he was parked. I got off the bike, yanked the helmet out of his hands and shoved it on my head, hard, immediately sorry that I used so much force.

"You know how to do this?" I motioned to the Triumph. Grinning from ear to ear, he jumped on the bike.

I climbed on to the rear seat. It felt weird to be on the back. I slipped my arms around his narrow waist, feeling solid abs under the bulk of his winter coat. It was a small consolation to allow someone else to drive my baby.

Max gunned the engine, and I held up my hand in a goodbye salute. Marcello had vampire speed, but he couldn't keep up with the Triumph. Frankie made sure of that.

CHAPTER 4

I sipped the piping hot coffee, enjoying the sensation of ice melting from my body. The coffee was out-of-a-vending-machine nasty, but it was hot, and I needed some heat. Riding a motorcycle was not the most prudent way to get around New England in the dead of winter. But fleeing vampires requires a level of speed and agility that most cars don't have.

I sneaked a peek at Max through the steam of my coffee. Even ruddy from the cold, he had a fantastic face.

We were at the Rhode Island Hospital ER, since I didn't know where else to go and needed to get out of the area fast. But Marcello didn't tail us, so we were good.

"You know, I was going to offer to use my car," Max said. He looked amused. Cold but amused.

"Consider tonight an adventure." I swallowed a mouthful of coffee.

Clearly the ER was the popular place to be at 2 AM on a Monday night in Providence. The place was packed. Gunshots, knife fights, beat downs, car crashes. The worst of humanity was staggering through the automatic doors. Muzak played softly in the background, adding a surreal quality to the blood and gore amplified by harsh florescent lighting. I was sure I looked like a damn goddess against the

30

bluish hues.

Honestly, all the blood was starting to get to me. I hadn't eaten in hours, and cravings were starting to kick in. I rubbed my beer-crusted head and tried to focus on my crunching hair and not my rumbling stomach. I would've killed for a rare steak, or even a burger. But at the rate things were moving, I wasn't going to make it out of there until way past breakfast.

I dropped my gaze to the outline of Max's muscular leg, snugly wrapped in his worn jeans. I could almost see the femoral artery pulsing through the curve of his thigh. I closed my eyes and considered what it would be like to sink my teeth into him, his blood warm and salty, slightly metallic.

"Want a candy bar or something?" Max's voice snapped me out of my gory daydream.

I opened my eyes to Max standing over me, watching me curiously. I nodded. The head move made me woozy. Not good.

Max felt my forehead. "Are you alright? You just went completely pale."

"Blood sugar," I whispered, closing my eyes again. I was having a hard time focusing. All I could smell was the coppery sweetness of fresh blood.

"I'll get you a candy bar." He ran his hand down my cold face. "Try to stay awake. Okay, Nina?"

I nodded and another rush of fresh blood hit my nose. It was a damn bloodbath in here. I wasn't sure a candy bar was going to cut it.

I took a deep breath and opened my eyes. Max turned the corner, heading towards the vending machines. There was a nurse sitting alone behind the front desk. I had to get out of the waiting room and away from all the free-flowing blood.

The few steps it took to get to the nurse felt like a mile. I kept my focus on her, the only non-bloody human in the room, as I inched my way through a gauntlet of open wounds. She looked up, eyes bored and tired. I didn't like doing what I was about to do, but her surly attitude made it so much easier.

"I need to see the doctor now," I said calmly, looking into her eyes.

"You have to wait your turn, honey." She snapped her gum and turned away.

I took her arm and turned her back to face me. "It is my turn." I glanced down at her nametag. "Jackie... Don't you think it's time for me to see the doctor?"

We locked eyes. Her shoulders dropped and her body relaxed. She looked down at her list of incoming patients, and smiled brightly at me. "Why, yes, here you are. It is your turn. Follow me, please."

"Max," I called as he rounded the corner, his hands loaded with about ten different candy bars. He nodded and followed behind.

I rarely use my ability to compel humans to my will. Generally speaking, I don't mind being part-vampire. But along with the blood lust, brainwashing another person to do my bidding makes me feel demonic. But I would rather compel someone than suck them dry. Tonight was about picking the lesser of two evils. I could live with that.

Jackie showed Max and me to a tiny room and left, still smiling sort of blankly at nothing in particular. The pang of guilt was quickly assuaged by no longer being surrounded by open wounds.

"I just wanted a bar, not a whole candy store," I snatched an Almond Joy from the pile of sweets Max dropped on the gurney.

"I didn't know what kind you liked." He looked a little sheepish.

"Thank you." I smiled, unwrapping the chocolate. I savored the first bite.

"You look a little better." Relief edged his voice.

"Yeah, I feel a little better. Maybe we should go," I suggested.

"Nope." His muscular frame blocked my exit. "You need to see a doctor, especially since you looked like you were about to pass out on me back there. Unless you want me to drive your bike again?"

I cringed. He ground a few gears on the ride over. I was worried about the transmission.

"So you are my ride back to my car," he continued with a smirk. "I need to make sure I am safe on the back of your Schwinn."

He had no idea how close he was to getting his blood sucked.

The doctor breezed in and Max flashed his badge. He went over the events of the evening with the MD, who proceeded to poke and prod my head and neck.

"Rusty blade gets an automatic tetanus shot," the doctor said as he pointed a flashlight in my eyes. "And you have a mild concussion."

Max looked vindicated. The doctor prepared the shot, and I looked the other way as he inserted it into my arm. I may be a bad ass, but I hate needles.

"Take acetaminophen and try to keep still for 24 hours," the doctor said. He swabbed at the puncture wound with an alcohol pad and then applied a Band-Aid, though I knew full well the needle prick already closed. "Can you do that?"

Twenty-four hours in bed? Good luck with that.

Max stared at me, "Yes, she will stay in bed for the next 24 hours."

"You sound pretty sure of that," I said sarcastically. I raised my eyebrows at him, and he held my gaze with such a fierce intensity that I looked away. My heart was pounding. I felt my blood rush to my pelvis.

I lost the staring contest. Max managed to fluster me, and he knew it. And he was savoring the win.

"Good," the doctor said absently, his nose buried in my chart. "We're all set here then."

He moved swiftly out the door. Max picked up the bike helmet and held it out to me. "Looks like I'm driving."

"The hell you are," I yapped, pushing the helmet into his stomach. "If you're worried about my driving, call a cab."

I stalked out of the room. I could almost hear him rolling his eyes as he followed behind me.

Frantic shouts interrupted our witty repartee. I pressed myself into the wall as a crush of medical personnel rushed down the hall surrounding a stretcher. They were moving fast, but not fast enough. Blood-soaked sheets were piled on top of a young male. The medics had the sheet pulled down to the man's stomach. One of the doctors had his hand inside the man's chest cavity, which was torn open. Shattered bones poked out, the jagged edges of skin and flesh hung down to meet his torso. I couldn't take my eyes off the carnage. A shudder ran through me and I felt my adrenaline boost. I wanted to throw up and have a snack all at the same time.

God, what is wrong with me tonight?

I shook it off and looked over at Max. His cell phone was chirping. Looking at the caller's name, he scowled. He strode down the hall to take the call. I was left cooling my heels.

I could hear the doctors and nurses rallying to save the man in a room down the hall. Machines beeped and voices called, getting louder and more frantic. "Damn it! We're losing him," a female voice cried out. The sound of shouts died down as the sustained beep of a heart rate monitor told me they lost the victim. A cold gust of wind slipped past. I shivered.

A man stepped right through the curtain and looked directly at me. He was dead, an apparition, and his body kind of rippled as he moved, not quite translucent -- I could make out his face, his eyes, his youthful physique -- but he was definitely not a solid form. I blinked and stared at time, dumbfounded. He was a ghost. I had never actually seen a ghost before. They don't physically appear to humans. Or vampires.

He was young -- I'd put him at 19, maybe 20 -- with a handsome, brooding face that carried several scars. His arms were inked with a mix of tattoos, including a giant cross on his bicep. But his eyes gave me a start -- they were haunting and old. He had clearly lived a life much longer than his birth years. And it didn't look like he was going to find much peace in death either.

The ghost's eyes went from haunted to determined. His form moved swiftly down the hall, and pushing towards me. I drew back, once again pressing myself against the wall. But it was too late. My body tensed up against the cold, wet thickness of ghostly goo that ran right through my own body. I shuddered. Gross.

Just then, Max returned, pushing his phone back into his pocket. He looked surprised to see me pressed against the wall.

"You okay?" he asked gruffly.

"Yeah," I peeled myself off the wall to walk to the exit. I lost track of the ghost.

"Will you be alright on your own?" he asked. "That was the Providence PD. There was another murder and a victim was found alive. He's here at the hospital. I am going to stick around and see if he's up for questioning after the doctors are done with him." He nodded at the room that the ghost came out of. Guess the ghost was the victim they thought was alive.

"He's not talking," I shook my head sadly. "He didn't make it."

Max turned and kicked the wall, frustration twisting his chiseled face.

"Want to drop me at a crime scene then?" he asked grimly.

"Why not," I said with a shrug. "It'll be the perfect nightcap to an evening like this."

CHAPTER 5

We headed to an abandoned dock at the Port of Providence, not far from the hospital. I forced to Max make a pit stop on the way to the crime scene. The candy bar did next to nothing to curb my hunger, and I needed a meat-like substance in my stomach before I snapped. There was a 7-Eleven about a block or so away from the crime scene, and I love hot dogs.

I squinted, my eyes adjusting to the harsh fluorescent lighting of the convenience store. The cashier had classic rock playing on the boom box behind the counter. Max studied the coffee. I made a beeline to the greasy "Big Bite" hot dogs spinning around on the rotating grill. Which one, or two, or maybe even three, wasn't sitting there all day?

I chose one dog and examined the self-serve toppings. After deciding on mustard only, the pump squirted a huge blob on the corner of my dog. I used the hot dog to spread the mustard out evenly, licking the mess off my fingers when I finished.

I examined the Slurpee selection. I missed the Slurpees of my youth. The flavor choice was limited for sure, but I missed the simplicity of grape and cherry. It was too damn cold anyway. Opting to live without the sugar rush, I grabbed a bottle of water from the fridge down the aisle.

"You want a coffee?" Max called out from around the microwave that was blocking us. I wrinkled my nose. Coffee from 7-Eleven? Gross.

"No thanks." I stopped and examined the fruit in the open refrigerator case. The poor little apple looked all bruised up. So much for healthy eating.

I maneuvered through the aisle to the register. The classic rock-loving clerk with three-day-old stubble stared at me from leaky red-rimmed eyes. Along with the dark circles, he looked like he hadn't slept in days.

"I got his coffee, too," I said, nodding at Max who was dumping at least 20 packets of sugar into his cup. I guess he was hoping to mask the taste.

"Ummm… Ahh… OK?" The clerk looked slightly baffled, like the idea of ringing up a cup of coffee halfway across the store was too taxing for his brain. Thankfully the register beeped loudly with each button he pushed, saving me from having to make awkward chitchat with a guy that was clearly stoned.

I dug out some cash from my jacket pocket, paid the man, and then stood by the newspaper rack, staring out of the plate glass window.

Absorbing the view of a flickering neon sign in the shape of a woman's extra large boobs, I bit into my hot dog, the slightly burnt skin giving my teeth a little resistance. I sighed in pleasure at the salty, nitrate-filled goodness. Max slipped up beside me, and stared out at the depressing landscape. A lone working girl was walking up and down the deserted streets, hoping for a date.

"Great atmosphere," he said flatly. "And how can you be a coffee snob but eat that?" He stared as I shoved a huge chunk of hot dog into my mouth.

"Don't knock 'em," I said through my chews. "These things hit a certain spot like no other questionable foodstuff."

Max laughed and wiped a bit of yellow mustard off of my cheek. With my hands hot dog free, I opened the bottle of water and chugged down about half.

"So explain this place to me," Max stared out at the Providence wasteland.

The area was pretty desolate, even though it was teeming with nightclubs a little over a block away. Of course, they catered to a decidedly seedy crowd.

"Several years ago, the city passed all sorts of ordinances that basically relegated the nudie bars to the area around the docks. We are on the strip of road that the locals called 'Fantasy Island,'" I explained. "This road runs parallel to the water. If you keep going north, towards downtown, the clubs and sex shops get more populous."

There was a club for every predilection, even of the illegal sort. There was the usual illegal gambling and prostitution, but there were also rumors of production on snuff films and other freaky acts.

Max raised his eyebrows. "Any of them any good?"

I snorted. "Yeah about as good as the hot dogs."

He laughed, and shoved open the 7-Eleven door. "How far are we from the crime scene?"

I looked over his shoulder as we walked out the door. I could see the blue and red cop lights flashing from the parking lot.

"It's right on the docks, just about a block that way." I pointed left, towards the light show.

"I'll walk the rest of the way," he said. "The cops probably won't let you much closer than this anyway."

I straddled the bike and strapped on my helmet, feeling awkward. "Are you going to be able to get back to your car later?" I asked.

Max nodded, smiling, and laid his hand on my arm, giving my bicep a squeeze. "You and your concussion OK getting home?"

"No problem." I smiled back at him and started up the engine.

Max nodded. "See you later." Then he thumped the top of my helmet and walked off in the direction of the red and blue flashing lights.

Once Max was out of sight, I started up the bike and followed him in the direction of the cop lights, cutting into an empty lot about halfway down the block. I killed the engine and dismounted. Then I ducked behind a scrap metal heap.

Because the Port of Providence was the largest exporter of scrap, mountains of twisted and rusting metal surrounded the docks. And in the valleys around these peaks, the garish signs from the strip clubs formed a neon oasis among the jagged metal.

There must have been a ship that went out earlier in the day. The pile wasn't crazy high; it was far from the Mt. Everest of scrap. I could easily scale it.

Since I saw one of the victims ghost out at the hospital, I wanted to get a bird's-eye view of this murder scene. If he decided to go full-on haunt, maybe I'd pick up some clues that could help a medium send him along to his next life. Since he died violently, there was a good chance he'd need a little help.

I carefully put my booted foot onto what looked like an old car bumper and pulled myself up. The pile shifted under my weight, but steadied right away. As quickly and as lightly as I could, I climbed my way to the top, tottering about fifteen feet off the ground, the metal groaning slightly with each step. I trained my eyes on the crime scene, wishing I had binoculars.

The dock was abandoned, but it was covered with about a foot of well-trampled snow. The seclusion, plus the proximity to the strip clubs, made it a good spot for illicit activities. From what I could make out, five bodies were arranged in a circle, with the feet meeting in the middle. It looked like they formed the spokes of a wheel. There was an empty spot that had a human shape indented in the snow -- my ghostly friend from the hospital. Max stood over the bodies, his shape casting a dark shadow where it blocked the police floodlight.

"Get out of the light, dammit," I muttered as the metal shifted under my weight. I readjusted my footing and a trickle of metal slipped down the pile. The uniformed cop by the crime scene tape stood a little straighter.

Max walked towards a man I assumed was a detective, allowing the light to flood back over the bodies. I gritted my teeth. Two men and three women. There were dark spots in the snow near the bodies -- blood spatter perhaps. But it was tough to make it out from where I was positioned.

Max huddled with the detective. He picked up a long, slender item. Murder weapon? It was hard to tell. This distance thing was a pain.

A flash of headlights pulled my eyes out of focus. I blinked a few times. When I looked again, my hospital ghost was standing in a disturbed area of snow near the corpses. That must have been where my little Casper went down.

He looked at the cops and looked back down at the bodies. He was growing increasingly agitated at what the cops were saying. His mouth moved rapidly, and his arms waved around, punctuating his silent words with an urgency that only I could see and sense. His defiance grew as the police continued to mill around the bodies. My hearing wasn't strong enough to pick up what the cops were saying, so I had no idea what had upset him.

He threw up his hands and aimed them at the floodlights. With a pop, the lights went dead and the dock was plunged into darkness. One of the cops let out a string of impressive curses and then chaos broke out as they scrambled to get the lights back up.

I shifted position again. The junk pile creaked under my weight. I lost my footing and slid several feet down the metal mountain, creating a loud crunching sound as metal scraped against metal. Landing ass first at the bottom of the heap, another pop sounded, and the floodlights unexpectedly came up again. I could hear more choice words as the sudden appearance of powerful light temporarily blinded the cops. It was a lucky break. The noise I made had momentarily piqued their interest. With the sudden burst of blinding light, they forgot all about me.

Sharp metal pressed into my left hamstring, threatening to cut through. I pulled myself gingerly off the pile, and slinked towards my bike, the cops forgetting about the collapsed metal as they refocused on the carnage in front of them. A chorus of angry voices broke the silence. It sounded like someone trampled the crime scene in the blackout.

My breath caught when my bike came into view. Casper stood by it. My heart pounded when I saw he wrote "vampire" on my gas tank in what appeared to be blood.

"That better come off," I snarled. My cheeks flamed with anger.

His eyes widened at my foul look.

40

"Yeah, Casper." My ghost scowled at me when I called him that, but I scowled right back at him. "Don't deface my shit with offensive graffiti. That's like a supernatural hate crime."

Agitated once again, he flickered in and out, jumping in front of me then fading away as I got closer to the bike.

He moved around so much that I passed through him by accident. The cold ooze moved through my body. I gritted my teeth and shuddered.

He stopped cold and stared at me. He looked almost familiar, but I couldn't place him. He had probably come into the bar once or twice. I felt myself soften. It's not easy being dead.

"Look," I said in a low voice. "You need to move on, my friend. There's no reason to stay here anymore. You're supposed to move on."

He became more animated, and his mouth began moving rapidly again. It looked like he was trying to speak, but I couldn't hear a word.

"Sorry," I muttered. "I don't speak ghost."

He looked exasperated and pointed at me and then at the bike. Then pointed at himself and the crime scene. Then me and bike. Then him and the crime scene. I was playing freaking charades with a ghost!

"Do what you need to do," I said with a shrug. Then I straddled my bike, turned the ignition and felt the sweet engine kick in between my legs.

And then he did it.

The cold plasma ooze of ghost dropped into me, but didn't slip through like before. I felt his presence drop into my body. Then a searing pain shot through my head, ricocheting off the walls of my skull.

I couldn't ride like this. I killed the ignition and gripped the handlebars. "Get out," I seethed.

"Can you hear me?" He had a deep voice, with a slight Spanish accent.

"Of course I can hear you. You are in my brain!"

"Need help," he said. He was struggling at the possession too, which made me feel slightly better.

"Hate to break it to you, but you're dead. Not much I can do." I pressed at my temples with my finger tips, as if I could squeeze him out.

"Behind you! Don't trust!" With those parting words, he jumped out of my body, leaving me shaking with cold.

I glanced over my shoulder and saw a uniform cop coming up behind me on foot. Once again, I turned the ignition on my bike.

"Hey!" The cop called out, rushing up beside me. I instinctively reached into my jacket but came up empty. I wasn't expecting trouble, so I wasn't packing any weapons.

"This is a crime scene. You can't be here." His voice sounded normal, but he didn't seem human to me. His movements were too quick; the color of his green eyes too vibrant.

"On my way out," I waved my hand and kicked the bike into gear.

He stepped in front of the motorcycle, and grabbed the handlebars. The back tire spun on the pavement but I wasn't going anywhere. Now that he was right in front of me, I recognized him. He had been outside of Babe's earlier, canvassing the neighborhood. He smiled, and his fangs flashed in the spillover from the spotlight. Damn it. I knew Marcello lurked in the shadows outside of Babe's. Was this the only one he turned?

The good news was he was a new vampire. A very new vampire. And I could handle a new vampire. It was the ones that had centuries on me that gave me the problems.

I killed the engine. Swinging my legs onto the seat, I quickly stood on the bike. I did a back flip off the bike as the Vampire Cop made a lunge for my legs. New vamps may be fast, but they are stupid, so they don't anticipate their opponents very well. I just had to keep him moving until I could arm myself with something.

Vampire Cop lurched towards me and made another grab. I

dropped to the ground in a push-up position. His arms wrapped themselves around air. I pushed my legs up and kicked out, nailing him right in the groin. He fell to the ground, whimpering.

I grinned. I loved that death didn't take that particular pain away.

While he was down, I hauled ass to the mountain of scrap metal and grabbed at the rustiest piece I could find. But the jagged piece I snatched sliced my wrist and blood sprayed out.

Vampire Cop forgot all about his aching testicles at the smell of blood. As I awkwardly wrapped my bloody wrist in my scarf, he rushed me. He pinned me against the metal mountain, which moaned when he pressed my body into it.

He gripped my neck with his left hand, and pulled my right wrist to his mouth. I yelped in pain when he bit down. His fangs pushed through my flesh and he began sucking.

I groaned as his opiate-laced saliva forced its way into my body, slowly turning the excruciating pain into intense pleasure. With my body limp, Vampire Cop raised his face, wiping my blood off his mouth with the back of his hand. He smiled. His fangs dripped blood. He dropped his hand from my neck and fumbled under my leather jacket. He ripped at my t-shirt, groping for my breasts.

Like most newly turned, Vampire Cop couldn't separate blood lust from sexual desire. They were linked. He pushed against me, and I could feel his erection through our layers of clothes. His extreme hardness was one more side effect turning Dracula. I had heard that it made sex unbelievable. But I wasn't interested in finding out if this was true, especially not from Vampire Cop. I preferred my dudes with a heartbeat.

With the lure of sex as a distraction, I made my move. My vampire metabolism pushed the drugs quickly through my system, so the opiate-induced pleasure wasn't as prolonged. I shuddered as his hand brushed against my nipple. I pushed my pelvis into his. Satisfied that he was fully distracted, I reached for the jagged metal that caused this commotion in the first place.

Gripping the metal tightly, I gave Vampire Cop a strong shove.

He stumbled back about three feet, looking stunned, his cock hanging out of his pants. Before he could react, I swung the piece of metal through his neck. The jagged teeth of the rusty metal cut into him, and then force took over. His head dropped to the ground, then his body crumpled down after it.

My legs gave out, and I slid to the pavement. Taking deep breaths, I tried to control my shaking. I still had more work to do. I was only halfway done to really destroying Vampire Cop. I still needed to cut out his heart and burn it.

Gathering myself together, I crawled to his body. Kneeling over the torso, I shoved my fist through the chest cavity with all my strength, shattering the ribcage. I plunged my makeshift metal weapon through his skin, digging out the heart. I reached in and pulled it out.

Still unsteady, I got to my feet and staggered to a barrel several yards away. I tossed in the heart, then went back to my bike and pulled lighter fluid and a match from my saddlebag. Returning to the barrel, I sprayed the fluid and dropped in a lit match. An inhuman shriek pierced the cold air, and Vampire Cop's body turned to dust, leaving a rumpled pile of clothes behind. At least that part of a vampire kill wasn't messy.

Tossing his uniform into the burning barrel, I said a quick prayer. I wasn't religious by any stretch, but it was the best way I could show respect. He was a human being once. There were people in his life who loved him. We were close in age; he could have been a friend. He could have hung out at Babe's. He didn't want to become a monster. It was forced on him. He was a casualty of war.

Pushing the senselessness of it all out of my mind, I straddled my bike. I could hear the cops telling grisly jokes in voices too loud, trying to ignore the depravity around them. Death hung in the air, threatening to suffocate all of us. They were already denying what was right in front of them. It was easy to ignore the noise of my battle with Vampire Cop. We really were just things that went bump in the night. Funny how the human mind can play tricks.

I turned the ignition. The engine purred. Passing 7-Eleven, I saw Stoner Clerk out front smoking a joint, staring down the road at the cop lights. He was so mesmerized, and stoned, he didn't notice me at all. The despair of the city weighed heavily that night. And, the cops looked like dinner. The fight left me with low blood sugar. Again. I had to eat something before I vamped out. I peeled off towards the blinking neon of Fantasy Island.

CHAPTER 6

It was close to five in the morning by the time I got home. I was grateful for the silence in my apartment. I was reeling from the events of the past few hours.

I dropped my helmet on the kitchen table, and pulled a bottle of water out of the fridge. I sighed longingly at the sight of my bed, tucked into the far corner of my loft. But instead of throwing myself on it, I gingerly walked around piles of unopened moving boxes to my ancient armoire styled with Gothic flourishes that held court at the foot of my bed. Promising myself I would unpack one more box tomorrow, I dropped to the floor and reached into a hidden bottom compartment and pulled out a long, narrow box. I took a deep breath and opened it.

The heavy iron dagger had an ornate silver hilt of entwined serpents shaped into an ancient Gothic cross. The blade, curved and sharp, caught the dim light with a glint as I unsheathed it. It was my father's dagger.

The dagger, like the armoire, was one of the few possessions left by my parents. The dagger was from my father's original family, forged somewhere in Italy during the time of the early Medicis. Babe had told me wild stories about it over the years -- that it was forged from the fires of hell or something. She never liked it, but she never really told me why. I had no clue if her hellfire stories were true, but I knew it was special -- magical in some way. And Marcello had its twin. It was rusted and dented and worse for wear, but I was certain it was the same mystical weapon. And it slashed me.

"I knew it looked familiar," I muttered to the dagger, as if it could talk to me.

I put the blade back in its sheath. But instead of returning it to the armoire, I slipped it into a special compartment built into my boot. I had no idea why I wanted it close, but I knew it was time to put it to work.

I headed to the bathroom and turned on the shower. I stripped out of my clothes and stood in front of the mirror to investigate the damage. My neck burned where the blade had cut me, and there was still a red mark where it sliced my skin. It was odd for a wound to linger that long, but maybe it was just rust. I'd have to see. Otherwise, all the bruises from the fight had healed. I'd clean up fine. I just looked exhausted.

I placed a bath bomb into the shower, stepped under the hot spray, grateful to finally be able to clean the stale beer out of my hair. I leaned against the cool tile wall of the stall and took deep breaths, inhaling the eucalyptus scent. It helped me focus.

It had been a crap night: attacked by a vampire, almost outed as a supernatural freak myself, sliced with my blade's twin, almost went all Dracula on Max in the ER because fresh blood was flowing. Oh and I had a run-in with a ghost.

What. The. Fuck.

I lathered up my hair, rubbing my head gently since I was apparently mildly concussed.

Assuming that Babe got a hold of Dr. O, and assuming he thought this merited a "drop everything" attitude, I could expect my team to get into Providence in the next 24 hours. Thinking of them made me smile. Apart from Babe, they were the only family I had.

After my parents died and my aunt realized that she couldn't care for a part-vampire baby, she took me to Dr. O, who had been working with my dad. Dr. Lochlan O'Malley was in charge of Blood Ops, our unit of the top-secret government program. It fell under the purview of the Department of Defense. BO. No kidding.

Most Blood Ops members lived on an army base in the middle

of the Nevada desert. That's where I was brought up, training for battle with all sorts of supernatural monsters and learning how to control my vampire instincts. I was "home schooled" by an elite team of educators, most of whom happened to be werewolves. Werewolves specifically were often extremely intelligent and had extraordinary discipline. Most other were creatures were as unruly as vampires.

Members of the Blood Ops unit watch for signs of supernatural crime. For example, most unsolved murders are usually the act of supernatural forces. But these cases don't necessarily go cold. Blood Ops investigates, and if the crime is supernatural, we dish out something closer to vigilante justice. Often a silver bullet, an incantation, or a stake takes care of the problem. Trial by jury and all that is impossible. The only way to restrain a rogue supernatural creature is to destroy it.

Did I stake a friend of Marcello's and now he's looking for revenge? No idea how he could connect it with me. Blood Ops members operate in the shadows, but then again, so do vampires like Marcello. The creatures we hunt are kind of aware we exist, but we are almost more like lore and legend then an actual, real threat. We are the fairy tales their maker's told them to keep them in check, sort of the "scared straight" of the preternatural world. Most of our bad guys are genuinely surprised when we show up to take them down.

So I wasn't convinced that Marcello had a beef with me because of my Blood Ops affiliation. But since it was where I spent the past 30 years of my life, what else could it be? I haven't been in Providence long enough to piss anyone off.

The Blood Op members that can mainstream, like myself, live among humans. I returned to my hometown of Providence, for instance, because it was turning into a hotbed of supernatural activity. That, and Babe wanted me to come home and help run the bar, which she co-owned with my mom. After Mom died, the bar became half mine. Moving to Providence was the first time I had ever lived away from the Blood Ops base since I was a baby. Weird that coming "home" was more like leaving home. I didn't really miss the desert, but I definitely missed my friends.

I tilted my head into the spray of the showerhead and rinsed my hair. The soapy water cascaded down my back. I picked up the bar of soap and began to lather my body.

I closed my eyes and for a split second imagined how Max's muscular arms would feel wrapped around my body.

Max was FBI. I was jarred back to reality. I wondered if that would make it harder or easier to hide Blood Ops from him. Relationships were complicated enough. I'd had a few one-nighters in my time, but I clocked more intimate time with my Rabbit vibrator than with a flesh-and-blood man.

A life like mine made it impossible to have any sort of relationship. It was hard to answer the "so what do you do" question. "Hunter of all things inexplicable" sounded a bit mad. "Blood Ops Agent" sounded absurd. And let's not even get into the vampire thing.

Relationships were definitely an issue.

I turned off the shower, grabbed a fluffy green towel off the rack and wrapped it around myself. Thinking about Max was way more fun than thinking about Marcello. But dealing with Marcello was clearly more important.

He was definitely after me, but there wasn't a clear reason why. Most vampires stayed out of the spotlight, attacking in alleyways and on deserted streets. Or they seduce you and attack in the privacy of your own home. An attack in the open was rare. Marcello seemed like a rogue. But more important, why was a rogue targeting me?

I padded back to my armoire and opened it again, this time pulling out an oversized t-shirt. After shimmying into it, I climbed into my bed, snuggling into my down comforter.

I suspected the answers about Marcello had more to do with me than with a vampire I staked. Wasn't it weird that I returned home after 30 years essentially undercover in Blood Ops to get attacked by a rogue vamp? I thought so. And then there was the knife -- a near replica of the one that belonged to my father. I had never seen one like it before, and then this clown shows up at Babe's, stabbing at me with the damn thing. I spent a lot of years hanging around Vegas, so I was a betting girl, and I'd double down on this having something to do with my murdered parents.

Babe, Dr. O and Frankie were my only links to my past. I hoped one of them had some answers.

My mind began to drift, and I fell into a fitful sleep.

CHAPTER 7

Babe was in her usual position at the end of the bar when I arrived by late afternoon. Plywood covered the hole where the window once was. A few regulars -- a bunch of old men who lived in the neighborhood, including Alfonso the drunk -- were dotted along the distressed wooden bar, nursing their drinks and chattering about crime statistics while they leafed through the newspaper. Babe's may be a college dive bar at night, but the daytime is reserved for the old-time neighborhood guys.

I poured myself a cup of coffee and plopped down on the stool next to Babe.

"Business as usual," Babe said with a nod. "Just a little more cave-like in here than we're used to."

"Well, you know I always appreciate that," I smiled. "Did you find Dr. O?"

"Said he'd fly out on the jet last night, while Frankie was still -- " Babe pursed her lips. "Able."

"Good," I nodded.

Frankie was full-vampire. The majority of them weren't depraved blood suckers. Hell, Frankie was descended from nobility.

Frankie and the rest of my crew would arrive once the sun went down, which was soon. The sky was already turning a vibrant pink, and a cold wind was kicking up.

I glanced up at the muted television. Ami Bertrand was back on the tube.

"Turn that up, will ya, Nina?" Alfonso hollered from his stool. I vaulted the bar and snatched the remote, turning up the volume. Then I gave him a refill on his beer.

Bertrand's voice was like silk in our ears. "It's a shame that the good citizens of this fair city, a city founded by a renegade, an outcast, have had to tolerate a political insider for all these years. He bought and sold your freedom ten times over..."

Alfonse blew a raspberry at the television.

"What do you make of that, Alfonso?" I asked.

"I don't like him, and I don't trust him." Alfonse sipped his beer thoughtfully. "But he'll win the special election."

His fellow regulars whooped and laughed at him.

Alfonso just shook his head and grunted. "What do you think, Senorita Babe?" he called out at the end of the bar.

"Al, you know I am way too old to be a senorita," she chuckled. "But you're right, he'll win."

"Shut that fool off, would ya?" Alfonso went back to his newspaper. I hit the mute button again and began slicing lemons for the night crowd.

"Nina, how are you feeling?" Babe looked at me over the rim of her glasses, which were sitting on the tip of her nose.

"Eh, okay," I sighed. There was no point in lying to Babe. She always knew when I wasn't telling her the truth. I hadn't slept well. Marcello kept invading my dreams, taunting me with images of a fire. I didn't recognize where, and I didn't see anyone in the fire, but I could hear screams. I wasn't sure if it was the mild concussion giving me nightmares or if he was getting into my head. Some of the older vamps could do that, and it was one of the abilities that freaked me right out. In case it was the latter, I pretty much stayed up all night.

"Once the gang arrives, you go home," Babe said firmly. "You

52

need time with them, and you need time to rest. You could've have taken tonight off, you know."

I knew, but I hated leaving her alone at the bar at night. Babe was a tough broad, but the neighborhood was a little rough around the edges, and she wasn't as young as she used to be.

"Promise you'll close up early if it's dead," I said, giving her a look.

"Yes, Boss." Babe grinned.

I didn't believe her. "I'll ask Dr. O to hang around and keep an eye on you then."

The door to Babe's flung open. I squinted at the motley crew who stood at the threshold.

An older gentleman with a tweedy coat and a professorial air strode into the bar. At his heels was a tall man with pale skin and long black hair that accentuated cerulean-blue eyes. With his long black leather coat, he looked like a rock star. That was Frankie.

I vaulted the bar and landed in front of them, Babe not far behind me.

"Nina," Dr. O said, pulling me to him and holding me tightly.

The tweed of his jacket was a little itchy, but the hug felt really good.

"You look lovely," Dr. O continued. "Being home has done some good, I see."

Babe turned in time to catch a kiss from Dr. O and their embrace lingered for a moment before she turned to hug Frankie.

With the greetings out of the way, we moved to the empty tables away from the bar.

Frankie slid his arm around my waist as we walked, a faint accent hinted at his European background. "What the hell is going on here?"

Frankie looked no older than me, but he was probably close to 500 years old and one of the most dangerous vamps I had ever come across. He was also a talented tinkerer and built my custom motorcycle. And he was one of my best friends.

"Where's Darcy?" I asked him, realizing that my other best friend was missing.

"That time of the month," Frankie smiled slyly.

That sucked. Darcy was our tactical support and resident computer genius. I was waiting for months for her to wire up my new Blood Ops home base here in Providence, and hook up my loft with some sweet electronics. But she was also a banshee, putting her out of commission for a few days a month so she could go somewhere safe to wail to her heart's content. Descended from the Tuatha De'Dannan, a race of Irish fairies, the myth is that banshees are the omen of death for one family. In truth it's the sound of the banshee's wail that kills a person who is suffering some sort of heartbreak. And in Darcy's case, it's usually men. Darcy finds the heartsick men and wails for them. It's a nasty business for her, particularly since the Blood Ops base was so close to Las Vegas. Hearts were breaking all over that city at any given time.

Knowing that they would be joining me here in Providence, I had a room next to Frankie's apartment built out for this purpose. Of course, I wasn't going to tell Frankie about it until it was too late. He'd piss and moan about having to listen to her shrieks, even though I had the rooms soundproofed. He'd claim vampire hearing, but that's sort of a load of bullshit. I spared no expense on the soundproofing. My dad was a 700-year-old vampire who amassed quite a fortune over the centuries. I was his sole heir. I could afford to build it right.

"Do you guys know a Marcello?" I asked as we settled down at a round table, not far from where Marcello attacked.

"Why?" Frankie asked. He looked like he was about to jump out of his skin.

"So you do know him," I said. I felt a small wave of relief. "He was the one who attacked me last night, right here. Spoke the ancient language to me. He knows what I am, and more importantly, *who* I am. But I know nothing about him, which puts me at a real disadvantage."

Dr. O shook his head. "So Marcello's here. I thought he might show up when he caught scent of you, but he put a lot of pieces together faster than I thought he was capable."

My patience was running thin. "So you *both* know him? Mind telling *me* who he is?"

Frankie hesitated. "He's a hit man."

"A vampire hit man?" I crossed my arms. Had the mafia taken over the vampire population or something?

Dr. O hesitated. "We think Marcello killed your parents."

I actually felt the blood drain from my face.

Dr. O continued. "Marcello didn't order the kill. That much we are sure of. He is simply a hired gun."

"So why is he after me?" I felt my fangs start to burst through my gums. Wrapping my arms around myself, I pressed my nails into my arms to force myself to stay seated. What I really wanted to do was run out of the bar, track Marcello down, and drive a stake through him.

"Because you came back. Apparently he has been waiting for you." Dr. O said, looking chagrined.

That response was infuriatingly cryptic.

Babe looked alarmed. "Nina, maybe you should go back to the Nevada..." She met Dr. O's eyes.

I sighed and reached for Babe's hand, pressing it against my cheek. "Auntie Babe, I love you. But I am so staying here to stake this bastard." I had been waiting for 30 years for this kill. It was all I thought about during the hours of the Blood Ops physical training. He was so mine.

"Nina, you have no idea what vampires like Marcello are capable of." Babe was edging towards hysteria. "And your dad was supposed to be unstoppable!"

I dug in my heels. "Dr. O, you agreed I could come home because some weird supernatural something is apparently setting up shop, remember? You said that the time had finally come for me to be here, to help out Babe, and keep an eye on the activity."

For two years, I wanted to leave the desert and come home. Home. I wanted to have a life outside of Blood Ops. I wanted to try to run my mom's bar. Babe was growing old, and I barely spent any time with her. My history was here, what was left of my family was here. And this is where I chose to be. Hell, I earned it.

"But that was before we knew that Marcello was still hanging around," Babe said, her voice rising. She wasn't giving in without a fight. "Now we know he's here, so I need you to go back to Nevada. Let them send another team out to deal with this other stuff."

It was all I could do to keep from stomping my feet. "You can't be serious!"

"You are your father's daughter," Dr. O said with a chuckle. "He wouldn't have passed up this fight either."

"Yeah, and look where that got him," Babe said. Her dark eyes were blazing with anger.

A far-off look on his face, Frankie spoke up at last. "But you need to know what to do after you catch him. At least I can help with that." He was filled with bitterness. I sometimes forget that Dad was Frankie's mentor and they spent centuries on the run together.

"I guess it's settled," Dr. O said, but Babe yanked him back to the table.

"Not so fast, Lochlan," she hissed. I had never seen Babe look so angry.

"Auntie Babette," I began, choking back tears. "I know what you did for me..."

"Do you?" Babe asked. "Really, did Lochlan tell you the whole story?"

"Babette..." Dr. O tried to stop her.

Babe refused to stop. "How we were on the run, how this thing and his so-called family kept finding us? How so many more were killed while we were running?"

I knew Babe had tried to take care of me, but I always assumed taking care of a half-breed had been too much for a young, single woman. I had no idea she was running from a vampire.

Babe was shooting daggers at Dr. O with her eyes. "So you

never told her how she ended up with you?"

Before Dr. O could answer, Babe stood up and stalked away.

Dr. O began to rise, but I stopped him. "Let her go," I stood. "I'll deal with her when she has a chance to think it all through. Let me get you guys something to drink. Beer?"

"Guinness?" Dr. O nodded and smiled appreciatively.

Babe stormed off to the stock room, and the bar was filling up with the post-exam college crowd. Talking to her would have wait. I filled a few simple draft orders from the college students filtering in before filling two pints of Guinness from the tap. I rolled my head from side to side during the slow pour. My neck and upper back were killing me from last night. And my neck was still red and raw from the knife wound, which was weird. I usually heal at warp speed.

I grabbed the pints and walked them over to the table, setting them down in front of Dr. O and Frankie. Dr. O was absorbed in conversation with two college kids. They sounded like religious studies majors, and since they barely noticed the beers in front of them, the conversation was probably getting heated. I headed back towards the bar, but Frankie caught my wrist.

"What's this?" He pointed to his own neck, while looking at mine.

"Nothing," I shrugged, and tried to move away, but he wouldn't let go.

"I don't think so." He raised his eyebrows.

"Frankie..." I warned as I tried to yank my hand away. Vampires and their goddamn death grips.

The door opened with a burst of cold air, and Frankie dropped my wrist. Since I was already pulling against it, the surprise release sent me stumbling backward at a good clip. Muttering several choice words under my breath, I ran straight into Max's muscular shoulder, bounced off of him and landed squarely on my ass.

"Ow!" I yelled, more out of shock than pain. But dammit now my tail bone was throbbing.

"Oh shit!" Max exclaimed, staring down at me. He rubbed his shoulder where my forehead met it. "You have a solid head!" He offered me a hand up.

"Sorry," I said, shaking my head. I wasn't ready to move just yet. I stared at the worn wood floor and hoped I wouldn't be picking splinters out of my ass later.

Max squatted down beside me, "You alright?"

I nodded, feeling a rush of air on my back. Frankie was now hovering, with a tiny smirk turning the corners of his mouth upwards.

I tentatively pushed myself up from the floor. Frankie grabbed me around my waist and hauled me to my feet so quickly that Max, who was still in his squat position, stared directly at my knees.

"Thanks," I said to Frankie, clearly not meaning it. He grinned and winked. Then he walked back to Dr. O, who was engrossed in some deep conversation with a student, beer untouched, completely oblivious to what was going on. Frankie dropped into his seat, a smug smile pasted on his face. He was so infuriating and he knew it.

Max was back on his feet and shot a look over in Frankie's direction. "You sure you're okay?"

I shrugged. "Yeah. Don't mind Frankie. He's an absolute shit sometimes."

"Nina, can we talk?" Max said, turning serious.

I nodded and motioned for him to follow me to the bar. Two frat boys ordered shots of tequila. After carefully checking their IDs, I grabbed two shot glasses and reached for the cheap shit.

"I don't think last night was a random junkie looking for some cash." Max spoke so matter-of-factly that I jumped. The tequila I was pouring missed the shot glasses completely and spilled all over my hand.

"No? So what was it then?" I tried to sound nonchalant, wiping my tequila-soaked hand on my jeans before sliding the shots over to the frat boys.

"I was hoping you could tell me." He pulled out his smart

phone, fiddled with it and held the screen towards me.

I took the phone from him and squinted at the screen. It was a picture of a gruesome crime scene. Four naked bodies, two women and two men, were laid out on the snow, their heads touching but bodies stretched out like a bizarre snowflake. It was a replica of the crime scene I took him to the previous night, only with fewer dead bodies. Their bodies were blue with cold. And there was a lot of blood.

Max swiped his finger against the phone's screen, and a new picture, even more graphic than the last, came up. It appeared that each body had a hole in the chest. It looked like the hearts were missing.

Another swipe, and there was close up on a weapon, but not just any old weapon. Against a blood-spattered snow background, a dagger exactly like the one Marcello used to attack me was painfully obvious.

I closed my eyes and feigned disgust. "Nasty. Why are you showing that to me?"

I hoped I sounded appropriately horrified. But my heart was racing. The dagger. Why was that damn dagger at a crime scene? And why would Marcello drop it? Could there be more than two out there, and this was just a really bizarre coincidence? I knew that was a giant stretch, but I really wanted to believe in coincidence right now.

"That dagger," Max began, his voice so damn even that it was unnerving me. "Is that the dagger from last night? The one that did this?" He ran his finger lightly over the scar on my neck. My stomach flipped and my skin tingled at his touch.

"Is there something you are not telling me?" Max asked, just as evenly as before. "Or not telling the cops?"

The sound of glass breaking was a welcome relief. "Holy CRAP!" Alfonso bellowed, but the words were slurred from one too many beers and sounded more like holly carp. "Open your eyes, people! Don't you see what that fucker is doing?"

I looked up at the television, and I saw Ami Bertrand leading a massive group of people up on the lawn of the state house.

"Al, it's just a demonstration," Babe rushed out of the stock room. The sound of shattered barware brought her out of hiding.

"Remember, we did that when we were kids."

Alfonso continued, his voice rising. "It's happening now. It's all happening, and we ain't ready. We ain't ready at all. It wasn't supposed to be now. We ain't ready for this yet. Not yet."

Babe went over to Alfonso and held his face in her hands.

"Al," she said firmly. "I am taking you home. Now."

She looked directly into his eyes, which were filled with tears. Then she whispered into his ear, he nodded and looked down, exhausted.

Babe grabbed her coat off the hook, and led Alfonso out the door. He was pretty drunk and leaned heavily on her narrow shoulders. Babe was even smaller than me, and she didn't have vampire strength. I was impressed that she didn't buckle under Al's near dead weight.

"I'll tag along. You know, safety in numbers," Dr. O said. Then he extracted himself from his conversation and nodded at Max as he shuffled past. "It's a rough neighborhood, right, Agent?"

Wait. How the hell did he know Max was FBI?

Max nodded slowly, his eyes following Dr. O.

"Do I know him?" Max muttered to me.

I couldn't respond. My focus was on Dr. O's half-drained beer. I felt a little light-headed, but probably because my nerves were shot. I swayed a bit.

Frankie suddenly appeared in front of me, catching me before I fell over. Of course, this made me feel even worse. Goddamn vampire speed wasn't exactly subtle.

"And you are?" Max glared at Frankie's hands, holding me firmly by the waist.

I was scanning my brain for a logical explanation for all this bizarre behavior, and came up empty.

"Frankie," he said, lowering his voice just a little. I caught a slight snarl at the corner of his mouth. Shit. He was showing off his fangs. Here. In my bar.

"Frankie, this is Max," I said weakly. "From the FBI."

"Feds?" Frankie dropped his snarl, looking slightly interested.

My ears started to ring.

"And where are you from, Frankie?" Max's question sounded almost like a challenge.

"At the moment, Nevada. Just flew in. To see our Nina." He grabbed me around the shoulders and squished me into him.

"And you two know each other from?" Max questioned.

"Oh, we've known each other for eternity." Frankie smirked.

"Eternity is a bit dramatic," I squeaked out. "We sort of grew up together."

My face flashed hot, and the bar began to spin. As ringing in my ears grew louder, Casper from the hospital appeared and stood by Dr. O's chair. He waved and then made a beeline towards me, slipping his cold plasma ooze into me before I could protest.

"Need to talk," his voice rattled around in my head. "Those pictures. Same vampire."

"Get out!" I doubled over as the pain in my head blinded me.

"Nina? Nina!" I heard Frankie say. He sounded so far away. Then blackness washed over me.

CHAPTER 8

I could hear worried voices expressing concern. Someone called out for a cold wet cloth and a male voice shouted, "They are on their way!"

Babe was laying down some very choice words in Spanish. Crap. I had been out long enough for her to be back from taking Al home?

Right before I blacked out, Frankie was causing a scene, Max was suspicious as hell, and Casper had reappeared. Even if I wanted to sit up, I couldn't. My body wasn't ready to respond yet, and given the situation, I wasn't in any real hurry to open my eyes.

The cool damp cloth hit my forehead, and I took a deep breath. I felt vaguely like I was floating. A hand grabbed my wrist, checking my pulse. Then someone pulled me up to a sitting position.

"Hold her head back," Babe's voice commanded whoever had hold of me.

My head tipped back, and some foul-tasting liquid dropped into my mouth and ran down my throat. About a second after hitting my stomach, my esophagus felt like it was on fire. My eyes shot open. I started to hack.

"What the hell was that?" I sputtered, coughing and grabbing at my chest. My entire body was burning. I reached out and Babe caught onto my hand, her face a mix of concern and triumph. Once my coughing subsided, I noticed she was holding one of her dusty cobalt bottles.

"Thank God," she sighed and stood up.

I leaned back and my head slammed against something hard. I turned and saw Frankie sitting behind me. Just over his shoulder, Max looked kind of pissed.

I tried to push myself up from the floor but fell back into Frankie's chest again. My head was still fuzzy and I felt like I was hovering slightly above my body.

"EMTs are on the way," Max said. He sounded authoritative and decidedly unfriendly.

"Call them off," I groaned. I was not going back to the hospital. "I just need some sleep."

"You need to get looked at," Frankie said.

"So THIS is what you two can agree on?" I spat out. "And, Babe, what the hell was that?" I would swear it was moonshine.

"Something that can kick your ass and wake you up." She was on the top of a step stool, returning the dusty bottle to its perch high above the bar. She moved her way back down and looked sternly at me. "No hospital for you," she said matter-of-factly. "But someone needs to take you home and you need to rest."

"I've got my bike...." My protest faded as soon as I saw her face. I felt five years old again.

"You are in no condition to drive, especially after what I just gave you," Babe said as she crossed her arms. "Max, take her home."

She huffed away and started clearing the dirty glasses from the bar. She was done talking about it, and so, apparently, were the rest of us.

Max strode out the door. "I'll pull my car around to the front."

Frankie wrapped his arms gingerly around my middle and began to haul me up.

"I can do it," I hissed at him.

"Really?" His amusement was grating, especially since he was right. I gave in and let him hoist me to my feet.

"Thanks," I muttered. With his arm still around my waist, we began to walk slowly towards the door.

The icy air stung at my face but it cleared the cobwebs out of my mind. I got my footing back and gingerly let go of Frankie.

"You feel that?" he asked, his eyes scanning the darkness.

I was about to tell him he was nuts when something hit me. My body began tingling and my heart started racing. I too began searching the darkness, but I saw nothing.

"He's out there," Frankie nodded into the blackness.

"Seriously?" This was kind of freaking me out.

Frankie shushed me. A moment later, a sly grin began to crack his stoic facade. "I think I know where he is," he whispered.

A black Suburban pulled to the front of the bar, and Frankie opened the door and lifted me up to the seat. Max was in the driver's side, looking concerned.

"Make sure she gets into her apartment," Frankie commanded. "Don't leave the house, Nina," he continued. "I'll swing by later." He squeezed my hand and I quickly caught his eyes. They were a bright, shining blue. He was ready to hunt. His body was a blur as he raced away from the SUV.

"I thought these were only for FBI agents on TV and in the movies. I didn't think you guys actually drove SUVs like this!" I said as I yanked the door closed.

"I see you're feeling better," Max said as he rolled his eyes at my comment. "So, where are we going?"

"You know where Olneyville is?" I responded.

"You really hang out in the nicest parts of town." He glanced at me and turned on the GPS.

I shrugged. My parents owned an old factory building that I was slowly converting into apartments. Apart from the small toy factory that rented the top floor space, I was the only tenant. Well, *used* to be the only tenant. Frankie was moving into his basement lair sometime before daybreak.

Max was right. Olneyville was a seriously crappy old industrial area. But the building was solid, my apartment was huge, and the area was pretty desolate, which was good for privacy. In terms of personal safety, hell, I was part vampire. The local thugs didn't scare me.

I looked into the side mirror, scanning the general direction where Frankie slipped into darkness.

"Want to give me the address, or do you want to keep sitting here?" Max tapped his fingers impatiently on the wheel.

"Sorry," I said, flustered. "50 Agnes Street."

"Now we're making some progress!" Max typed into the machine. Once the address was in place, he pulled onto Wickenden Street and headed towards the highway.

Now settled into his car, I glanced in the back seat. The seats were down, and I could have sworn there was a surfboard taking up space in the back.

"There's a storm coming in, and I heard there could be some decent swells." Max grinned sheepishly as he pulled onto the highway.

"I had a feeling you surfed," I watched the cars whiz by on Route 95. "But you may want to rethink your surfing plans. It's not just any storm. They are talking nor'easter. Those are no joke."

Max eased the car onto an exit ramp to a secondary highway, "A little storm doesn't scare me."

"You want the Olneyville Square exit. It's coming up," I warned as Max whipped around cars like a NASCAR pro.

He tapped the GPS and glanced at me. He slowed as he eased onto the exit ramp, and stopped at a red light.

Olneyville was like a ghost town. On the edges of Providence, it was once the manufacturing hub of the state. But as factory jobs dried up, so did this pocket of the city.

Max made a left turn into the desolate industrial area. Old factory buildings lined both sides on the street, stark gang symbols graffitied onto the old, red, brick walls. Some buildings were crumbling in on themselves.

Max hooked another left and braked in front of the smallest of the factory buildings, as the GPS sing-songed, "You have reached your destination." I reached into my bag and pulled out a garage door opener. With the press of a button, an industrial garage door opened.

"Go on -- pull right in. It's safer for your car." I pressed the button again once the car cleared the doorway.

Inside was a small parking garage. Since I was the lone tenant, Max's was the only car there. With it parked, I led Max through a doorway that opened onto a hall, pulled out my keys and unlocked the fire door. With a satisfying whoosh, I pushed the door off to the side and walked into my apartment.

I motioned for Max to come inside, and he followed me down the dark narrow hallway. Once we reached the end, I hit the light switch, illuminating the airy loft.

Max looked around and let out a low whistle, taking it all in. A galley kitchen spread down the wall on the left. On the gleaming countertop sat a lit Our Lady of Guadalupe candle, just like the one at Babe's. Running the length of the kitchen was a large rustic wooden table, with benches on either side.

Directly in front of us was a living area, with two deep purple couches facing each other; a distressed wood coffee table sat between them. On the far wall was an office, although it looked more like a space shuttle command center with all the computer equipment, most still unplugged, on the oversized desk.

The living room area separated the kitchen from a huge workout area in the corner. There was a treadmill, free weights, a spin bike, and a heavy bag. A pull-up bar hung from the ceiling.

In the other corner, my large four-poster bed sat at a diagonal angle. Long pieces of silk snaked down the posts, ready to shield the bed from the rest of the room. The armoire stood to the left of the bed, and a small changing area was to the right. The changing area was separated from the space by beautiful Japanese screens.

My private bath was off the narrow hallway, just behind the kitchen. It was large and while not exactly luxurious, an old claw foot tub gave it loads of character.

And strewn about the apartment were random boxes of my still-unpacked life.

Max took me up on the invitation to sit down on one of the overstuffed couches. Then he raised his eyebrows and nodded. "No wonder you live here."

"Did you want a beer? I think have some Raging Bitch in the fridge." I headed into the kitchen.

"Thanks, I'd like that," Max said with a smile. Damn, he had a nice smile.

I opened the fridge, and the cold air felt good on my now flushed face. I dug out his beer and slammed it against the edge of the counter to remove the cap.

"Don't cook much, do you?" he asked.

I turned to see him looking at my immaculate kitchen. Only the burning Veladoras was on the counter. My mouth tugged up at a small smile and I shook my head.

"Look, Nina," he paused, collecting his thoughts. "I really could use your help with this case..."

"I am just going to take a quick shower." I felt pretty wrecked after the past few days. "Then I will have a beer with you. And you can ask me three questions."

"Just three?" He looked a little crushed when I nodded.

I lit a few candles before making my way to the bathroom. There were very few overhead lights in my apartment -- the florescent bulbs made my head ache. But the space was loaded with candles, including a giant candelabra with five tapered candles at the entry to the living room. It cast a warm glow around a good portion of the loft. Moonlight streamed in from the old factory windows, causing the shadows to dance seductively with the bluish light.

Once in the bathroom, I turned the faucets. The sound of water rushing out of the showerhead immediately set me at ease. I stripped down, giving the water a minute to heat up, and then I stepped into the hot spray.

I really was not up for talking to Max about the damned dagger, and I wished the weapon could have been an easy-to-find hunting knife. But the truth was, these daggers were ancient and rare. As I understood, there were only five left, three of which were supposed to be in Europe. The vampires that held those three never made the trip over. My father had the fourth, the one now in my possession. I heard the fifth was entombed somewhere in Egypt.

I didn't have time to tell Dr. O about the dagger, and now Max was expecting me to chat about them. I rubbed shampoo into my hair with gusto, my frustration growing the more I thought about him. I liked him, dammit. And I had no interest in layering lie on top of lie. But I had no choice.

I rinsed the shampoo out of my hair, bubbles circling the drain. Maybe this borderline obsession with him was due to a long dry spell. I hadn't been on an actual date in like five years. Of course, I had hooked up a few times, but the last time was maybe a year ago. Frankie and I went to Chicago for a few days to blow off steam. He was hot and in a band.

If I could just get this out of my system, maybe I would be clear to focus on my work once again. It was, after all, a matter of life and death.

I turned off the water and grabbed a towel. I padded out of the bathroom, towel wrapped around me.

"Let me just throw something on!" I called out. Then I swept towards the changing area.

Behind the screens, I stripped off the damp towel. I pulled out an old white tank top and a pair of torn sweat pants from the dresser and yanked them on quickly.

I went back to the kitchen, pulled out another beer, and

cracked it open on the counter.

I sunk down onto the couch across from Max and took a long swig of my beer.

"So," I said. "You're a Federal Agent? You don't look like a Fed."

"What's a Fed supposed to look like?" He was mocking me but he was good-natured about it.

"Not a surfer," I smiled.

I liked the way his eyes lit up when he smiled.

"I'm not from around here."

"No kidding," I chuckled. "California or Hawaii?"

"California." His smiled broadened.

"Okay, so why Providence? It's freezing, and the surf sucks in the Atlantic."

Max laughed. "I'm here helping the police department with some gang trouble. Apparently, I am considered a gang expert. I wrote a book on it once."

I didn't want to give him the satisfaction of knowing he had just impressed me.

"What about you?" He leaned towards me, his arms on his knees. I was grateful for the coffee table between us. "You from around here?"

I shrugged, took an exaggerated gulp from my beer and looked down at my bare feet. I wasn't ready to answer that question yet.

Max got up and negotiated his way around the coffee table. He sat down beside me.

"You went through something pretty terrifying last night, and I don't blame you if you don't want to talk about it, but the dagger at my crime scene today looked an awful lot like the one that did this." He brushed his fingers softly along the raised pink scar that was oddly not healing.

"I'm fine," I croaked out. If the slight quiver in my voice didn't give away how I was feeling about Max, my sudden shiver did. I closed my eyes briefly and imagined kissing him. Bad idea. A fire in my belly roared. My eyes snapped back open.

"So, can you tell me anything?" he shifted a bit closer.

I took another gulp of the icy brew, hoping that it would cool me down a bit. "Show me those pictures again," I said, steadying my thoughts. I needed to take another look. If that was indeed the dagger, it was too much of a coincidence.

Max pulled out his phone and handed it to me. I tried to look disgusted by all the gore, but the composition of the pictures was intriguing. The bodies laid into the shape of a star, similar to the bodies I saw last night. Just less of them.

"What do you think the dagger was used for?" I asked, my eyes still taking in the crime scene. "Stabbing?"

"We think it was used to carve their hearts out," he said methodically.

"Was that cause of death?" I asked. My tone was almost as clinical as his.

"Waiting on the autopsy," he responded, eying me warily.

"Did they bleed out?" I squinted, looking intently on the images.

"We think so." Max pursed his lips. "Why?"

"That's not a lot of blood for four victims." I immediately kicked myself. Oh yeah, I just own a little dive bar.

"I would assume, you know, puddles..." I tried to recover from my gaff.

"You're right." He looked slightly impressed. "And you know this, how?"

"I watch way too much TV." I laughed a little nervously when I realized that there was no television in my apartment. "At the bar. Alfonso loves those CSI shows."

I took another swig. My hands were shaking.

"Sorry." Max noticed my discomfort and took the phone out of my hands, then he reached over and held them. "Are you alright?"

I closed my eyes and, for the first time since all this crap began to happen, felt completely exhausted.

The mysterious Marcello, the ancient dagger, the spike in "unexplained" phenomena that drew me back home. The supernatural forces were building in this City, and I was here to battle them. But I wasn't expecting these forces to hit so close to home. Everything was about to change. This could be my last night to feel more human than beast.

Max touched the side of my face. "Why don't you try to lie down?"

"Will you stay?" I was too tired to hold on to my bravado.

Max picked me up in his muscular arms. I wrapped my arms around his neck and he carried me to the bed. His touch was strong and reassuring, but also surprisingly gentle.

"I'll stay as long as you want," Max stroked the side of my face again.

"Thanks."

Our eyes locked. I willed myself not to pull away this time, and he bent into me.

I parted my mouth and he slowly slid his tongue in. We began exploring each other gingerly, and then our tongues began to dance with greater urgency.

I yanked at his t-shirt and he smiled and pulled it off. I drank in his golden, rock-solid form, chiseled to perfection by years spent chasing the waves.

I wrapped my hands around him and pulled him on top of me. He moved his hands down the sides of me body, feeling each curve from my breasts down to my hips.

I guided his right hand under my tank top and to my breast. Running his fingers lightly over it, he caressed me softly, teasingly. My mind was screaming at me to get off this runaway train, but my body refused stop.

I trained my hand lower until I found his zipper, and began pulling at it. My hands fumbled a bit at my urgency. It finally relinquished. As I began to slide it down, a knock on the door interrupted us.

Max stopped and eyed me curiously. I shrugged and ignored it.

The banging became louder, and then Frankie's voice called out, "Come on, Nina! Open the bloody door!"

I sighed and pulled away from Max. Talk about a mood breaker.

Adjusting my disheveled clothing, I strode across the apartment and flung open the door.

"What, Frankie?" I growled.

"That's a hell of a greeting, Love," Frankie took in my appearance and smirked. "Aren't you going to invite me in?"

"I have to think about that." I glowered at him.

"That's a fine thank-you for bringing your bike home." He dangled the keys.

"Shit, Frankie, where'd you leave it?" This was a crappy neighborhood and the bike could get stolen.

"Relax!" He moved aside and I saw it gleaming in the hallway.

"You rode it down my hallway?" I shook my head, incredulous. I suppose scuffmarks on the recently restored hardwood floors were better than a stolen bike.

"Now doesn't that merit an invitation?" He laid on the puppy dog eyes a little thick.

"Frankie, please come in," I sighed and walked down the hallway into the kitchen. Max was pulling on his shirt. His expression darkened when he saw Frankie behind me.

"You leaving?" Frankie grinned at Max like a Cheshire cat,

72

shrugged his backpack off and plopped himself on the sofa. He unzipped the bag and began pulling out large, leather-bound books that were a few birthdays short of ancient. "Because I need Nina's help...with...work."

Frankie nodded at me, like he was looking for some sort of expression of gratitude for not blowing my cover.

"Did you want coffee?" I pulled a bag of coffee from the fridge.

"No, thanks," Max said, eying the strange tomes. "I'll let you get to it."

I followed him to the door. "Sorry about this." I motioned towards the living room where Frankie was flipping through a magazine.

Max turned and leaned against the doorframe. "Make it up to me."

"How?" I smiled slightly, and felt my lower body tingle.

"Let me take you to dinner." He snaked his arms around my waist, and I leaned into him and nodded.

"I'll pick you up at 8:30." He kissed me on the forehead and walked towards the garage. I enjoyed his perfect ass for a minute, then shoved the door closed.

Frankie and I had work to do.

CHAPTER 9

I shuffled lazily back into the living room, yawning. It wasn't that late, but I was exhausted. Frankie hid behind one of his enormous books. I could sense the smirk even if I couldn't see it.

I thought to pick up where I left off with the coffee idea. A full pot would be good. "Anything interesting in there?" I called to Frankie over my shoulder as I headed towards the kitchen to finish the coffee.

"Actually, yes," he said, tilting the book towards me. I squinted at the page.

"Holy shit," I crossed back to the living room, picked up the book, and promptly dropped it on Frankie's toe. It was heavy.

"Sorry!" I said, as he winced. I picked up the book again and held it out to him. He flipped through the pages, to the one he was reading.

There was the dagger. And below it was loads of writing. In a language that looked familiar but not really.

"This isn't vampiric tongue, right?" I asked.

Frankie shook his head, "No. The ancient vampiric is different from today, but there are usually enough similarities between them that

74

we can decipher ancient texts. I can't place this, though."

"What about the book?" I closed the volume and looked at the cover. "Where'd you get it?"

"After I lost Marcello's track, I went back to Babe's and I was mucking about in her attic. I found them in some sealed boxes." Frankie shrugged. "They were with your parents' stuff. She said she forgot they were there or she would have given them to you."

"Anything else in those boxes I'd be interested in seeing?" I was a little pissed that he didn't bring the whole haul with him. But you can't exactly transport moving boxes on a motorcycle. Besides, I had enough unpacked boxes in my apartment anyway.

"You'll need to see yourself." He shrugged again, clearly wanting to stay out of the family drama. "What did the G-Man want?"

"A knife just like my dad's was dropped at a crime scene," I was trying to push past my annoyance. Babe didn't forget about those boxes. I knew she was only trying to protect me. And I loved her and knew she had her reasons, and Frankie shouldn't be caught in the middle. But the five-year-old me wanted to pinch him.

"One doesn't just drop a dagger like that at a crime scene," Frankie said incredulously.

"And a dagger just like it did this to me last night, too." I pointed at my neck.

Frankie cocked an eyebrow.

"Any chance there are more out there than the five we know about?" I asked. For all we knew, this could have been the top-selling item at the Wal-Mart of ancient times. Although I seriously doubted it.

"There's always a chance," Frankie said. "But I'd say the chance was slim."

I yawned and got up off the couch to head to the kitchen again. Maybe this time I would actually get the coffee started.

"How far were you able to track Marcello?" I asked. The dagger was leading us down a dead end.

"A bit, but then he vanished," Frankie said. He looked worried.

"How far did you get?" I filled the coffee carafe with water, raising my voice of the running faucet.

"To downtown, and then I lost him by that big hotel." Frankie was clearly frustrated. He rarely lost someone's trail.

"Which hotel?" I asked, already knowing the answer.

"The one with the old glass elevator that's stuck between floors."

I knew it. "The Biltmore. They have been seeing some seriously supernatural activity since I arrived, and it feels stronger every time I pass by."

"Coincidence, then?" Frankie winked.

I snorted. Neither of us believed in coincidences. I turned the pot on.

The Biltmore Hotel still had a hint of elegance hidden beneath the shabby exterior. The historic old hotel sat in the center of downtown Providence. Built in the Roaring 1920s, it made headlines for installing a grand glass elevator that offered breathtaking views of the Capitol building. For decades, it was the toniest spot in town. A post-work cocktail at the Biltmore was de rigueur for the moneyed set that ran the City and the politicians they ensconced into office.

But even something as grand as the Biltmore can fall apart. Buildings collect memories, and as the city of Providence fell further and further into decay, so did the once-stately hotel. Too many years of corruption, murder, and cover-ups bled into the walls and floorboards.

The landmarked building now appealed to a seedier sort. Busted businessmen drank cheap whiskey in the off-key piano bar, while bored prostitutes tried to make a quick buck. The hotel had regressed to include mostly SROs, or single room occupancies, where residents on the same floor shared bathrooms and kitchens. Every now and again, some ignorant, unsuspecting out-of-towner who relied on an out-of-date guidebook or their own memories of the hotel's grandeur, checked in. Their expression -- a mix of fear and shock masked with a tart politeness -- said it all and said it best. But with nothing more to do and not wanting to embarrass themselves, they let old Jeeves (yes, that was indeed his name) cart their luggage along the dusty carpets into decrepit rooms with cracking plaster and peeling paint.

And so the Biltmore was perfect for occupation by supernatural entities. They could sit shoulder-to-shoulder at the bar, their energy feeding on the desperation of the down-on-their-luck businessmen and the hookers that loved them. Sometimes these poor women left with something more than a date, and returned as poltergeists or vampires. Even more troubling, some simply didn't return. I wouldn't count out some psycho attempting to Bride of Frankenstein some of their bodies. Yeah, I dealt with that level of depravity.

There was a lot of weirdness happening in the vicinity of the Biltmore, too. A concentration of bars and nightclubs behind the old hotel gave police a way to explain the pile up of dead bodies in the adjoining alleyways. From drunken brawls to muggings to gang turf wars, this tiny city had so much violent crime in a few downtown blocks that it was turning into that old movie, "Fort Apache, the Bronx."

"Did he go into the hotel?" I pressed Frankie for more details.

"Don't know, Love." His nose was back in the book, his expression twisting as he tried to recognize what the archaic language contained.

I crossed my arms and let out a puff of air. Frankie looked up and raised his right eyebrow.

"Would you like to go down there and look for yourself?" Frankie offered, somewhat sarcastically.

"Yes, I think I would," I said, pouring a mug of coffee.

"Will you be wearing your bunny slippers, then?" The corners of Frankie's mouth twitched up. He looked me up and down, not even pretending to conceal his amusement that I was essentially in my pajamas. "Or would you prefer to put your boots on?"

"Screw you, Frankie," I muttered. I put my mug on the counter and I stalked to my armoire. I yanked it open and grabbed whatever was closest -- a black tank top, old faded Levi's and a flannel shirt. My selection made Frankie laugh harder.

"Going lumber jacking?" he scoffed.

"Since when did you become Beau Brummel?" It was not an

accident that I hoisted a reference to the famous British dandy.

"You know, even his blood tasted a bit prissy." Frankie smacked his lips.

Of course he knew Brummel, and of course he drank his blood. Probably at an opium party.

I swirled around to say something smart-ass at him. But as my gaze caught his bright cerulean eyes, my heart accelerated and felt my gums rip as my fangs pushed through.

Before I could even react, Casper flashed in front of my eyes. The ooze of him pressed at my body again. A searing pain shot through my head. I thought it was going to split open.

My knees buckled, and I dropped to the floor. Frankie leapt over the couch and coffee table and was down beside me before I could process what was happening. I fought to catch my breath, and the room began to spin.

"Frankie?" I whispered into the blackness.

CHAPTER 10

My head throbbed. I knew if I opened my eyes, light would pour in and make it worse. I could hear faint whispering somewhere in the room, but I couldn't make out the voice. It wasn't familiar, and I strained to make out what it was saying, which made my head ache even more.

"I can't hear you," I muttered.

Then I felt the cold thickness of plasma melt into my body. "No no no no no! Get out of here," I growled. "I will not share my body with a ghost."

I was trying to keep my emotions in check and be firm about it, which was hard to do. Ghosts thrive on the adrenaline that pumps through humans when emotions run high, which is why possessed people are usually angry. But if you appear too weak, the ghost could try to push you into submission to keep the shell. Dealing with a ghost inside a body was delicate. I was not thrilled that this was happening.

Now that the ghost was inside my body, I could hear him loud and clear. "I need your help," he said.

"And I should help you... Why?" I took a sharp intake of breath when a searing pain sliced my head like a razor blade. Casper felt it too -- I felt his plasma push out of me for a brief moment.

"Please," he said sounding scared. "You're the only one who can see me. And hear me."

"Oh come on," I moaned. "Find someone else to haunt."

"No, you're it." His fear was giving way to annoyance. "Believe me, I tried."

Well crap. I had heard about ghosts attaching themselves to people, but I had very little experience with it. When Blood Ops came across possessions, we'd call in an exorcist and leave it to the professionals. But he was body-jumping, not possessing, so he obviously wasn't interested in controlling me.

"Why are you attached to me?" That thought was kind of creepy. "Does it have something to do with the hospital?"

"I was murdered," he pushed on quickly.

"Well, duh." I felt bad and all but my head was killing me. I hated being possessed.

"He'll kill more of us," he said as panic edged into his voice. It wasn't helping my head at all.

"More of who?" I asked. Did he know the connection between the victims? "How many more of you are there?"

"Not me. More of *us*!" His frustration at me ricocheted through my head.

"Us?" I pressed my hands against my forehead. "Who is us? Friends? Relatives? What?"

I felt him try to shake his head. Well, he was really trying to move my head and I was not going to let him do that. My brain would rattle.

"What do you want me to do about it?" My headache was making me more short-tempered than usual. Plus, I had a freaking ghost in my body. I was allowed to be bitchy.

"I want you to stop it, Nina," he said testily. Clearly he was in bad mood too. Of course, he was just brutally murdered, but I think my headache was bothering him too.

I took a deep breath, hoping the extra oxygen would help ease our pain. "Whoever you are, this is a human problem. I can't interfere."

"Not human. El curandero," he panted. "From Veracruz."

"You?" I asked, startled.

"Us. All of us."

My heart skipped. He was a curandero, a healer, a Mexican white witch. This must be serious if he was coming to a vampire to help. There wasn't a lot of love between vampires and witches, particularly el curandero. And I doubted those feelings changed in death.

Babe's salty Spanish curse punctured my ears, and I felt the plasma lift out of me. I smiled slightly, relief flooding my body as Casper left me. I rolled onto my side. A wave of nausea hit me, and I quickly rolled onto my back again, groaning.

A cool, damp cloth scented with ginger was gently applied to my forehead. It inhaled the soothing scent and carefully opened my eyes, expecting to see Babe's worried face. Instead Frankie was beside me, gently pressing the compress to my head. The centuries-old vampire looked a little scared.

"What happened?" I murmured, not daring to speak much louder.

"I have no idea," Frankie shook his head and squeezed my hand, which I didn't realize he was holding. It was cold, not uncomfortably so but slightly jarring.

I groaned as a tried to sit up. His arm flew across my chest, and gently pushed me back down.

"You just went pale and passed out," he stroked my hair. "You've been out cold for over an hour."

"When did you eat last?" Babe chimed in. She sounded far away.

I shrugged.

"Great." I could hear her tap-tap-tapping her nails on the kitchen counter. The noise sounded like it was inside my throbbing head. "Lochlan, why is this happening? This is not supposed to be happening."

I squinted open my eyes to look at her, and the dim candles felt like a blinding spotlight. I snapped them shut immediately.

"What's not supposed to be happening?" I muttered.

"Your blackouts, Love," Frankie whispered back. "Vampires don't blackout."

"But humans do, Frankie. Half human, remember? I think I just need to eat more or something." I tried to focus on slowing my breath. It kept my mind off the dull ache in my head that the ghost had just left.

Babe's tapping stopped suddenly.

"Did you feel that, too?" Dr. O's resonant whisper carried across the room.

I forced my eyes open very slowly and looked at them. Babe was frozen, only her eyes moved, searching the room. Dr. O cocked his head, listening. He took a few tentative steps, feeling the air around him.

Babe released the breath she had been holding. "We are old and paranoid," she muttered. The teakettle began to sing, and she busied herself making tea. Dr. O sat down at my long redwood slab dining table. He looked exhausted.

I knew my headaches were from Casper body-jumping into me, and maybe my blackouts too. But I didn't want to mention it to them yet. I didn't want them to freak out and try an exorcism. Witnessing a real live exorcism in LA three years ago kind of put me off of them. Besides, if Casper knew something about the murders, he needed to stick around.

"What time is it?" I closed my eyes again, wondering if my friendly ghost would return.

"Getting on to 3 AM, I believe," Frankie said. He rearranged the wet towel on my forehead, finding a cool spot.

"Did you get a chance to check out your room?" We were still a few hours from dawn, but I wanted to make sure Frankie was okay. Better to know now if something was wrong with it.

"It's lovely," he pressed the towel a little too firmly.

"Frankie!" I pushed at his hand and opened my eyes, breathing through a wave of nausea. "You didn't even check it, did you?"

When I took over the building, I built an apartment in the basement specifically for Frankie. It was as safe as he could get without being truly underground. And he hadn't bothered to give it a glance. I built a special room next door to him for Darcy's banshee wailing. If he had seen his apartment, he would have noticed the room, and he would be whining about his sensitive vampire hearing.

I was fairly certain that no sunlight could get into his apartment, but I would have felt better if he had given it the once over earlier, in case we had to come up with a Plan B to make adjustments to the space.

"Nina," Frankie sighed. "I trust you. You know what you are doing. I am sure it's fine."

Babe crossed the kitchen and placed a tray with a teapot and mug on the coffee table in front of the couch. She poured out the pungent brew, while Frankie helped me into a sitting position.

"You will drink this, and you will like it," she said firmly.

"What is it?" I asked timidly. Did I really want to know?

"It will make you feel better, that's what it is." Babe looked stern.

Wrapping my hands around the mug, I inhaled the steam, wrinkling my nose at the peculiar smell. I looked over at Dr. O. His lips twitched as he stifled a laugh. Babe pulled herself taller, put her hands on her hips, and pursed her lips. I sipped it cautiously. My nose wrinkled involuntarily. It tasted awful.

Dr. O couldn't hold his tongue any longer. "It's henbane."

I spit a mouthful of the tea back into the cup. "You gave me poison?" I gasped.

"Oh for Christsakes," Babe crossed her arms and tapped her

foot. "Yeah, it's poison. But the quantity won't harm you and it'll make your headache go away."

"Along with all other feeling," Dr. O said, looking pointedly at Babe.

"Lochlan, please. Back in the day, your people put this in beer and drank it for kicks." She rolled her eyes. "God, it's the tiniest of tiny amounts."

Dr. O shook his head at her, grumbling "henbane" while he followed her to my kitchen.

"Who were you talking to, Love?" Frankie took the mug from my hands. He sniffed the brew. "Oh, that's awful!" Wrinkling his nose, he placed it on the coffee table, out of arms reach.

"When?" I slipped back down to a horizontal position on the couch.

"Just now, before you woke up." Frankie lifted my head gently and shifted a bit. He placed my head back down, resting it in his lap. Pressing the compress against my skin again, he reached out with his other hand and grasped my fingers.

"I guess it was a dream?" I said cautiously.

I didn't want to tell him about Casper yet. I never had any affinity for the dead, never showed any aptitude in dealing with spirits or poltergeists. Humans sure, but not the dead. Not only could I see a ghost, but he could body-jump me so easily? Even mediums with the innate talent to channel the dead couldn't do it without their rituals. Yet here I was, just channeling a dead guy whenever he felt like a chat.

"Quite a dream," Frankie said. He played with my fingers. "Someone was following you, someone was murdered. And I'd swear you were talking to a dead guy."

I sat up quickly, and the room rolled. I groaned and gripped Frankie's knee as a wave of nausea hit me again. "In case you didn't notice, things have been a bit stressful around here."

"Nina!" Babe rushed from the kitchen. "Put your head back down!"

My stomach twisted. My battle with the nausea lost, and I stumbled to the bathroom.

"I blame the henbane!" Dr. O called after me.

CHAPTER 11

It was just past 9 AM when my eyes fluttered open. I snuggled deeper into the covers and shut my eyes again. Certainly, no one would blame me if I spent the day in bed. It had been a rough night, for sure.

The enticing aroma of coffee wafting from the kitchen proved a stronger pull than my soft and warm bed. Let's hear it for auto-brew! I rolled out from under the covers, pulling a throw blanket over my shoulders, and shuffled, still a little unsure of my footing, into my kitchen and towards the heavenly scent.

A note with Frankie's beautifully embellished script was propped against the coffee maker. I admired the carefully calligraphic lines. They don't teach writing like that anymore.

Notice I remembered the coffee. I hope I did it right.

I'll see you tonight. We have work to do.

I smiled. He finally mastered the coffee machine.

I poured my first cup when my cell phone chirped. It was Babe.

"Hola, Auntie," I smiled into the receiver.

"Auntie yourself," Babe sighed. "You gave us a hell of a scare, Nina."

"I know. Sorry." I poured some cream into the coffee and watched the color fade to a lovely caramel. I sipped the hot liquid carefully.

"Are you in bed?" A rhythmic tic, tic, tic of Babe tapping her nails on the phone made me wince. That woman was a bundle of kinetic energy.

"No." I rubbed my scalp and yawned.

"Lochlan wants you in bed." Babe was firm about this.

"Like that's even possible," I huffed into the receiver. "Did you know there's a pile of books on my living room floor in some weird language that no one can read?"

I could hear Babe clicking her tongue. "Of course I know about the books, Nina."

Babe's reaction took me by complete surprise, and I spilled coffee all over the kitchen counter. I grabbed a dishtowel and started mopping up the mess, the phone cradled in my shoulder.

"What are those books, Babe?" I asked.

"I just didn't think they mattered..." She sounded a little distant, distracted, and I could hear pages turning in the background.

"What are you hiding?" I felt last night's migraine twinge at my temples.

"Look," she snapped back to attention. "I'll explain it all once I figure it out myself. But Frankie and Lochlan agreed that I need to deal with the books first."

I was spectacularly annoyed now. The throbbing at my temples was beginning to pick up a techno beat. "Am I going to be the last to know?"

"I promise to tell you everything, but not now." Babe was trying to be soothing. It wasn't working. "Look in the fridge, there's a steak in there. Lochlan said to cook for breakfast. He thinks the headache was triggered from not enough protein and wants you to eat more of it. It's been marinating all night, just the way you like it."

I sighed. My annoyance slipped away. It was hard to stay mad at my aunt, especially when she marinated my steaks in tomatoes with cumin, garlic, chilies and the other smells that reminded me of my too-brief childhood spent in Catemaco. I didn't remember a whole lot from that time, but that marinade was unforgettable.

"How do I cook it again?" I was hopeless in the kitchen. Babe claimed it was for lack of trying. She said genetically speaking, I should be a five-star chef.

"Grape Seed Oil on the grill pan, heat it until it's sizzling. Sear the steak for a few very short minutes on each side. Two minutes each should keep it nice and bloody," she rattled off her usual directions. "And don't forget to let it sit for a few minutes before you cut into it. Make a few eggs while you are waiting."

"Got it," I said, pulling the grill pan out of the cabinet and placing it on the stove. If bloody beef gets rid of these headaches, I'll happily sear away.

"I'll call you later," Babe said. "I have some research to do myself."

"Right." I was slamming the cabinets, looking for the oil.

"Cabinet to the right of the stove, up top." I could almost hear her roll her eyes.

"Got it, thanks." I grabbed the bottle of oil, and in a very slick second, it slipped out of my hands. Vampire reflexes kicked in, and I caught it on the way down without missing a beat. "Do you need help at the bar today?"

"Don't worry about the bar. I have it covered."

And she clicked off the line without a goodbye.

Babe sure was acting peculiar. But she left me a marinating steak, so she definitely still loved me.

CHAPTER 12

Babe told me to stay in bed, but after wolfing down an amazing steak and egg breakfast, I felt like I could conquer the world. The protein infusion took the migraine away. Now I felt dangerously invincible, a bit more vampy than usual. I wonder if age was evolving my vamp nature. Or maybe I wasn't getting enough sleep.

Given my sudden invincibility, I decided it was time to collect a little intel from the field, starting with the area around the Biltmore Hotel. If Marcello was lurking in the neighborhood, something had to be there.

I rolled the Triumph out of the hallway -- Frankie was going to clean up the damn skid marks on my beautiful hardwood floors--and into the blinding December sunlight. Strapping on my helmet, I noticed a dog skulking across the street. I straddled the bike and turned the ignition – kick-starters are definitely cool, but they aren't exactly foolproof when trying to escape from the baddies. The dog didn't flinch at the sound, but continued to sit and stare at me. She was a skinny thing for a Rottweiler.

I eased my bike onto the deserted street, turning in the direction of downtown Providence. It was below freezing, but I had my thick leather jacket and long underwear under my jeans. Plus the engine threw off a fair amount of heat.

While the ride would be shorter, highway driving would also be much colder. So, I opted to take the scenic route through Federal Hill, Providence's very little Little Italy, and straight into Downcity, which is the fancy name the urban planners gave the downtown area in an attempt to revitalize it. Traffic was surprisingly light considering Christmas was only about two weeks away. Out of habit, I did the sign of the cross as I passed Holy Ghost Church, which stood like a religious centaur at one end of the Hill.

I came up to the stoplight where Dean Street crossed Atwells Avenue, slipped the bike into neutral and planted my feet on the pavement. A short man with a goatee and a shock of white hair peeking out from under his hat stopped and stared at me. He was wearing a track suit that belied the fact that he was about as wide as he was tall. I am used to stares when I ride, particularly in subzero weather, but something was a bit unsettling about his gaze. It was too familiar. The light changed and I kicked the bike into gear. Engine roaring, I pulled away. The old man tipped his Borselino fedora at me and gave a small bow. Funny but weird.

A few frigid minutes later, I idled the engine in front of the Biltmore Hotel. The outdoor skating rink across the street was all but abandoned, save for a few drunks sliding around on the ice with their paper bag–covered bottles. A handful of sad-looking people pushed through the revolving doors of the hotel, while two frightened tourists came rushing out. Guess they had used the same old guidebook.

My creep-o-meter was running on high. I made a sharp right on the street that ran between City Hall and the hotel, and found an open space to park. Street parking felt safer than going into the Biltmore's parking garage. I backed into the spot, killed the engine, and hopped off the bike. I removed the helmet but tucked it under my arm. I headed up the block, and away from the hotel.

The neon from a Quizno's sandwich shop brightened the shadows cast by the large, mostly vacant buildings that created a wind tunnel down the street. My nose twitched as I caught the scent of something decidedly not sandwich oriented. The cloyingly sweet smell of anise permeated the air.

Across the street was a line of abandoned storefronts. A lot of shops were boarded up, dusty "For Lease" signs hanging forlornly in the windows. One with a cluttered front window stood out. I quickly crossed the street, and the sound of my boots on the pavement echoed down the near-empty street. The smell of anise was getting stronger as

I got closer to the cluttered store. I stopped in front of its old wooden door, black paint peeling away. There was no signage except for a weird, almost rune-looking symbol painted in red near the top. A table filled with animal skulls, feathered headdresses, three-foot plastic replicas of Saints and other paraphernalia was visible through the grimy window.

It was a botanica, a witchcraft store. Santeria, Voodoo, and Wicca were all represented in the crusty window. I shivered and stared at the relics. Could this be where Marcello was going when Frankie lost his trail last night? Too many supernatural shenanigans were happening in a very concentrated area. It could have easily thrown off Frankie's ability to track Marcello. Get too much supernatural energy in one place, it becomes like radio interference.

Would Marcello come to a botanica? Witches and vampires don't exactly hang out. There are centuries of turmoil between the two groups, from wars to political coups to plain old bad blood. That infamous feud between the Hatfields and the McCoys? That was a classic vamp versus witch war.

The botanica's old wooden door creaked open. I ducked into the doorway of the empty store beside it, tripping over a junkie with a needle still stuck in his arm. He moaned and rolled over, splayed halfway onto the sidewalk. I pressed against the cold metal door and held my breath as heavy footsteps thudded down the sidewalk in my direction. A familiar shock of golden blond hair crossed in front of my line of sight. What the hell was Max doing here?

I shrank into the shadows as he negotiated his way around the body. Once he passed, I slid out of my hiding place and, keeping close to the doorways, followed him down the street. He turned into the parking garage attached to the Biltmore. I gritted my teeth and continued after him, just catching sight of him using the hotel's back entrance. I slinked to the doorway, pulled it open and looked into the hallway. I caught a fast glimpse of Max turning down the hallway. I paused at the threshold, an uneasy feeling growing in my belly. Pushing it aside, I continued to follow.

The once-empty hallway suddenly filled with all manner of spirits. And like a cavalry charge, they rushed straight for me. Instinctively, I crouched, knowing full well that the position would do no good against the ghosts. The cold slime of ghost plasma oozed along my body as the entities swarmed. Swatting them was useless.

They began to slam into me, their combined force so great that I fell backward and sprawled on the floor.

Looking up, I saw more entities swirling above me. They looked almost like translucent people, but they were horrific. What used to be flesh was rotting off their bones. Coarse hair, sparse but wild, was floating around heads that were little more than skulls patched with skin that hadn't yet rotted out. Their sockets were dark voids. Looking into those eyes was like looking into a frightening abyss. I caught the foul stench of death as one of them exhaled too close to me.

Seven of them nose-dived right at me. I tried to roll to avoid impact, but these things were quick. They crashed into my chest and stomach, trying to find their way into my psyche but unable for some reason. Several bounced off, but three remained stuck like suction cups. I felt their ooze creep around my body as octopus-like tendrils wrapped themselves around my torso, binding my hands and plastering me to the floor.

The largest ghost hovered just above, his rank breath skimming my face. He unzipped my leather jacket and, finding exposed skin, he whipped a tendril down onto it, searing my skin. I yelped, a mix of surprise and agony. He was freezer-burning my skin! A second hit and I could feel blisters start to well up. Crap.

I kicked out at the poltergeists and, of course, hit nothing but air. I felt another slam of ice on my chest, my skin pulling away as he whipped the tendril off. Another ghost began to snake its ghostly appendages over my face. Its fingers felt like razor blades slicing into my skin. Blood began to drip down my face.

I had never encountered malevolent ghosts before. Hell, I had never actually seen a ghost manifested until Casper in the hospital. Now I was seeing them everywhere. I had no idea how I was going to get out of this mess. God I hated the Biltmore.

Just when I thought it could not get any worse, I felt another hit of cold plasma, and this time the ooze dropped right into my psyche. My nerves went into overdrive when I felt the sharp pain in my head. Then a familiar voice echoed in my ear.

Casper sounded a little panicked. "What the hell did you do this time?"

I never imagined I would ever feel such relief at the familiar migraine that exploded in my head. "Help me," I panted, forcing the words out. Between the poltergeists cutting and searing into me like prime beef, and my ghost-induced headache kicking in, I wasn't in the mood to explain myself.

"Trying!" Casper wheezed out. He handled possessing me about as well as I handled being possessed. God I hoped he could help.

Casper tried to push my eyes down. "Hey!" I protested.

"Trust me," he pushed again, and, sensing his exasperation, I grudgingly clamped my eyes closed.

Then, Casper took over my mind's eye, and I saw his brooding image clearly. His arms were moving in quick but elegant patterns. My arms, completely out of my control, followed his movements. Faintly, he muttered words I could not make out, the pace of our arms quickening. Energy swirled around him, and he raised his chiseled face towards it. His dark skin glowed and his black curls appeared taken by a breeze.

Casper's hands were moving so rapidly now they were just a blur. I sensed the ritual was reaching its peak when his commanding voice intoned, "Stamus exitium praesenti. Eieci malum!"

Then nothing. And nothing was a good thing. The weight of the ghosts on my torso disappeared. The cuts on my face began to knit back together. My freezer-burned skin started healing. I opened my eyes and stared at the white ceiling, no hideous ghost faces blocking the view. Casper forced me to my feet. We stumbled down the hall and back into the parking garage.

"What the hell was that about?" I examined the areas of my body that were freezer-blackened by the ghost.

"They couldn't get into your body." I could sense him grinning through his exhaustion.

"And why is that?" I asked.

"'Cause I am a possessive little freak. Put a spell on you," he boasted. "I am the only ghost getting into your pants."

I snorted. The kid was funny. "Thanks, I guess. Why'd you do that?"

"I may be a ghost but I'm not a moron," he deadpanned. "It's protecting you. Promise."

I frowned. "Why do I see them now?"

I rubbed at my temples. Now that the poltergeist assault was over, the pain of sharing my head with this kid was grating again.

"Because we need you, mi pequeña vampira."

"Who needs me?" I asked sharply. "And how the hell do you know...?"

But Casper oozed out of my head before I could ask him how he knew I was a vampire. And why did he insist on hanging around?

Casper didn't leave right away. I turned to where he hovered by me, ready to assault him with questions. The greenish cast of his face stopped me. He favored his left arm, a hand pressed over his bicep.

"Show me." I motioned towards his arm.

He took his right hand away, and I gasped. I couldn't help myself. His flesh, turned a black and purple color like a bruise, dripped away from the bone. Like the poltergeists that attacked, his ephemeral body was rotting away.

I reached for him, and caught nothing but air. He disappeared.

"Thank you, I guess," I whispered into the air. A gentle gust of cold air brushed the back of my neck in acknowledgment. With my battered body on the mend, I staggered towards the street. I didn't care that I lost track of Max. I was so done with the Biltmore.

Stomping through the parking structure and muttering the string of Spanish curses learned from Babe, I walked straight into Max. Literally. After impact, I skidded away from him, nearly landing flat on my ass. Me falling on my ass was clearly becoming a thing where Max was concerned.

"Nina?" Max gripped my arm to steady me. "What are you doing here?"

"Shopping." I eyed him. "You?"

"This is where I am staying," he said with a smile.

"Here?" My eyes narrowed to slits.

He nodded. "Yep, the Biltmore."

Crap. That wasn't good. I suddenly felt a weight press down on my chest, and I knew that some bad juju was spilling out of the hotel again. I turned on my heel and began to walk quickly back to my bike, Max almost running to catch up.

"Wait! Where are you running off to?" He caught up and touched my shoulder. A jolt of electricity shot down my arm. I half-expected to see sparks shoot out of my fingers.

"Coffee!" It was the first thing I could think of.

"My treat?" Max smiled. "But you pick the place. And Dunkin Donuts is a little too played out around here."

I motioned to the Triumph. We crossed the street and I handed him my helmet. I straddled the bike and Max got on back and wrapped his arms around me. I felt relief as I tore down the street, away from the Biltmore and out of site of the botanica. I headed south, back to Federal Hill. An espresso at Venda Ravioli sounded like a good idea. And I needed to find out what Max was doing in that botanica.

CHAPTER 13

Venda Ravioli is an old-school joint that is a mix between Italian bakery, butcher and corner deli. It serves up prepared foods like a deli, has some of the most sensational meats like a gourmet butcher, and has some of the best espresso and Italian pastries on the planet. We settled into a table and I inhaled the glorious cappuccino steam. I had a plate of ricotta cookies to nibble on, and a slab of ground beef wrapped up to take back to the stray dog that was lurking around the building this morning.

I bit into a cookie and tried not to think about the fact that Max went into a botanica in the middle of spook-ville. It wasn't working.

"So, Max," I began, determined to take it a little slow. "Do you go to botanicas often?"

"Only when I am working cases." He looked at me curiously, sipping his cappuccino, which had a dusting of cinnamon on top. I watched his eyes light up on his first taste. "Oh you are right, this is amazing."

God, he had no clue. I nodded and smiled. "Well, it's...kind of creepy, don't you think?"

Max let out a hearty guffaw. "Don't tell me you believe in all that hocus pocus stuff! That crap is all in your head."

My face went hot, and I pressed my cold hands on my cheeks to temper the redness before it set in. "What if it's not exactly hocus pocus?"

"Nina, people cannot 'spell' other people," he said, using air quotes. "Kill them, yeah. Spell them, no." He shook his head.

"Yeah, weird people go to those places! Weird!" I gave a little extra force to that word. "And maybe dangerous. In the non-hocus pocus sort of way."

Max just nodded at me, eyebrows raised. This conversation was not going well.

"Nina, I am the go-to agent for gang murders. Botanicas are part of the job." He shook his head. "I am a little surprised they freak you out. You seem like the type that would have checked out a botanica or two in your teens. Try out a Ouija board, that sort of thing."

"They don't freak me out," I lied, picking up another cookie and biting down on it. "So, did the lead pan out?"

"Yeah, it did." He sipped at his coffee. "They had a replica of the knife left at the murder scene."

I choked on my cookie.

Max reached over and gave my back a few whacks. I coughed out cookie bits into a napkin.

"You okay?" The corners of his mouth twitched up.

I shot him a dirty look, which only made him smile more broadly. I slugged down more cappuccino, the hot liquid smoothing the rough edges on my abused throat.

The door swung open and a cold gust of wind caught our attention. In walked Ami Bertrand, the mogul gunning to be Mayor of Providence. He was in his late 50s, with a full head of thick dark hair, brushed away from his face, graying at the temples. He was much shorter than I imagined -- he had maybe an inch on me, making him 5' 2" at the most, and he walked with a limp. Even wearing a heavy, camel-colored coat, I could see that he had an athletic build. For an older dude, he looked muscular. He carried an expensive walking stick, the silver handle molded into a snakehead.

Close on his heels was the white-haired, goateed gentleman that I had seen earlier this morning. Bertrand was walking straight towards us. He extended his hand when Max stood.

"Agent Deveroux." Bertrand's voice was smooth and rich like chocolate ganache. "Good to see you enjoying the best cappuccinos in Providence! Be sure to tell your friends about it when you get back home. Are you enjoying your time here?" Bertrand eyed me and smiled. It made me squirmy.

"Mr. Bertrand." Max smiled back at him. "This is Nina Martinez. She co-owns..."

"Babe's on the Sunnyside," he finished Max's sentence. I found that annoying. "Of course, everyone knows Babe's."

"I don't believe I've seen you in there, Mr. Bertrand," I said as politely as I could. I didn't like him.

"No, I have not made it to your fine establishment yet, Ms. Martinez, but perhaps I will soon." He smiled and winked at me. Ew.

I nodded at his expensive looking coat and scarf, and his ridiculous walking stick. "Leave your cashmere at home. Our patrons are a bit more rough around the edges."

"Yes," the goateed man interrupted. He had a faint Italian accent. "I heard you had some trouble there the other night. Anything you would like us to look into?"

"Nope, no trouble." I smiled curtly. "Sometimes bad things happen in bars. Occupational hazard and all that."

"Indeed," Bertrand said. He smiled again. "Well, I want to make sure our small business owners are taken care of. They are the lifeblood of our city."

He drew out the word blood, lingering on the vowels a bit longer than necessary. On a creep scale of one to ten, this guy was off the charts.

"Thank you, Mr. Bertrand. I'll remember you said in the voting booth." I hoped he couldn't read that as a lie.

"I appreciate the sentiment, Ms. Martinez," he said as he

elegantly removed the gloves from his hands. "But I am certain we will win, with or without your vote."

So he was a human lie detector. I smiled at him coolly.

"Tavio," Bertrand turned to the goateed man. "Make a note to visit Ms. Martinez's alehouse, perhaps Friday night?"

Alehouse? What century was this?

My cheeks ached from the forced smile that was glued onto my face. Babe was going to kill me. She had no use for people like Bertrand, and didn't want our bar used as a campaign stop. I hoped Alfonso stayed home. If he had a few in him, things could get ugly.

Actually, thinking about it, it might liven things up a bit.

"Wonderful idea, Mr. Bertrand!" Tavio smiled and helped Bertrand off with his coat. "It's been a long time since I saw your aunt." He smiled at me, almost kindly. There was that familiar feeling again, but I couldn't place it.

Familiar or not, I didn't trust it. I picked up my helmet.

"Lovely to meet you," I said through my plastered smile. "But I gotta run. Alehouse and all. Max, do you need a ride back Downcity, or did you want to stay and catch up with your friends?"

Max stood up, pulling on his coat. "I should get back to the station, too. It's an easy walk."

"How is the investigation going, Agent Deveroux?" Bertrand's voice was velvet. "Hard to believe that such a small city can have such big city problems. If I'm not voted in, I worry that we'll turn into Detroit."

"Gangs are everywhere, Mr. Bertrand," Max said matter-of-factly. "Urban areas, rural areas. Even wealthy suburbs are seeing gang symbols scribbled in the bathroom stalls at the high schools."

"Well, we're lucky to have such an esteemed federal agent helping our city in our time of need." Bertrand waved his hand, turned his back, and with that we were dismissed.

I could not get away from Bertrand fast enough, and almost took the door off its hinges in my rush to get out.

I turned on my heel and rounded on Max. "So you and Bertrand are chums?"

"Whoa!" He held up his hands. "Back off. He knows my boss, and called when the murders started getting out of hand. He's the reason I am here."

"But--" I huffed.

He dropped his voice. "I think the guy is creepy as hell. But he owns this town. Better to ride the waves, you know."

Much as I hated to admit it, he had a good point.

"Be careful, okay, Max?" I gave him a faint smile and pulled on my helmet. "Things feel a little off right now. So watch your back."

"Wait a minute." Max touched my arm and I felt voltage. "Does this mean you give a shit?"

"It means I want that dinner you promised me tonight." I slid onto the bike and turned the ignition. The engine growled to life.

CHAPTER 14

I eased into the right turn by my building and looked across the street. The dog was there, pacing along the wall of the dilapidated building.

I came to a stop and killed the engine. She looked at me warily, hunched over a bit, head down and eyes up. I surveyed her in a similar manner.

For a big dog, she was a scrawny thing, all legs and ribs where she should have been solid muscle. Without taking my eyes from her, I swung off the bike, reached into the saddlebag and pulled out the package of ground beef from Venda Ravioli.

Both of us yelped in surprise when the building's door crashed open and a stocky man sauntered into the noon sunlight. I had never seen him in the neighborhood before, and I eyed him warily. Apparently, the dog wasn't too keen on him either.

He stopped when he caught me looking at him, and smiled, a gold bridge covering his front teeth. Bristling, I snarled at him, exposing my fangs.

I wasn't the only one snarling. The dog's growl suddenly caught his attention. She advanced on him, showing her teeth too, the growl getting louder and more intimidating. She inched forward, hair bristling, a hungry look in her eyes. The man was too scared to move, which was probably for the best. The dog would have given chase.

If I looked half as scary as that when I was pissed off, vamps like Marcello would beg for a stake through the heart. The power the Rottweiler was throwing off was awesome.

Slowly, I walked towards the dog. By now, she had the gold-toothed man almost cornered. He had his hand back on the door, ready to bolt back inside. Which he immediately did when I called out "Hey pretty puppy!" and she turned to stare me down.

Ears back, she cautiously padded her way towards me. At least she wasn't showing me her teeth. Progress!

I rested on my haunches to meet her on her level. She circled around me, leaving several feet between us. I ripped open the package of raw meat, and pulled out a chunk. I held my hand out, palm up, with the ground beef on top and waited.

Her nose twitched. She cautiously moved towards me, eyes never leaving my face. She tentatively sniffed at the meat and then snatched the whole piece into her mouth and swallowed. Just as fast, I grabbed another wad and held it out. She gobbled it up. We repeated this until she downed the whole pound of ground chuck.

"Sorry, girl," I said soothingly, wiping my hands down the sides of my pants. "I am all out."

I stood and walked back to the bike, and she followed along a few feet behind. I turned and looked at her. Her ears were now forward -- alert but friendly. Her panting almost looked like a smile.

I didn't want the sound of the bike to spook her, so I pushed it towards the garage without starting it. With a press of a button, the garage doors on the loading dock raised, and I walked the bike into the building. I could hear the tip tap of her nails come in behind me. I stopped with my back to her. She walked up to me and nuzzled my hand. We were friends.

Dropping to one knee, I stroked her head while looking her over. Her eyes were bright and alert. Even once she bulked up, she'd still be small for a Rottweiler. I checked her ears -- dirty but no mites. No fleas either -- the one bonus of living on the street in the winter months. Underneath the grime and matted fur, she was a beautiful dog. Too beautiful to leave on the street.

As if she were reading my thoughts, she pushed her wet nose into my face and licked. Then she turned and trotted back out the garage door and across the street to continue her patrol along the opposite building. She clearly had something on her mind, and didn't want to leave the street just yet. I was worried about her, but she made her choice. I'd pop out later and give her some steak.

I closed the garage door and made my way to my apartment. The building was quiet. Frankie was in the basement, well hidden from the sunlight. I unlocked my apartment door, and breathing deeply, entered my sanctuary of an apartment. After removing my ass-kicking boots, I walked to the living room, and stared at the mess of books on the floor. I grabbed my laptop off my desk and dropped down to the couch. Firing up my computer, I figured I would try good old Google translate. It was a reach, but I had nothing to lose for trying.

If Frankie were awake, he would have laughed me out of my apartment. There were many modern things he refused to believe in, and one of those things was the Internet. For all the tinkering he did with electronics and his spectacular ability to build just about anything, including my fabulous bike, his abhorrence of the World Wide Web was pretty shocking.

Once the site loaded, I opened to a random page in one of the old tomes. I pecked out C-O-Q-U-O-E and hit return. I blinked and a correction popped up. "Do you mean C-O-Q-U-O?" I clicked yes and a translation popped up. "Boil." It was Latin. Sort of.

DUH.

Frankie and I both missed the obvious. Of course, it wasn't Latin exactly. It was easy to misread it as something else.

I tried another word. C-I-C-U-O-A-T-E changed to C-I-C-U-A-T-E translated to Hemlock. Boil poison? Lovely. What the hell was I reading anyway? D-E-A-V-O-T-I-O-U? It was really "devotion," an incantation used to imbue the poison, apparently from the days of Caesar. These books belonged to my parents? That was weird.

I stuck a scrap of paper into the book to mark the page and stretched. The sun was low in the sky, ready to slide away to the horizon. I had my date with Max in a few hours, but needed to work off some aggression and clear my head. My little gym in the corner was calling to me. It was time to channel some vampire angst.

CHAPTER 15

Drenched in sweat, I pushed the weight up for the final rep of the bench press. Weight-training helped clear my mind, especially when I was frustrated.

I climbed on a chair to reach my pull up bar. "Control the negative" I reminded myself, through gritted teeth, at the top of the movement, and slowly lowered my body back down. Repeat. After 20 pull-ups, I dropped to the ground. Chugging water, I walked in circles to catch my breath. But my mind refused to slow down.

My lineage traced back to ancient Greece. My dad was a descendant of the Empusa, a demigoddess who seduced young men and sucked their blood. Since so many vampires had been vanquished over the years, particularly during the Victorian age when vampire folklore ran amok, there were not many left directly descended from the original vampires. This made my father one of the most powerful vampires in the world when he was alive. His powers apparently passed down to me, but would never be fully realized until I turned into a full vampire, which wouldn't happen until I was dead.

According to Dr. O, I was one of the few true vampire children in the world. Vampires are made, not born. So I was a freak phenomenon. I don't think my parents even considered that I would have vampire in me. With a human mom, it was hard to imagine that they thought I would be born anything but human.

My mom was a student at Brown University, a double major in religion and folklore, when she met my father. Being from Catemaco -- where there's a witch on every corner, and the supernatural is part of everyday life -- she was fascinated by him. According to Babe, my dad finally found love after searching for it for 700 years. They didn't think about the consequences of trying to live a traditional life. Who would expect that there would be consequences?

Could this be why someone wanted my parents--and me-- dead? I never asked Dr. O what happened to the few other vampire babies, and he never told me. I just assumed they lived their lives, died and were reborn as vampires. They either remained in the shadows or they were staked.

And how does my dad's knife tie into all this? Is Max right? Does Marcello have something to do with these murders? And the victims weren't vampires. Casper was a witch. It was possible the others were too. Was Marcello targeting witches? Vampires and witches hated each other. Maybe they were just grudge murders while he waited to off me.

I grabbed a jump rope and used the remote to turn up the music. While Flogging Molly vibrated off the walls, I exploded off the floor. After several months without Blood Ops, I was soft. I needed to get back into fighting shape. Frankie and I used to beat the crap out of each other daily. Based on the other night, I could hold my own with Marcello but I wasn't sure I could take him down.

I felt a hand on my shoulder, and with the speed of a puma, I swirled the rope around and hit the intruder in the chest, knocking him back. He leapt away, moving so fast that I lashed out again at a blurred outline, this time with a roundhouse kick that connected to his jaw.

He grabbed my foot on its way down and flipped me to the floor. "Nina, stop!"

"Ow!" I fell to the floor with a thud, landing hard on my back. "What are you doing, Frankie!"

"You need to learn how to lock your bloody door." He helped me to my feet, and then turned down the music.

I shrugged. "What do you want?"

"I wanted to make sure you were alright." He looked worried.

"When I left you at sunrise, the vomiting seemed to have stopped."

"I really don't remember too much." I mopped my sweaty face with a towel.

"Yeah, you were a regular Linda Blair," he said, punching at the heavy bag in the corner of the room. I hoped he didn't punch a hole through it.

"Babe's damn henbane." I had little recollection of drinking it, but I assumed that was the cause. "Guess it was good to barf that crap out."

"How's the head feel?" he asked.

"Fine, actually. Beyond 100 percent," I said. I was a little surprised about that, considering that I had been sick and blacked it out like a college kid on a bender.

"Good," Frankie said. He took a mock swing at me, and I ducked. "Score one for Babe's poison. Cure worse than disease and all that."

"And while you were lazing around in your coffin," I said, sending a punch out towards his chin, "I figured out the language in those books." My punch missed of course. Frankie was across the room before it even got close to landing.

"You know I don't sleep in a coffin." He reached out and grabbed me around the waist, flipping me onto my back without breaking a sweat. "So, are you going to share?"

"Latin-ish." I pushed up to a squat position.

Frankie roared with laughter at the "ish." I took advantage of his momentary mirth to sweep my leg under his feet, and down he went beside me on the mat.

"The Latin is old," I explained, still feeling a little smug. "So it's not the easiest Latin to recognize, but it's some form of Latin."

He shook his head. "I bet it's Etrusian." After living for half a century, Frankie knew a bunch of arcane languages, but this one had him stumped. "So, how did you figure that out?" Now he refused to get up, lounging on the mat.

"Google." The shit-eating grin on my face spread.

Frankie waved his hand dismissively. "I refuse to bow to the Google gods."

"Well ancient Etrusian is not going to help me destroy Marcello." I wanted to refocus on our task. "I don't know that I am strong enough to battle someone his age."

"You sure about that?" Frankie smiled, rubbing where I kicked his jaw.

"Frankie, I get some good shots at you, but I have never been able to take you down." I looked at him sideways. "It was the same with him the other night."

"What you need to do is train up." Frankie's voice was stern, but his look was mischievous.

I was halfway up from the floor when he pulled my feet out from under me. I went down in a heap. He was still lounging on the floor.

"No fair!" I growled while Frankie laughed at me. "I am a half-blood; not that quick."

"Nina, you have to learn to do it." He pulled me up to my feet. "Marcello doesn't give a shit if you're a half-blood. And the faster you can move away from him in a fight, the better."

I definitely saw that logic. But there was no way I could best a full vampire in the speed department.

"Try it," Frankie encouraged. "Look at me, and imagine coming at me at the speed of sound.

I screwed up my face as I looked at him.

"What's that?" he asked, copying my expression. "You look constipated."

"I can't do this," I said. I dropped my shoulders.

"No," Frankie said calmly, and then he tripped me again and moved to the other side of the room before I could even lash out at him. "You refuse to do this. You are a vampire, Nina. Stop being so

107

damn scared of it."

"I am *half* vampire, and I am *not* scared of it," I barked.

"You've always been scared of it," Frankie goaded me on. "Ever since you were a kid, you were petrified of it."

My face grew hot as my anger hit a boiling point. From the floor, I glared up at Frankie with such fury that even he stopped.

My eyes caught on a pile of over-sized art books on a bookshelf above him. I imagined the lot of them landing on his head.

In a split second, the heavy volumes slammed straight down on him, sending him off his feet. He landed on the floor with a loud crash, the books sprawled beside him.

My eyes were as large as saucers.

"What the fuck was that?" Frankie stared at me as he rubbed his head, looking at the bookshelf still attached firmly to the wall.

"I don't know." I shrugged. It was definitely weird. "Maybe I didn't install the book cases right."

We booth stood, and Frankie moved in on me. "You are such a girl."

His eyes flashed, and he gave me a fangy smile.

I crouched into position, ready to leap. He held up his hand.

"Condition," he said. "You have to be fast."

I rolled my eyes. It was enough for Frankie to get the first shot in, a kick right to the stomach. He knocked the wind out of me.

I back flipped to my feet and rushed at him, pushing my palm straight into his nose. I heard the satisfying crunch of bones breaking, and blood poured out.

Frankie looked up at me, but it wasn't Frankie anymore. He moved closer, his fangs glistening. His blue eyes blazed.

"Oh shit," was just about all I could gasp out. He was just inches from my face, and he grabbed my arms, crushing them against my sides, pulling me towards him. I started to squirm, my pulse pounding.

"Don't fight me," he begged. We went too far. He was losing control. I gulped in air and tried to calm down. I closed my eyes and willed him to stop.

Something heavy pushed into Frankie. He dropped me as he flew backwards across the room. He hung pinned against the opposite wall, arms and legs splayed, for about ten seconds before he dropped to the floor.

I stared at Frankie's crumpled body across the room. I had watched him turn vampy on me and wasn't sure what to expect now. He didn't move.

Crap. This was my best friend. I refused to be afraid of him. I crossed to his slumped form and knelt down beside him.

"Frankie?" I poked at him carefully.

His eyes popped open and he grabbed my shoulders and pushed me to the floor, pinning me down. He looked almost scared.

"What was that?" he held my shoulders for a second too long, his blue eyes, only a twinge of red remained, staring into mine. It made me uncomfortable, so I looked away. He released me and we both stood up.

"Time for a drink," I replied, wiping sweat off my face.

"No, what _was_ that?" he repeated.

"Why don't _you_ tell _me_ what that was!" I spat out. "You lost control, Frankie."

I walked to the fridge, grabbed a beer and popped the top open.

"I knew what I was doing." He was totally lying. "I had control the whole time. I was trying to scare you."

"Well it worked." I didn't want to fight with him but I knew there was no way he was in control of himself.

"What pinned me to the wall?" Frankie's eyes were intense.

"Did you feel it?"

"I thought that was you." I squinted at him and took a swig of my beer.

"No, no, my love," Frankie crossed his arms. "That was all you."

I leaned against the counter, watching him look at me with a curiosity I had never seen before. I wasn't sure I liked it.

He walked to me, and I caught him breathing in my scent. I pushed him away. "Don't sniff me!"

"Nina," his voice was measured, like he was explaining something to a defiant five-year-old. "That was most definitely you. I don't know what it was, but I think those may explain." He looked at the books that he had procured from Babe's attic. "Time to pay a visit to Auntie Babe."

"Don't be stupid," I huffed. "I am not running to Babe because you lost your shit. She'll hit the roof. Besides, I have a date. And I don't intend on breaking it."

"Date?" Frankie looked up. "With that FBI guy?"

"Maybe..." I felt my cheeks blaze again.

He shook his head. "Tell you what, I'll go visit with Auntie Babe, you enjoy your...date." He snorted.

What the hell was his problem?

"Frankie!" I yelled at his backside as he stalked to the door. He hesitated a minute, and then a rush of wind blew through the apartment as the door opened and closed quickly. I heard the dog bark, low and vicious, outside. Good. I hope she scared the crap out of him.

CHAPTER 16

My taut muscles finally relaxed when the hot spray of the shower hit my back. I closed my eyes and tilted my head back; water rushed over me. I grabbed my shampoo, and began to slowly work it into my hair.

I had a date, a real date. I hadn't been on a real date in, like, ever. Raised in the sheltered environment of Dr. O and an army base, I didn't even know about dating until I was allowed to assimilate into the outside world as an adult. I had had hook-ups, sure, but never a bona fide date.

But my mind kept wandering back to Frankie. Never mind that he went all fangy on me. Did I really push him into the wall like that? He was hanging in the air, there was no way I could have done that. Right? Unless I developed some weird superpower. The thought of it made me laugh out loud. Or was that why Marcello wanted me dead?

I forced it out of my mind. I didn't need Frankie's vamp out adding to my stress. I was looking forward to being completely and utterly human, even if it was only for one night.

I finished the shower and stepped out of the steam into a chilly bathroom. I gave a little shiver and wrapped myself in my fluffy towel. I slinked over to my giant armoire, threw open its doors and stared. Panic slammed into me like a brick. I had nothing to wear.

Yay for dating.

After 20 stressful minutes, I settled on a pair of fitted gray cargo pants and a form-fitting black sweater that scooped to the edge of my shoulders, just enough to show the outline of my upper back. I debated on the shoes. High-heeled ankle boots would finish the look. But I couldn't fit the knife into the fancy boots, and I didn't want to go out without it. I decided to wear a knife holster around my calf. It would be slightly uncomfortable, but I really didn't want to go out unarmed. I just hoped my feet would survive a night in those heels.

A touch of makeup, and a little product to give my hair a lift, and I was ready. And early. By a good half an hour. Crap. Thirty whole unencumbered minutes for my nerves to try to psych me out.

I sighed and walked to the fridge and extracted another beer. "Here's to liquid courage," I said. Then I popped off the cap, raised the bottle and took a swig.

With nothing left to keep me occupied, my mind began to wander. What if he asks those inevitable questions about childhood? How does one explain a vampire family? How does one explain being taught to fight all the shit that you don't believe in on a top-secret military base until the age of 18?

The front-door buzzer made me jump. He was early.

I took a deep breath and buzzed open the front door. His footsteps echoed down the hall and I leaned against the door, trying to calm my nerves. He knocked and I pulled the door open. His piercing green eyes caught mine for a split second. He was damn good-looking. His slightly overgrown dark blond hair curled down the nape of his neck. I could see his muscular chest outlined under a crisp, blue, button-down shirt.

"Did you want a beer before we go?" I asked, awkwardly aware that I was still holding my bottle.

Max smiled. "We'll be late for our dinner reservations." He took the bottle from me, winked and raised it to his lips. I suddenly felt very warm. If we didn't leave soon, we probably never would.

"Then we'd better go," I muttered, and reached to take the bottle back.

He grabbed my hand, and pulled me to him. I bristled, my back tensed at the sudden movement. He pulled me tighter, and leaned down to kiss me, his tongue slowly tracing my lips as he pulled away. My body relaxed into his, and I smiled at the pressure I felt against my thigh. Glad I wasn't the only one thinking about skipping dinner.

"You look beautiful," he whispered into my ear as we slowly pulled apart.

"Oh, you!" I mocked punched him in the arm. Oh God. So dorky.

I turned tail and clipped to the kitchen to leave the beer bottle on the counter. I picked up my leather jacket and purse, and shook my head to clear it a bit.

A quick visual sweep of the apartment, and we were out the door. Our footsteps echoed down the hallway. He pushed the building door open, holding it gallantly as I passed. I spared a glance at the building across the street. The dog was gone. I hoped she found someplace warm to go.

The air outside was bitterly cold, and it felt good against my flushed cheeks. Max opened the door to the passenger side of his black Suburban, and I slipped into the leather seat. I watched him walk around the car, and get into the driver's side. He started the ignition and looked over at me.

"We are going to have a real date," he said matter-of-factly. "Right now, I want to go back inside your place and throw you on that bed and rip your clothes off. But I think we need to have a real date first."

I grinned. I really would not have been disappointed to bypass the date thing and go straight to the clothes ripping. But his tone was so charming, I had to go along with it. "So where are we going?"

"A surprise," he said as he pulled away from the curb.

Max maneuvered the car through the narrow streets and then eased onto the highway. We were traveling south, out of the city. I smiled slightly and stared out the window at the blur of cars we raced past. I guess FBI agents didn't get pulled over for speeding.

There wasn't much south of Providence -- a few malls, lots of chain restaurants and, eventually, the beach. Max didn't strike me as an Applebee's sort of a guy, and of course there was that surfboard still laid out in the back. I didn't need to be a super-sleuth to figure out our destination.

"I'm not dressed for December surfing," I teased. "I hope you brought along a wet suit for me."

Max grinned, the oncoming headlights illuminating his handsome face. His smile made my heart melt a little.

"You," he said, reaching for my hand, "should consider a career as a detective. You certainly kick ass like a cop."

We sat in a weird, uncomfortable silence for a minute. Hurrah for first dates!

"So," I cleared my throat. "Are you from Southern or Northern California? You strike me as more San Diego man."

"So close!" Max laughed. "Yes, I am from Southern California, but the City of Angels. I grew up in Long Beach but now live in LA proper."

"Ah, Long Beach," I smiled. "Love the airport." Not a lie. I loved the fabulously retro Long Beach Airport, with its outdoor luggage carousel. The few times I few into Long Beach, I was transported to 1950s Cuba.

"You fly to Long Beach?" Max laughed. "Are you from Las Vegas or something? That's the only reason to fly in or out of Long Beach. The cheap Vegas flights."

That caught me off my guard. Where I grew up -- that one could be tricky.

"I spent time out West," I said vaguely. "So, how long have you been a G-man?"

"About 15 years," he said, not seeming to notice the abrupt switch in conversation.

"Like it?" I asked.

"It has its moments," he replied. "Like right now. Wouldn't be here with you if it weren't for the Bureau."

"They must miss you in LA," I mused.

"Not enough to call me back yet." He sighed. "Actually, I am pretty sure they are happy to have me across the country for a few weeks."

I knew he was on loan, but figured it would be longer than a few weeks.

"So when are you going back?" I hoped I sounded casual.

"When the case wraps." He eased the car onto an exit ramp. "I'd like to have it cleaned up in a few weeks time."

"Getting close, then?"

Max just shrugged. I should have felt relieved that he would be out of the state so quickly. His sticking around could complicate things. But it was hard to ignore that my stomach suddenly dropped.

"We have reached our destination," Max announced grandly.

I looked out the window and squeaked. We were across from the Coast Guard House, the most spectacular restaurant in the state. It overlooked the ocean. Just before storms, magnificent waves crash into the windows that flank the dining room. It's the most thrilling place to be. And the impending nor'easter meant that the ocean would be at its most merciless. I could hear waves pounding into the rocks already, the roaring water as heart stopping as a rock concert.

The freezing wind caught me off guard as I got out of the car and I shivered. "Welcome to New England," I yelled to Max over the noise of wind and waves. His California good looks appeared stunned by the brutal cold.

We rushed into the nearly empty restaurant and were guided to a table by the expanse of windows overlooking the ocean, which was churning and frothing right below.

The view of the powerful Atlantic Ocean was breathtaking. The sound of the water the smashing the rocks made me feel exhilarated. I always found the power of the ocean thrilling, which was why living in land-locked Nevada didn't agree with me.

"Incredible," I whispered.

"Isn't it?" Max looked a little awestruck himself. "I am happy Rhode Island is by the ocean. It's damn cold, but it's got waves."

I grinned at him, and felt almost giddy. So this is what a date felt like! It was pretty nice, I had to admit.

A waiter came over with a bottle of Sauvignon Blanc. Max expertly tested the wine, giving it his approval. The waiter poured out two glasses, and I inhaled its crisp scent, trying to relax my grin so I didn't look like a simpleton.

"So...." Max cleared his throat. "Tell me about your time in Las Vegas. Were you a showgirl?"

I choked. My mouthful of wine sprayed all over the table, and Max.

"Oh! God!" I gasped and wiped up the mess with a napkin. "I am so sorry." I winced a little as he wiped at his face.

"I was too young to be a showgirl." I tried another gulp of the wine, and this one actually found its way down.

"Ah, so you were raised in Vegas!" Max looked almost smug. Clearly he loved piecing together a mystery, like a good federal agent.

I gave in. "I was raised near Vegas."

"And what are you doing in Rhode Island?" Max pushed gently, as a waiter placed two steaming bowls of clam chowder in front of us. I guess he ordered beforehand, and for me too.

"I have family here... Babe... We both own the bar... Together..." My voice went hollow.

"And your parents, are they still in Vegas?" Max didn't seem to notice my awkward stammering. He just dug into his chowder.

"My parents..." I hesitated. "My parents are dead."

Max looked up suddenly. "I am so sorry."

"It's okay," I said, shaking off the thought. "You didn't know. I was very young when it happened. My aunt tried to raise me on her own, but she was young herself. So I was sent to live with a family friend."

The carefully rehearsed story came out of my mouth easily, the familiarity soothing. And it wasn't a complete lie. The broad strokes were true. Many kids have lost their parents and been sent to live with friends of the family. I just left out the part about the friend being a government operative on a top-secret military base that dealt with supernatural crimes.

"That must have been terrible for you." It was Max's turn to flail around. Dead parents can be such a conversation killer, especially on the first date.

"That's life." I smiled. "What about you? What made you join the FBI?"

"Living with gang violence," Max explained. "Long Beach is a rough city with a lot of gang activity, and growing up in that environment...I knew from a young age that I just wanted to stop it."

"That's pretty righteous, Max." I was impressed. "And now you are the authority on gang violence. So then gangs are here? In Rhode Island?"

"Looks that way." Max looked out over the water.

"Now say it like you mean it," I prodded.

He laughed. "That obvious?"

I nodded.

"Honestly, I am not sure," Max played with his napkin. "You have gangs here, absolutely. Every place does. But I am not convinced that these murders are the work of a gang. Or, I am not convinced *yet*."

A steaming plate of mussels was placed in front of me. I inhaled the delicious smell of white wine and garlic. My eyes widened and I went at them with gusto.

"It's refreshing to take a woman out for dinner and have her actually eat." Max looked amused.

I popped a perfectly cooked muscle into my mouth. "Wait until it's time for dessert!"

Max reached across the table and grabbed my hand. Startled, the flush from my face moved slowly down my body.

Dates were kind of fun. I would have almost felt badly about what I missed over the past 33 years, but I was too content, enjoying this moment of pure normalcy. I was just a regular woman out on a date with a super hot guy, not this weird vampire/human mutant that was supposed to save the world from stuff no one believed in anyway. Being normal was...simple.

Then something out of the window caught my eye. Bile rose in my throat, and I closed my eyes and silently willed what I thought I just saw away.

After a small shake of my head, I opened them again. My heart raced as my adrenaline surged.

"Oh crap," I blurted before I could stop myself. Max's head snapped around, following my gaze.

Marcello. He was standing on top of a rock in the middle of the water. He looked like he was calling the fury of the ocean by the movements of his arms. The waves became more violent, and a huge one came barreling towards their window. Marcello's shrill laughter pierced the air.

"He can't do that!" While he could influence the weather, he certainly could not call upon the sea to do his bidding.

I wasn't sure if I said that out loud. I couldn't hear anything over the crush of the waves.

My vampire instincts took over. Bounding over the table, I grabbed Max by the collar, pulling him with me as I bolted to the front of the restaurant. A massive wave crashed through the window, shattering glass everywhere. I threw us both down on the floor, behind the wall of the coatroom to block the wave's impact. Water rushed over us and then receded quickly.

Spitting out seawater, I sat up and looked over to where we were sitting. The window was shattered. The table and chairs, along with the poor waiter, were swept out to sea, leaving a gaping void over the craggy rocks. I vaguely felt Max grab me from behind and drag me out of the restaurant as another wave came thundering towards us.

CHAPTER 17

Max hauled me like a sack of potatoes out of the Coast Guard House. He didn't put me down until we were well across the street, and at that point, he dumped me rather unceremoniously on my ass.

He stared at me. "What the fuck was that?"

I shook my head slightly. I was about a half of a second away from panicking. Marcello was out there somewhere, and he had some weird control over the weather and the ocean.

I had no idea how much Max had seen. Marcello definitely saw me with Max. The expression on his face made it completely clear how much he would enjoy killing both of us.

I stood up and started pacing around the parking lot, oblivious to the fact that it was brutally cold and I was drenched in seawater. My purse. My leather jacket. Those were swept out to sea. Shit. I loved that leather jacket. How was I going to replace that leather jacket? Dr. O, I had to call Dr, O. He'd know what to do. I reached for my phone.

"CRAP!" I shouted. It was in my purse.

Max grabbed me by the arms and spun me to face him.

"I need to know you are alright." His voice was calm but forceful. "I have to go back and see if I can...help."

I gripped his arm for a second. My nails sunk into his flesh. Was it safe for him to go back in there? Sirens were approaching. First responders would be here soon. I nodded.

"Stay here!" he shouted over his shoulder as he ran back into the restaurant.

The wind picked up. There was a flash of lightening, followed by a huge crack. Then, someone tackled me from behind, sending me five feet forward, and then pushing me face-down into the pavement. I felt my skin tear away from my palms and heard the fabric on my shirt rip, as the road burned white hot into my flesh.

I pushed up and flung the weight off of me. I jumped to my feet and turned, ready to strike, and came face to face with Frankie.

I lashed out at him. "What are you doing?"

"Saving your life," he pointed behind him. A tree branch the size of a small car was laying where I had been standing.

"You. You?" I asked, shock still coursing through me. "Wait. Were you *following* me?"

"Nina, Love, this is not the time to discuss it." Frankie looked up as another crack of lightening hit the light pole just across the street from us, plunging the area into total darkness, save the pink and orange sparks arcing up from the transformer.

"Nina!" Frankie was yelling now, to be heard over the surf that began crashing again, rising over the sea wall. "You need to do something!"

"Me? What can I do? Marcello's out on some rock in the middle of the friggin' ocean, Frankie!" I could see the first responders running into the Coast Guard House. I didn't think the building would hold up if another wave hit.

"I need you to trust me on this one, Nina!" Frankie yelled above the howl of the wind as its strength pulled me several feet towards the sea wall. He grabbed my arm and pulled me back. "What you did to me tonight, you need to do it to him right now!"

"What are you talking about?" I gripped my arm around Frankie's waist to keep from blowing back towards the water again.

Sleet was now driving down from the sky, piercing into my skin like a thousand sharp points of needles.

"Please, Nina! Trust me!" Frankie cupped my face and looked deeply into my eyes. "Trust yourself."

I broke away from him and sank to my knees. I thought of Max and all the other first responders still in the building, it teetering on the edge of the sea. Fear welled up inside me. I closed my eyes and saw Marcello, standing on that rock, calling up another wave.

"Don't you dare," I growled.

Marcello just laughed, as though he could hear and see me, and then released more of the ocean's fury. Freezing cold seawater crashed down on me, chocking me, pulling me back with it. I felt Frankie's strong grip on my ankle, keeping me with him. He anchored onto a cement post with his other arm. As the water receded, I heard voices rise in panic from the restaurant.

In my mind's eye, I witnessed Marcello's triumph. I could hear his laughter. I could taste his elation. And now I was pissed.

"Ventus pulsus eradico," I began chanting. "Ventus pulsus eradico...." I had no idea what I was doing, or why I was doing it, but I couldn't stop.

The wind began to whip again, and the trees around us cracked. I let out a guttural scream that normally would have scared the hell out of me. I felt like I was locked in a trance. I screamed again, and the gulls mimicked my cries. A cacophony of screams blew over the ocean.

That wiped Marcello's smug expression right off his face. It was his turn to be shocked, maybe even scared. The water began to churn and swell around him. This time I was the one harnessing the power of the ocean. He raised his hands over his ears trying to block out my rage. My primal screams echoed again and again, the water frothing as I conjured a 30-foot swell. Marcello spun off the rock and disappeared in the wind. I dropped the wave with a crash and slumped into myself.

The water receded back into the ocean. Everything was suddenly, inexplicably, still.

After a minute, I opened my eyes and saw Max running towards me. He stopped dead several feet away, staring at me. He looked horrified.

Still kneeling on the pavement, I quickly glanced around. Frankie was gone.

"You should take me home now," I said softly. I was freezing, soaking wet and exhausted. I didn't know if I could stand on my own and used the side of a car to pull myself to my feet. I leaned against it, shaking.

"Yeah." Max walked slowly towards me. "That's probably a good idea."

Max steadied me and we moved towards his car. He dropped my arm when he saw I could stand on my own. The silence between us grew as ice cold as my skin. I turned the events of the past few minutes over and over again in my mind. I had no idea how to explain to Max what had happened. Would he believe it was a couple of rogue waves?

I caught him looking at me, a strange mix of curiosity, confusion and disgust. I suspected that the rogue wave idea wasn't going to fly.

It was only until we were in the relative safety of the car, with the heat blasting, that Max let loose.

"I'm gonna ask you again: what the fuck was that?" He didn't look scared anymore. He looked pissed. Very pissed.

I didn't know what to say, so I kept my mouth shut. The tires screeched as Max pulled out of the lot. I closed my eyes, and almost wished I was still locked in battle with Marcello out on that rock. Somehow that fight felt easier than the one we were about to have.

Max was weaving in and out of traffic, one eye on the road, the other on the rear view mirror. I was checking my side mirror every once in a while too. I wondered if we were being followed, either by Frankie or Marcello.

"You realize we are running away from a crime scene," he spat, breaking the silence, his voice angry.

I wasn't ready to agree that it was a crime scene just yet.

122

"Are you going to tell me what happened?" Max asked through gritted teeth. "Or do you want me to believe that I lost my mind?"

I breathed in sharply. Guess he saw what I didn't want him to see. I closed my eyes and pressed my fingers into my temples.

"Do you want to tell me who that guy was? And what the hell you were screeching out there?"

My silence sent Max into conversation overdrive.

"Are you going to tell me that was Pig Latin?" he shouted. "You know there are these bizarre murders happening all over this town, and you refuse to tell me what the fuck that weirdo scenario was back there?" Max was on a roll now. He came face to face with an inexplicable tragedy, and simply walked away. I think his talking, angry as it was, kept him from going into shock. "Makes me think that all these bizarre things are linked. And maybe *you* have something to do with them."

More silence. I couldn't answer him. I didn't know what to say.

"Do you?" Max challenged me.

I let out a deep breath. "I am sorry Max, but this is complicated."

I watched his strong jaw tighten. I knew it wasn't the answer he wanted to hear. But there was no way he'd understand the truth. And, right now, there was no way I could explain it. I had no idea what happened out there. Marcello was not capable of conjuring a natural disaster. And I should never have been able to stop him like that.

"You know what, Nina?" he spat out at me. "FUCK YOU!"

I cringed. This was not going well.

"Max," I responded evenly. "It's better if you leave this alone. Please. It's my fault. I should have never come with you tonight. I think it's best if we just stop this."

"Maybe it's a little too late for that," he said through his teeth, still gritted tightly.

I shifted uncomfortably in my seat. What if it was too late? Would Marcello just ignore him now? If Marcello was behind these murders, then Max was hunting him as well. Of course, hunting him for entirely different reasons, but hunting all the same.

And what would Max do if he caught Marcello? Handcuff him and read him his rights? Do I warn him to bring some Holy Water and a wooden stake to work along with his gun and bulletproof vest?

Frayed nerves and a mental image of Max, Vampire Hunter -- complete with a chain of garlic around his neck -- sent me into a fit of inappropriate giggles. I tried to suppress them with a coughing fit.

Max looked at me sideways. He pulled off at the next exit, and stopped at the side of a quiet road.

He took a breath. "Nina," he said, his voice was calm, but I could hear his heart racing under his shirt and he refused to look at me. "No matter what you tell me, I will believe you."

His sympathy was forced, hoping to coax an explanation out of me.

I felt my eyes well up. What could I possibly tell him? I closed my eyes, shook my head and willed the tears away.

Max slammed his hand on the steering wheel.

I jumped.

"Damn it," he said in frustration. "I think I deserve an explanation. Don't you?"

I bit my lip. I wanted to tell him. I had carried around this secret my entire life, with the safety of Dr. O's protective circle being the only companionship I knew. I longed to tell him everything. The family I was born into, how I was orphaned, where Babe sent me to live and why. But it was such an extraordinary tale that he'd probably drive me to the nearest mental hospital and have me committed.

Vampires, Druids, demons, ghosts. These were the stuff of horror films and best-selling books. They were built up in modern fairy tales. They were mythical creatures that were given Hollywood sex appeal, a mystique that made them even more dangerous. When vampires are romanticized heroes, a blood-thirsty and vile beast like Marcello was exceedingly treacherous.

I looked at Max. He didn't look angry. He looked hurt. "Please, Max," I whispered, reaching for his arm. "I need you to trust me on this."

He pushed my hand away. Shaking his head, his face shifted to pure anger. Why should he trust me anyway? I only almost got him swept out to sea.

CHAPTER 18

I felt lightheaded and wobbly, as if I were drunk on champagne, when I stepped out of Max's Suburban. I wasn't sure if it was from his NASCAR-inspired driving or the impromptu tsunami Marcello and I blew through the Coast Guard House that left me so unsteady. Probably both.

Since I spent the ride with my eyes closed, I needed a minute for my sight to adjust (not to mention my legs) to the unfamiliar surroundings. We were in a parking garage. As I stumbled behind Max, blindly following him to the exit, I felt a weak surge of energy grow stronger with each step. I came to a dead stop when I realized that we were in the parking garage of the Biltmore.

Max, aware that my staggering had abruptly stopped, turned to look at me finally. His exasperated expression softened only a little as he took in my shivering, wet-dog appearance.

"You okay?" he asked gruffly. He was still pissed.

I squinted my eyes at him and gritted my teeth, mostly to keep them from chattering. "You can just take me home."

"I'll take you home, but I have to pick up a few things first."

I crossed my arms in front of my chest and raised my brows. It was all I could do to not stomp my foot like a petulant child. He didn't budge.

I weighed my options. I could walk home, but I was still soaked through with seawater, it was cold, and it was one long-ass walk. I could wait right where I was, but being alone in desolate parking garages at night Downcity was never a good idea. Or I could deal with the psychic onslaught that was exploding out of the hotel.

I sighed and willed myself forward, bracing myself against the creeptastic energy that was about to overpower me.

Max yanked open the door to the back lobby, and the rush of energy almost knocked me on my ass. I hesitated. Holding my breath I stepped over the threshold. Immediately, I heard whispers of spirits desperate to communicate. I was trying to shut down my mind, but it wasn't going to be easy.

We made it into the lobby proper, and a grand staircase leading up to the broken glass elevator, once the crown jewel of a magnificent hotel, loomed in front of me. The polished brass was tarnished green. The ghost of a bride, her white wedding dress soaked in sticky red blood, repeatedly tossed herself down the stairs.

I looked over at Max. He charged up the stairs, seeing nothing out of the ordinary. Apparently, I was the only one getting an eyeful. I slowly stepped past the unlucky bride. She halted her repeated tumble and reached a blood-stained hand out to me. She opened her mouth, her teeth cracked and broken like a delicate porcelain teacup that dropped to the floor. An otherworldly moan escaped from her mouth, then her lips fought to form the word "help."

I shook my head at her and whispered, "I can't." A mournful-looking bellboy with a gunshot hole in the center of his forehead pushed her from behind. Down the stairs she went.

His smile at me was devoid of humor. The fashion of his bellboy outfit was clearly from the opening days of the hotel. He had dark hair and olive skin. He was handsome once. I guessed he was around sixteen when he was killed.

"The Mayor would like to see you in his office," the bellboy said. His accent was thick. I placed it as Italian, which made sense. Providence experienced an influx of Italian immigrants in the 1920s.

"What Mayor?" I demanded in a hushed tone.

He turned and walked back up the stairs. His brains leaked out from under his cap. The bullet that killed him must have exploded. I stared at him, horrified. This seeing dead people thing was no fun at all.

A cold hand grabbed my elbow and turned me around. I did a double take as I faced Max. His tanned skin took on a greenish cast. His eyes sank into their sockets. He looked thinner, almost gaunt.

"Why are you talking to yourself?" he asked, steering me by my elbow up the stairs and towards a floor of guest rooms.

I tried to wrench my arm out of his grip, which was unnaturally strong. For a split second I wondered if I could take him down if I needed to. "Where are you taking me?"

Damn it, he was possessed. The hotel was feeding energy to the ghost that captured him, making him stronger. I wondered if it was also killing Max.

"We're going up to my room for a minute," he said in an odd monotone. "I told you before that I have to pick up some things before we go."

I dug in my heels. "I will not go any further," I growled softly, hoping to keep the ghoulish things from overhearing.

Max raised his hand and tried to knock a blow to my face. My vampire reflexes kicked in, and I blocked him quickly but not as easily as I hoped. His movements were stiff but strong. He was like a living zombie. Whatever possessed him was clearly in control. Max was unreachable.

I twisted his arm around his back and, now behind him, sent a forceful knee into his kidneys so that he knew I meant business.

"We are walking out of here now!" I reached around him and snatched his cell phone from his pocket. No bars. Dammit.

I pushed Max back down the stairs, one more time past the suicide bride. A wisp of air rushed past me. The bellboy blocked us in the middle of the staircase.

"The mayor will see you now," he intoned.

"I'm busy." As much as I didn't like it, I walked through him with Max in front of me. A feeling of cold slime encased my body. It

128

made a weird sucking noise as I pushed both Max and myself through his ethereal form.

Another rush of wind, and the bellboy was in front of me again. "He doesn't like to be kept waiting," he warned.

I had only made it down five steps.

"I'm a busy lady. He needs to make an appointment first," I said. I pushed through the cold slime, once again coming out the other end in a giant "thwack."

Another rush of air, but I was already down on the ground floor and rushing Max through the lobby. Frightened tourists flitted around nervously, eying the unsavory characters walking through the lobby in various states of mania or undress or both. A prostitute wearing a PVC latticework dress and not much else put on her best sexy face as I rushed past. It was Max's turn to dig in his heels, and I smacked right into him.

"Max..." she purred, slipping her arms around his neck.

She *knew* him? Oh man. I had to get him away from this hotel.

I shoved her backwards, and her eyes flashed red. Her tongue lashed out towards me, green and forked. I barely dodged it.

The door to the street swung open with the arrival of a group of rowdy drunks singing what sounded like a dirty sea shanty. I caught Max by the scruff of his neck, and pushed him out the door. He went airborne and splat-landed face down on the sidewalk. I grabbed him by the middle and hauled him up while the drunks applauded. I shoved him head first into the back of a taxi.

"Wickenden Street. Babe's on the Sunnyside," I barked at the driver and shoved my hands into Max's front pockets looking for cash. Max was pretty out of it; he looked half asleep. But the green tint was starting to slip away from his complexion and he was beginning to look at lot less gaunt.

He grabbed my hand as I stumbled through his pockets. "What are you doing?" He was groggy. "Where the hell are we?"

"I need money for the cab," I explained calmly as I felt gravity shift a bit. Great. The driver was taking us up College Hill. He thought we were loaded and was trying to scam a larger fare. I slammed on the plastic partition. "You took the long way, asshole!"

He just grinned and shrugged.

"Why are we in a cab?" Max groaned as he rubbed his head. He probably felt hung over and slightly carsick. Having your body possessed will do that to you.

"How much do you remember?" I held my breath. If the possession affected his short-term memory, maybe I could get myself out of this.

"We were having dinner and then you...*You*!" His eyes almost bugged out his head.

So much for forgetting. I exhaled slowly. "Right, well, you blacked out, and now we are in a cab."

"What did you do to me?" he demanded.

I was losing my patience. "I *saved* your ass, that's what I did."

"Where are you taking me?" he asked anxiously.

"Got it!" I huffed and sat back, a wad of cash in my hand. "We are going to Babe's."

He looked startled for a second and reached down to his ankle. He pulled out a small gun from a holster, checked it and held it in his lap.

"You brought a *gun* on a *date*?" Well this was insulting.

His eyes narrowed. "Apparently, I need a gun around you."

Technically I could see where he was coming from. I did have a knife planted in the same general location. I didn't want to tell him the gun would do him no good.

"Put that thing away," I grumbled as the taxi pulled up in front of Babe's. I dug through Max's wad of cash looking for just enough to cover the fare and a crappy tip. I hated being scammed like a tourist.

I glanced at the digital clock in the taxi's dashboard. It was 11:48PM. The door to Babe's swung open, and a burst of Irish folk music preceded a group of college kids on their way out. Looked like Babe was trying to close up early anyway.

Max still looked pissed but followed me into the bar. The gun was now in his pocket, but his hand was still on it. We walked in on Babe and Dr. O doing a weird jig behind the kegs, while Alfonso laughed. They looked like they were having a ball. It was time for us to be the party poopers. Their eyes went wide with disbelief when they saw us. We still weren't completely dried out.

Babe reached for a remote to shut the music off, and she turned on the overhead lights. "We're closed!" she yelled. The few remaining customers stared in shock.

"It's not even midnight!" Someone protested.

Babe shot him a look. He slammed down the rest of his beer, and nodded at her. "Goodnight, ma'am."

We sure could clear a room. Within minutes, the place emptied. Only Alfonso remained in his corner, sipping a whiskey.

Babe turned the lock on the door, drew the shades, and looked at me. "Are you okay?"

I shrugged.

"What about him?" she nodded at Max, who was sitting at a table in the corner with Dr. O.

"Not sure." I shrugged again. "He's been staying at the Biltmore."

She raised her eyebrows and crossed her arms. "What happened?"

I shook my head. "Marcello.... Babe, I never saw anything like it. It was like he was controlling the ocean."

Babe shifted uncomfortably. I told her the story, about Marcello on the rocks, and the waves crashing into the restaurant, and about how I threw the waves back into him seemingly with just my mind. I went on to explain the bizarre stop at the Biltmore, and how Max had been possessed, and not for the first time. I shuddered, and she pulled out a bottle of the good tequila from under the bar and

131

poured out two shots, one for each of us.

The tequila burned its way down my throat. The heat from the drink felt good. I was still cold from the mess of a night. And I seemed to shake less with the alcohol.

"Lochlan!" she called out over her shoulder. "It's time."

"Upstairs," she ordered.

I followed her, with Max and Dr. O behind us. Alfonso intercepted Max, offering to buy him a drink first. We trudged into the back room and up a small staircase to Babe's apartment above the bar.

Babe's apartment had the architectural flourishes typical of the historic buildings in the neighborhood. Built-ins and ornate woodwork, along with sloping large-planked wood floors made the place feel comfortably old.

The staircase from the bar led to the back door of the apartment, which opened to a hallway before the kitchen. A long, butcher-block counter ran along its length. It was filled with herbs under grow lights. The hallway led to her kitchen, with copper pots hanging from the rack overhead. Apart from a toaster oven and coffee maker, Babe's lit Veladoras was the only item on the kitchen counter. The kitchen led out to a combined dining and living room on one end, and two bedrooms on the other.

Babe motioned us into the living room, which was filled with rough-hewn wood furniture and other antiques, along with a big comfy couch piled high with afghan blankets. I stood stiffly by the fireplace, aware that I was still pretty wet, as Dr. O kindled a fire.

Babe followed us in, carrying a clean tank top, black yoga pants and an enormous blue plaid flannel shirt. She handed them to me without a word, and I headed off to the bathroom to change.

The overhead light in the bathroom was unforgiving. I looked pale and tired. Dark circles surrounded my eyes and drips of mascara had dried along my cheeks. I pulled off my salt water-stiff clothes. The shirt was ruined, torn to shreds along the left shoulder and down the right side by my abdomen. I examined some fresh bruises, and then pulled on the soft cotton tank and yoga pants. The bruises would be gone by the morning, but the scar along my neck was still red and angry. I ran my finger on its edge and flinched. It still burned.

I rinsed my face, rubbing at the dried mascara. My hair hung lank and snared, like the start of dreadlocks. I considered rinsing it out in the sink, but the sound of Babe's teakettle whistling caught my attention. I could use a cup of something hot. I pulled on a pair of warm wool socks, gathered up my wet clothes and headed into the kitchen, where I placed my boots on the radiator to dry. I neatly folded my salvageable clothes and placed them on the table. I mourned my shirt and dropped it in the trash.

"Go in the living room," Babe said. She poured steaming water from the kettle into a teapot. "I'll be right there."

I skulked back to the living room. Frankie arrived while I was cleaning up. He and Dr. O were talking in hushed tones by the fireplace.

"Hey," I gave a little wave as I plopped, exhausted, onto the couch. I slipped an afghan over my shoulders. I wanted to rest my head on the arm of the couch, but knew I would fall asleep in an instant.

Frankie sat beside me and pulled the blanket tighter around my shoulders, looking intently at the scar. His fingers touched it gently. The scar ignited again, fire surging through it. I shuddered and instinctively pushed his hand away. Frankie nodded at Dr. O. He gave my hand a squeeze.

Babe walked into the room, balancing a tray filled with a teapot, mugs, and a plate piled high with hastily prepared sandwiches. She poured out the tea and passed the mugs around. My fingers curled around the hot mug as peppermint steam filled up my nose. I started to relax.

Then I noticed that Babe, Dr. O and Frankie were all looking at me intently. If felt like an intervention.

"What?" I picked up a sandwich and took a bite. Ham and cheese.

"Nina, we need to talk," Babe said gently, motioning for Frankie to move so she could sit down next to me. Dr. O nodded encouragement at both of us, as Frankie moved back to the fireplace, shifting uncomfortably from foot to foot.

I shrank back a little. "About?" This felt weird.

"About your mom...." She twisted her lips.

"And my dad?" I finished for her.

"No, about your mom." Babe held her breath for a minute. "And me..."

"Am I going to need the tequila for this?" I squinted. Frankie nodded and bolted into the kitchen. I heard his heavy boots clomp down the stairs to the bar.

"Nina, honey, I didn't want to say anything until I was sure," she began. She twisted her moonstone ring around on her finger. "Okay, there is no other way to do this than just tell you. Your mom...and me...well...we're witches, dear."

I blinked. "Witches. Like broomsticks? And pointy hats?"

Frankie returned and placed the tequila bottle and four shot glasses on the table. He poured out shots.

Babe sighed. "Now, Nina, that's like saying Frankie here is Dracula."

He raised his eyebrows and smiled just enough to show his fangs. Yeah, he could be a bit of a cliché.

"Seriously? And you didn't tell me because?" I crossed my arms and glared at them.

Babe sighed again and looked at Dr. O. "You can blame me for that, Nina."

Dr. O sat on the coffee table, across from Babe, making sure to keep some distance between us. "I wanted to see if you had the gene first," Babe continued. "We weren't sure, with the vampire gene so pronounced in you, that the witch DNA would manifest. We really did not think you could carry both and survive."

"That's a shitload of power in that little body, Nina," Frankie offered enthusiastically as he raised his tequila shot. "Cheers!"

"And that's exactly why we didn't think it was possible," Dr. O chimed in, giving Frankie a dirty look.

"And now you think that it can...because?" I sipped the tequila.

I felt a little nauseated and lightheaded by the news, so slamming down the shot was out of the question. Unfortunately.

Babe reached over to me and gently touched the scar on my neck. "Because of this. You heal rapidly, Nina, but the knife? The scar? You were struck by a witch's blade. That this scar isn't healing tells me that the witch in you has manifested."

I shook my head. "I don't get it. Why would this knife affect me any different than any other? You can buy the damn thing at the botanica Downcity. They sold one to Max! And he's no witch. Or wizard. Or warlock. Or whatever."

I finished the shot of tequila. Frankie dutifully poured another.

"Believe it or not, on a molecular level, witch DNA is stronger than vampire's," Dr. O said, putting his hands over Babe's. She was shaking. "That your body cannot heal the knife wound is the witch DNA rising to the surface."

Plus," Frankie jumped in, "when I told Dr. O about our sparring match, that pretty much sealed the deal. Nina, you were fighting me with your witch power, not your vampire power. How else could you pin me to a wall without touching me?"

"So those books in the attic...." I trailed off. My eyes felt as wide as saucers.

Babe nodded. "Those are our family's Grimoires."

"Our family's what?" I asked.

"Grimoires. It's our books of magic, passed down through the generations. I hid them away after your mother died."

God, this was so weird. "So, Auntie, you are no longer...witchy?"

Babe laughed softly. "I am still a witch, Nina. I just practice simple, easy spells. I don't want to attract attention."

"Attention. Right." I pounded the second shot back, and motioned at Frankie to refill my glass.

"Remember how Christina Tucci broke out in that rash when she refused to pay her brother's bar tab?" Babe nodded knowingly.

"That's a good hex. I have to remember to teach you that one."

My circuits were overloading. I dropped my head in my hands. I was a living vampire and a witch. My Aunt Babette was apparently a witch, able to cause embarrassing rashes and fell vampires. I was so far removed from normal.

Frankie perched next to me on the arm of the couch and gave my shoulder a squeeze. "For the record, I think it's cool. And I say that knowing full well you could probably kill me without a wooden stake."

"So there's a rainbow in all this?" I rolled my eyes.

Frankie grinned.

"Do I get a wand?" I asked sarcastically.

"No," Babe sighed. "You know vampires are stereotyped. Why would witches be any different? No wands, no pointy hats. Definitely no broomsticks. Please, I don't need you falling off the roof thinking my kitchen broom can zoom you down the block."

"OK," I sighed, "So I am a witch. Can we move on now?"

"Not quite," Dr. O replied. He looked deep in thought. "Marcello is here, and we think he's being assisted by witches. As a vampire, he should not have been able to touch that blade."

"Wait? Vampires can't touch the blade?" I asked. "How can I touch my dad's? How could he have touched it?"

"His was spelled so vampires could," Babe explained.

"How?" I pushed.

"We don't know." Dr. O stared at Babe. "But a witch must have spelled Marcello's blade."

"So those two women he was with the other night were probably witches," I mused, my brain beginning to kick into gear.

Babe nodded. "He hit you with that blade for a reason. Now they know who you are, and after tonight, what you are capable of doing."

"Tonight?" Dr. O looked at Babe quizzically.

136

As Babe got Dr. O up to speed, I slipped into the kitchen. I dug out a can of cheap beer and a grabbed a bag of salt-and-vinegar chips off the counter.

"Are you okay?" Frankie followed me. He was leaning against the doorway, his lanky six-foot plus frame filling it.

I nodded and popped open the beer. I didn't really care that I'd wake up with one hell of a hangover tomorrow.

"Babe just rocked my world." I took a swig. "But yeah, I am okay. I think."

"So, what now?" He took the beer out of my hands and helped himself to a fast chug. "Babe trains you up a bit, maybe?"

I shrugged and held out my hand for the can. He handed it back just as a huge crash from the bar boomed up the staircase. I jumped at the noise and dropped the beer, which sprayed all over the floor.

"Shit," I groaned. "And I forgot about Max!"

I raced downstairs and skittered to a stop in front of Alfonso. He was standing over Max, who was out cold. One of Babe's mysterious cobalt bottles was on the bar next to him.

Babe's voice called down the stairs. "Al, what happened?"

"I gave him the stuff, just like you said!" Alfonso yelled back at her.

"Bring him up here!" she ordered.

Alfonso raised his eyebrows and looked at me.

He grinned and said, "Lumen." The lights in the bar dimmed.

Hot damn. Al was a witch too. One word of Latin and he could turn off the lights.

Al headed up the stars, leaving Max crumpled on the sawdust-covered floor. I stared at him, my mouth hung open in absolute shock.

"Don't worry, Nina," Frankie's voice echoed down the staircase, pulling me out of my stupor. "I'll clean up your beer mess."

I took a breath, heaved Max's limp body over my shoulder and hauled him up the stairs. This was going to be one long-ass night.

CHAPTER 19

It took less than an hour to sort out a short-term plan, just enough time for Babe to cook up an antidote for whatever Alfonso had given Max to make him pass out. We all crowded in her kitchen since she insisted I watch her. I had to get comfortable working potions, she said. But it looked like she was boiling some freaky soup that smelled like old socks. I stared at her while she worked up the spell, but didn't absorb any of it.

Frankie and Alfonso took Max back to the Biltmore with one of Babe's cobalt bottles filled with the antidote and a few spooky-looking talismans. They were wards designed to keep the supernatural mob that convened at the hotel out of his room, she explained. Since Frankie and Al were supernatural themselves, they risked being attacked. And as I learned firsthand, pissed-off poltergeists were no joke. There was a reason why we called in the priests to deal with them.

Babe gave Frankie and Al very specific instructions on where to set up the talismans and what Al needed to chant. They were to tip the liquid in the bottle into Max's mouth right after and then come back to my apartment building to meet up with us.

We needed to regroup there since the sun was going to be rising soon and Frankie needed to get underground before daylight. I assumed he could feed at one of the clubs near the hotel -- there were always willing donors around places like that, especially when Frankie laid on the vampire charm.

I was stuffed into the back of Babe's Fiat 500, a giant pot on my lap. Oh who are we kidding, it was a goddamned *cauldron*. It was a welcome-to-the-coven gift from my aunt.

The cauldron balanced on top of more giant Grimoires that Babe insisted on returning to my possession. I sulked the entire ride back to my apartment.

My crankiness melted a bit when the light from the garage illuminated the bright shining eyes of the stray dog I'd fed earlier. Her pink tongue hung out panting, as if she had just run a marathon. I unfolded myself from the back seat, stuffed the pot along with the oversized books into Dr. O's arms, and walked out of the garage and knelt by the scraggy ball of fur. She stuffed her head under my chin and nuzzled into my neck.

"Hey Dog," I said sweetly. In absence of a proper name, Dog would have to do. I extracted her head and scratched behind her ears. She felt wet. "Rough night for you too, huh?"

She licked my hand.

"Well, come on." I stood and walked back to the open door. This time, there was no hesitation as she trotted right next to me into the building. I closed the garage door behind us.

Babe gave me a funny look as we passed her and headed down the hallway and into my apartment. She and Dr. O trailed behind us.

Once inside, I filled a large bowl with water and put it on the floor in the kitchen. She lapped it up happily as I dug through the fridge looking for something to feed her, coming up empty.

Dr. O warily knelt down to get a better look at Dog. "When did she show up?"

Babe was hovering by the stove, grinning.

"The other night," I said with a shrug.

Dr. O smiled at Dog who gave him a little lick and pawed playfully at his hand. He nodded at Babe.

She stepped toward Dog with her hand out. Dog gave it a sniff and then let Babe smooth the fur along her strong head. "You have a Hell Hound as your familiar."

I burst out laughing as I looked into the expectant brown eyes gazing up at me. Hell Hound. Please.

Dr. O sighed. "You didn't pay much attention in my mythology lectures, did you?"

I cringed. Truthfully, I spent much of his mythology lectures plotting ways to kick Frankie's ass, who was my fight instructor at the time. I figured ass-kicking would be more useful in the field than mythology.

"If you had been paying attention you would have known that this beautiful animal is indeed a Hell Hound, and that Hell Hounds are not necessarily evil." Dr. O crossed his arms.

I hate it when I disappoint Dr. O, but I was still feeling a little rebellious. "I thought she was a Rottweiler. And what's all this crap about 'a familiar?'"

It was Babe's turn to sigh and look annoyed. "Apparently, you weren't paying much attention in your history of witchcraft courses either."

"Well, actually," Dr. O said, looking positively chagrined. "I didn't push too much witchcraft on her."

Babe's eyes were so wide I thought they were going to pop out of her head. "How *could* you?" she choked out. "You knew she could show witch tendencies."

"There was such a slim chance..." Dr. O trailed off as I cleared my throat.

"Yeah, you guys can argue about my education later." My patience was wearing thin. "What's 'a familiar?'"

"A familiar is an animal that is a witch's closest companion. They are different things to different witches, and looking at the size of yours I'd say you have a protector." Babe pointed at Dog, whose ears perked up at the attention.

"Great," I replied. "What do I do with her?"

Babe looked angrily at Dr. O.

"I bet you taught her all about Druid history," she snapped

before turning to me. "She's your ally. She will try to keep you safe, serve as an extra pair of eyes and ears. She will be the most trustworthy partner you could ever want."

Dr. O nodded in agreement. "She is actually the best familiar you could ask for." He smoothed her fur and felt her muscular physique. "She is a Church Grim, a guardian spirit. This dog will fight for you to the death."

Babe snorted. "Of course she is. Familiars are always well matched to their charges."

"But Auntie, you don't have any pets," I blurted out.

Babe's angry eyes softened. "What about Cookie Puss?"

"The *bar* cat?"

Cookie Puss was a tiny black and white cat that let out monster hisses if anyone who wasn't Babe tried to go near her. She was so feral every veterinarian in the state refused to see her.

"She's more than a good mouser," Babe smiled.

I looked at Dog, who by now was sick of all the talking. She made herself comfortable on the couch. And before I could boot her off the cushions, she stretched out and yawned. I flopped down next to her and she dropped her huge head in my lap.

Absently scratching her ears, I thought about Casper. He claimed to be a witch. A witch's blade was found at his murder scene. And I, apparently, was a witch.

"Babe," I began, closing my eyes in hopes that the exhaustion would pass. "Did these serial killings happen before I came into town?"

Babe shrugged. "I don't know. You've been here what, four months?"

"Since the start of fall semester, so yeah, about that."

"I think they started about a month after you arrived. Yes, closer to Halloween," she said, growing more certain. "I remember thinking it was fittingly frightening for the civilians given the season."

"I think someone is targeting witches," I said. I continued

petting Dog absently.

Dr. O steepled his fingers together and looked at me intently. "Why do you think that?"

"Because a spirit of one of the victims is hanging around." I didn't want to say the next part out loud. "Talking to me."

Babe laughed. "Nina, you know spirits can't talk."

"They can communicate in your head if the ghost jumps in your body." I shuddered as I said it.

It was Babe's turn to look alarmed. "You've been possessed?"

"Well, when you put it that way, it sounds bad," I said, feeling indignant. "He's just trying to communicate."

Dr. O looked more excited than concerned, so I focused on him. "Well, what did he say?"

"That he was a curandero. And that everyone murdered were witches. And I think he knew I was a witch."

Dr. O looked at Babe. "Did you know any of the victims?"

Babe shook her head. "No. Al and I pretty much stick to ourselves. The covens popping up are usually just New Age wiccans, no one with true witch blood. But curandero? That is Mexican. And that means Catemaco."

I nodded. "He said he was from Veracruz."

Babe sank down into the couch across from me. Catemaco was where my grandfather — Babe's and my mother's father -- was from. It was the place she took me to briefly after my parents were killed.

Babe suddenly looked very old and tired. "Any idea how old your ghost is, Nina?"

"Young. Around 19, 20 maybe. I didn't see him alive, and it's kind of hard to judge when they are ghosts. Why?"

"Because you are rather famous in Catemaco," Dr. O said. He

settled in next to Babe and put his arm around her slumped shoulders.

I stared at both of them. "Why am I famous in Catemaco?"

Babe looked defeated. "You know I tried to take you there after your parents died."

"Yeah," I said. "And you hated being back in Mexico and couldn't take care of me on your own and my grandparents were too old to help."

"All lies," Babe sighed. "Marcello followed us, followed *you*, to Catemaco, but I thought that on our ancestral lands, the power of my family could destroy him. But while we were able to protect you, he started killing other infants."

She choked back a sob, so Dr. O continued. "The Veracruz witches were frightened and angry. They knew you were born of a vampire. Their city was warded to keep vampires out, so they didn't believe there could be a vampire in their city. So they thought you were sucking the blood from the other babies. They were going to kill you. Babe called me for help, and a Blood Ops team was able to extract you."

"If Veracruz was warded, how did he get in?" I asked.

"That was the question, wasn't it," Dr. O gave a small humorless laugh. "He was aided by witches. He had to be. Just like now."

Dog sat up and growled, the hair on her back standing on end. The temperature dropped suddenly and I caught -- not sight exactly, more like a feeling -- of Casper.

"Oh no you don't!" I stood up as pressure blasted at me. I tried to push him away, for all the good that did me. Dog continued to growl, by then snarling and showing off some pretty impressive fangs.

I felt Casper's ethereal body push directly into mine. A sudden explosion of pain ripped into my head as the usual ghost-induced migraine took hold.

"Do you have to do this now?" I asked through gritted teeth.

"Sorry." I felt him shrug. "Only way to communicate."

I growled at him, just like Dog. "Then what do you want?"

"Hotel." His urgency was quickening my pulse. "Problem."

"What problem?" I was trying to breathe through the headache. It was very hard to focus.

"Spirits angry. Talismans."

Right, okay. They don't like the talismans. No surprise there.

"Your friends. Are. Trapped!" He began to push against me, forcing me to my feet. Between the momentum and my headache, I promptly fell to the floor.

I needed more information. "Trapped where?" I asked.

"Room."

Trapped in a hotel room?

"What will free them?" He better know, because I sure as hell didn't.

"Chant," he said, pushing me to my feet. "I know it."

Great. I guess he was coming with me.

"Will you get out of my head at least so I can drive?"

I felt a whoosh of relief as he pushed himself out of my body.

I opened my eyes and blinked against the light. Dog was still growling but was much more low-key about it. Babe and Dr. O were just staring at me incredulously.

Dr. O broke the uncomfortable silence. "Well, I haven't seen a possession quite like that in a long time. What did he want?"

"It sounds like Frankie and Al ran into some problems at the Biltmore. The freaks don't like your Talismans."

"Dammit!" Babe muttered. "Al forgot to cast a shielding spell on them before they walked in."

"We've got to get there and get them out." I walked to my armoire and yanked it opened. "We're running out of night, and

Frankie has to get underground before he fries." Vampires and sunlight don't mix.

I pulled my gear out of the armoire and stripped off Babe's yoga pants and flannel.

I threw on a chain mail shirt, which made knifing me or, even more important, staking me difficult. Layered on top of the chain mail was a fitted leather vest that had tons compartments to hold paraphernalia -- a bottle of Holy Water, blessed wooden stakes, and a container of salt. I slipped my sterling silver cross over my head, wincing at the sting on my chest when it hit my skin. I could wear the cross but my vampire genetics made it burn a bit going on.

Next were wrist sheaths Frankie made for me when I graduated from training. Adjusting the well-worn leather cuffs onto my arms always made me smile. The narrow, sterling silver blades snugged into them were soaked in Holy Water and blessed by a priest. But Frankie was the consummate tinkerer so the blades were spring loaded. They tucked up into the sheaths and with the press of a button they shot out over my hands, keeping the blades secure (and my hands free to grab) as I used them. They were my favorite weapons.

I pulled on black cargo pants and loaded the pockets with more stakes, extra bullets, and a few shuriken, or Japanese throwing stars, also made from sterling silver and doused in Holy Water.

I loaded a new clip into my 44 Magnum -- four sterling silver rounds rotated with four hollow point wood bullets that were filled with Holy Water. I shoved this into the vest's built-in holster nestled into the small of my back. I didn't sense any were-animals in town, but I didn't want to take any chances. Frankly, I didn't know what to expect anymore. Once I was suited up, I put on a cargo jacket to hide it all. My ass-kicking, steel-toe black boots completed the look.

"We should take the dog," Babe said. She nodded at my beast, who was still alert, eyes following something we couldn't see. I was pretty sure she had her sights on my Casper.

"We?" I asked her.

"You aren't going in alone," Dr. O said firmly. "We don't know enough about this ghost to trust it. We'll take the Mini."

Great. Dog and I could cuddle up in the back.

CHAPTER 20

Once again, I found myself in that damn parking garage attached to the Biltmore, staring at the back entrance and dreading walking through. Dog sat at my right. Her low, throaty growl told me she was as on edge as me. I could hear Babe and Dr. O coming up behind us, and before I could turn to look at them, goddamned Casper just dropped straight into my body without any warning. I staggered backwards and landed flat on my ass.

"Goddamn it!" I groaned, stifling an angry shout. Pain began to flood my head again, and I closed my eyes against the fluorescent glare of the parking garage lighting.

"You need me to help you fight the ghosts," Casper reinforced his reason for the body jump.

Babe and Dr. O were beside me, reaching for my arms. I took a breath and drew myself up on all fours. How was I going to accomplish anything with Casper in my body giving me such a migraine?

Babe and Dr. O each gripped one of my arms and hoisted me to a standing position. I opened my eyes just enough to squint. It was like being in a fun house. Since there was an extra person in my body, my vision was completely distorted. Sort of double vision with a case of really bad seasickness. I willed myself not to hurl.

With Babe and Dr. O holding me sort of steady, we made our way into the haunted hotel, Dog stalking along at my side. The back hallway into the Biltmore was deserted, but sounds of clinking glass and slurred voices echoed towards us. The bars outside had closed two hours prior, but the Biltmore patrons had no use for the Blue Laws. The seedy watering hole pretty much never closed.

With Casper guiding me, we made our way as quickly as we could to a back elevator. I wasn't sure how the ghosts missed our presence, until I noticed that Babe was clutching a rosary and muttering to herself. This must have been the shielding spell Alfonso forgot to cast. Without it, the super freaks knew that he had protection talismans for Max's room, which probably precipitated their attack. Of course Babe wouldn't make the same mistake.

When the doors opened, we rushed into the elevator, and at the ghost's instruction, I pushed 14 to get to Max's floor.

"They are in the room, right?" I asked my Casper.

Babe and Dr. O looked at me oddly, and I pointed to my head. This was taking some serious getting used to.

Casper must have nodded, since my head bowed in response, kicking off a throbbing sensation.

"It's a yes," I groaned at them. Dog licked my hand in solidarity.

The ding of the elevator opening its doors did not make my head feel much better. With their grip back on each arm, Babe and Dr. O guided me out of the elevator and we stumbled down the hall. Casper stopped me in front of Max's room.

Dr. O gripped the doorknob. "Ready?"

I nodded, breathing in sharply from the pain.

Dr. O turned the knob and pushed the door open. A shock of bright light exploded from the room, and I shielded my eyes, cursing that I didn't have my sunglasses. I walked boldly in, blinded by the light. Just past the threshold, Casper put on the breaks. My vision adjusted and I shrank back in horror. The room was filled with snakes.

I leaped onto the bed and started screaming like a little girl.

Okay, wait. I need to point out, it wasn't me screaming. That's what Casper forced me to do. This tough-assed, tatted-up Mexican witch was afraid of snakes.

I would have loved to enjoy a laugh at his expense, but I was a little freaked-out myself. The snakes were everywhere. On the floor, on the bed, slithering all over Alfonso, who was knocked out on the floor. Curiously, they were not bothering Max, who was lying face up on the bed, snoring.

"Nina!" Babe had jumped onto the bed too, and she slapped my face, hard, pulling me (well, Casper) out of hysterics. She pointed at the source of the blinding light, and my heart stopped.

Frankie lay in the center of two bright tanning lamps. His beautiful face was blistered, and his arms were dark, blackened by the UV light. Dr. O struggled to reach him, kicking snakes all over the room. But it was futile. The lamps wouldn't shut off. The switches didn't work, and they weren't plugged into any outlets, so cutting the electricity wasn't an option. The poltergeists didn't want to kill Frankie and Al, or else they'd be dead. But they were feeding off the pain and misery, making the spirits stronger.

I leapt off the bed and popped my blades out of my wrist sheaths. Dog joined me. She forced the snakes between me and Frankie to retreat, while I swiped the blades through them as they moved to the side. I could hear a hiss each time a head came off, and judging from Casper's little party going on in my head, I was killing the spirits along with the reptile bodies they were inhabiting. Score one for me!

When I reached Frankie, I re-sheathed the knives and tried to yank him out of the lights. But his skin was so fragile from the burns that it slid right off his bones. Moving him was impossible. This was not good, and I was close to panicking. His eyes fluttered open, and he looked at me.

"Bloody hell, Nina. Why were you screaming like a little girl?" He croaked.

The light from the lamps was strong, and my skin turned lobster red. Great, now I was going to get a sunburn, or worse if I didn't hurry up -- part vampire, and all that.

I squinted at the two sunlamps, which really looked like four in my double vision. I couldn't pinpoint exactly where they were. I drew

150

up my leg and connected with the lamps with a long, smooth roundhouse kick. They collapsed to the ground and the bulbs busted and glass shattered everywhere.

Frankie let out a groan. "Took you long enough."

He tried sitting up without his charred skin oozing off. He looked like barbecue.

"Now. Time." Casper was urging me. I pulled out the Holy Water as more snakes slithered over Alfonso and towards me. Dog successfully pushed some away from me, but we were outnumbered. The snakes latched onto my ankles and began to twist around me, trying to pull me down. I took a swig and felt the water burn my mouth like scalding-hot coffee before I sprayed it out and over the snakes. They scattered when it hit them.

"Exunt corpus, licentia corpus, dimitto corpus," my voice repeated the words, each invocation becoming louder and more forceful as the snakes began to.... Well, burn up is probably the best way to describe it.

With a satisfying popping noise, the snakes disappeared from the room in flashes of flame. Babe rushed to Alfonso, placed the rosary on his forehead and murmured "espíritu de salida." He opened his eyes, sat straight up and shrieked, before dropping back to the floor. She gave his body a nudge with her foot. "Zote," she huffed at Al, calling him an idiot.

Casper laughed, causing my head to vibrate.

Dr. O went over and helped Alfonso stand up. Something knocked him out, but luckily he hadn't been possessed.

"Isn't it time you left?" I muttered to the ghost inside my head.

"I need your body to get out of here," he sounded surprisingly stronger. Good for him. But I felt like shit.

"Why?" I really wanted to have my body back.

"Trapped here without you," he said. "I weaken when I leave your body. The spirits want to trap me here, and it's harder for me to fight them."

I dropped to the bed and looked at Max. He slept through the whole damn thing. What the hell was in that potion that Al doused him with?

Babe began placing the talismans around the room, whispering in Spanish as she dropped each one.

Frankie, now leaning against the bed, reached up and squeezed my hand. Vampires sure could heal fast. His charred skin was shedding, being replaced with flawless, alabaster skin. The blisters on his face were still there, but they were beginning healing over, too.

"You alright?" he asked.

"I will be when Casper gets the hell out of me." I closed my eyes. Now that the adrenaline was leaving my body, my head was going back to throb mode.

"What happened to sleeping beauty over there?" Frankie nudged Max's foot.

Babe was perched on top of the bureau, shoving a talisman into the ceiling, and muttering an invocation. She looked down at us when she was finished.

"Now we clean up and give Max the antidote," she said very matter-of-factly as she wiped her hands on her thighs.

"I got to get this guy out of my head," I moaned. I felt useless. I was in agony with even the slightest move.

"Frankie and Al, you boys clean up your mess," Babe barked. "Nina, I'll get you outside and we can get rid of your friend. Thank him for his help tonight for me, would you?"

"Ow! He said de nada." A wave of nausea hit and I rushed to the bathroom before I vomited all over the floor. I could hear Frankie laughing at me as I heaved.

When I was empty, I staggered out of the bathroom.

Babe hooked her arm in mine and helped me out of the room. "Let's get you out of here."

When we entered the hallway, the impact of the Biltmore hit me full force. Even Babe looked a little green with all that was happening. Lucky for me, Casper the Witchy Ghost was the only ghost that could possess me. I suppose it's better the ghost you know and all that. But poor Babe had no such protection, if you could call it that.

"Aren't you going to cast a spell or something, to keep the ghosts from messing with you?" I whispered.

She shook her head tersely. "I broke the incantation off in the room, and I can't start it again with all these spirits around. They keep blocking it. Give me the water."

I handed my flask of Holy Water to her, and she opened the top and took a gulp. I felt the cold breeze of ghosts flashing past us even before I saw them. They didn't look happy. A few of the more modern spirits gave us the finger.

We managed to wind our way through the hallway and down the creepy stairwell without incident. When we got back into the parking garage, I felt Casper crawl out of me, and my body ached with relief.

He paused beside me at the moment, grinning. His grin turned sour, however, as he looked past us. And with a little wave, he simply disappeared.

Behind us, someone was clapping, slowly. Babe and I both turned in the direction of the noise. Babe grasped my hand. Crap. It was Marcello and he was wet. And really, really angry.

A giant puddle was pooling around Marcello, his hair stringy and hanging past his shoulders, and a gleaming, brand-new witch knife in his hand.

"You made it out, you little bitch," he said, flashing his fangs at me.

"Back at you," I said, flashing my fangs too. They obviously didn't impress him because he lunged at me immediately.

"Sorry!" I yelled as I pushed Babe, hard, out of the way. I ducked down and did a somersault under his arm, coming up behind him.

He turned. With Babe at his back, I could keep his eyes off of her. I nodded my head back towards the hotel, and she nodded and began to make her way to the door.

"Not so fast, witch. Confuto!" He barked "restrain" at Babe, shifting his arm towards her for less than a moment.

Babe froze on the spot. But I could see her mouth moving. She wouldn't be frozen for long.

"Why don't you confuto me, you fanged freak?" I called out. Diverting his attention wasn't that difficult.

"Because you, fanged freak, are not that easily stopped," he hissed, and made another lunge at me. I jumped back, and his knife barely missed my stomach as it whooshed past.

I lifted my leg and gave Marcello a quick front kick that slammed him right under the chin. His head snapped back and he lost just enough balance for me to land a second kick at his arm, forcing him to drop the knife. I dropped to the ground and scrambled for it, but he was quick. He flung himself on top of me, the weight of his body crushing into mine. I felt the hilt of the knife press into my stomach. He might've been on top of me, but the knife was under me. I was still in the game.

He pulled back my hair, wrenching my head back to expose my neck. "I could bite you right now, little one," he whispered into my ear as I pushed my hand under me, searching for the knife. "I can hear your heart -- it's moving very fast. Your blood is rushing just under here," he added with lick to my neck. He was dangerously close to my jugular vein.

I refused to flinch and forced my arms further under my body to reach the knife.

"I could slip my teeth into you. It could be ecstasy for both of us. Or just one of us." He pressed his groin against me harder. Ewww.

Of course, I didn't think sinking his teeth into me was part of his master plan. But not only was Marcello pissed, he was showing clear signs of blood lust. A pissed off, lusty vamp could easily forget about his big, master plans.

He pulled my head back further, and I felt his fangs brush against my neck. This time, I couldn't help it. I flinched.

The barest hint of pressure was on my neck. His teeth began to slide down, pulling at the skin on my neck. I felt my skin split open, and a small moan escaped his mouth as he barely broke through the skin and then stopped.

Taking advantage of his hesitation, I pulled the knife out from under me with my right hand, twisted around and swung it away from my body and up my left side. I plunged it into the side of his neck. I hit him with so much force that he flew off me and slammed into a parked car about 15 feet away.

I jumped to my feet, feeling the small trickle of warm blood slip down my neck. I brushed at it, a smear streaked down my hand. Marcello stood on the car, the knife protruding from his neck. He smiled and pulled the knife out, pointed it in my direction and winked.

Marcello was centuries old, so he was strong and he was fast. He rushed towards me, the bloody knife lashing quickly as he attempted to cut me to ribbons.

Then I heard a roar behind me.

I fell to one knee as Marcello sliced at my neck. I ducked just in time. Dog sailed in the air, over my head. She sunk her teeth into Marcello's arm, the one holding the knife. I heard bones snap and the sound of metal skidding on pavement as the knife landed on the ground.

Bone protruded from Marcello's arm as Dog snarled at him. He slowly retreated from her. I snatched up the knife, and slipped it into my weapons vest. Marcello put a few feet between him and Dog, then, moving swiftly, he vanished.

I dropped to the ground, shaking. Dog padded over to me and licked at my face. I hugged her tightly around the neck.

"You are the best Hell Hound ever," I stroked her ears.

She flopped down beside me and rolled on her back, her feet kicking about in the air. In return for saving my ass, all she wanted was a belly rub.

Footsteps came up fast behind me. Babe, Frankie, Alfonso and Dr. O rushed to us. Babe looked worn out.

"Guess you reversed his curse?" I asked her.

"It wasn't a very good curse either. He may be a powerful vampire but he's an amateur witch." She sniffed. I kind of loved that my aunt was a magic snob.

Dr. O plopped himself down on the other side of Dog, stroking her head. "He isn't meant to be a witch. He's getting help from somewhere."

"He had another knife with him," I said. I plucked the weapon out of my vest. "Could that be what's aiding him?"

"I'm not sure, but it's a consideration."

Frankie was staring at me intently. "What's with you?" I asked.

"You were bitten." He pointed at my neck.

"Just a small puncture. I'll heal in an hour," I said casually.

Frankie knelt beside me and pushed my head to the side, looking at the wound. His fingers brushed it lightly. It sent chills through my body. He cocked an eyebrow at me and crossed him arms.

"I am *fine*," I muttered.

"Right then," he nodded, standing up. "So when did you get a dog?"

I smiled and stroked Dog's jet-black fur. Frankie tentatively reached out to pet her too, but her body stiffened and she responded with a low growl.

He yanked his hand back. "Well, I guess that's that then," he said clearing his throat. "Shall we go home? I think I have had enough for one night."

"Nina's not going home," Max's voice boomed behind me. Before I could turn around, he reached around and grabbed both of my hands, twisting my arms behind my back. The familiar snap of handcuffs echoed in the parking garage, and my wrists immediately itched from the metal. Dog's growl turned downright vicious, but, at the shake of my head, she held back.

"What the hell?" I craned my neck around, hoping to catch

Max's eye. He wasn't serious, was he?

"I have to bring you in, Nina." His voice was low, gruff.

"For what?" This was ridiculous. I just helped save his ass and now he was hauling me in?

"I need to bring you in for questioning for 16 separate murders," Max said in the most measured, almost clinical way.

Frankie leapt to his feet. "Oh come on!"

"Now, Max, really," Dr. O said, reaching into his pocket. I caught the corner of his Department of Defense badge peeking out.

Shaking his head, Max pulled out his Glock, training it between Dr. O and Frankie. "Hands where I can see them. Both of you."

In the distance, police sirens were blaring, the noise getting closer.

"Forget it, Doc," I said flatly. "Let him bring me in. They have nothing."

"We'll get you out in an hour," Babe said. She glared hard at Max.

Frankie nodded in agreement.

"Just get Dog home and fed, okay?" I asked.

Tires screeched. With his hands on my arms, Max swung me around and pushed me toward a waiting cop car.

"You just made the biggest mistake of your career," I muttered.

"Really?" he snorted.

"Really," I responded. With his hand on my head, he guided me into the back of the police car and slammed the door shut.

"See you at the station," he said to no one in particular. He knocked twice on the roof of the car and motioned for the cop in the driver's seat to go. We peeled out of the parking garage.

I leaned back and closed my eyes. Was it really just a few hours ago that I was all dolled up and ready for a fancy dinner with this guy? Now I was soaked through with Holy Water, snake snot, ghost goo, and, of course, blood. And my date was escorting me to the police station on murder charges.

See why I don't go on dates? Someone always ends up in handcuffs, and not the fun kind.

CHAPTER 21

I was stripped of my weapons as soon as I entered the building. The cops raised their eyebrows at my gun and wrist blades. They laughed out loud at the wooden stakes.

My police escort dumped me in a dingy, gray interrogation room. I stared at the mirror, looking past my rather scary reflection. After battling an older-than-dirt vampire twice and a hotel full of ghosts, I looked pretty beat up. I was sure Max was studying me from behind the safety of the one-way glass. I was tempted to stick out my tongue.

The staring contest lasted a good hour before he came into the room. The handcuffs made my wrists itch, and I was desperate for some cold water. A cup of coffee wouldn't have hurt either; I was exhausted. But Max came in empty handed.

He sat down opposite me. "You sure pack quite an arsenal."

I shrugged. "I am legally permitted to carry those."

He shifted forward. "I didn't see any paperwork."

"Babe's bringing it." I smiled tensely. "Is she here yet?"

"Right now, I ask the questions."

"Then ask me a question," I shot back. I was tired and testy.

"Okay then. Why were you carrying a small armory on your person?"

"Have you let me call my lawyer yet?"

"You aren't under arrest. Yet."

"Then I suggest you charge me with something."

He stormed out of the room. I dropped my forehead on the table and groaned.

When Max came back, he dropped a knife that looked like the one Marcello pulled on me.

"Do you recognize this?" He leaned on the table with both his hands, peering down at me.

"Yes, it was in the crime scene pictures you showed me."

"Have you seen it anywhere else?"

I shrugged. "It was used on me tonight. Max, you have no idea--"

He slammed his hands down on the table. "What don't I know, Nina?!"

I looked at him in silence.

"What I do know is that we both almost got killed tonight, I blacked out a large chunk of the evening, and when I came to, I see you and that weird skinny guy getting awfully close in the parking garage. So now you tell me what I don't know."

"I was being attacked. Again. My god, just uncuff me, will you?" I slouched back in my seat.

That made him snort.

"Seriously, Max. Let me out of these cuffs."

He ignored me. "Where else have you seen this knife?"

"You got this all wrong." I twisted my hands around, trying to satisfy the itch from the cuffs.

"This has been linked to at least one murder scene, and it was just like the knife used in the attack on you at the bar. So what aren't you telling me?"

"I am telling you to let me go."

"Damn it, Nina!" He slammed his hands down on the table again. It made me jump. "I am trying to protect you."

I didn't mean to laugh. Honestly. But I was so tired that it was exactly what I did.

"This is protecting me? That's fucking rich."

Max paced the room, agitation in every footfall. "Cut the bullshit, Nina."

"No, Max, you cut the bullshit. You know damn well that I was at the ER with you two nights ago when those murders happened. So there is no way you can pin any of this on me." My patience had officially worn thin.

"But you know what this knife is, don't you?" He kept on fishing.

"Yes, it's the knife that was used on me in the bar attack. Are we done here?"

"No. Why did I find this knife in a botanica?"

"Because that's where they sell them?" I offered.

But now he caught my attention. I always thought my dad's antique knife was a rare artifact. And it was being carried in a crappy downtown botanica?

He dropped it on the table. It clanged and bounced like it was made of a cheap metal, not the heavy iron that my dad's knife was forged with.

"How did this cheap piece do so much damage?" I forgot myself and said it out loud.

Max's expression changed from pissed off to self-righteous. I expected him to bellow "ah ha!" at any moment.

"You're right." He smartly held back his I-told-you-so. "That's the only difference. The metal on the knife found at the crime scene was pure silver. This is a silver plate replica."

"And a replica means the original is some sort of antique?"

He scoffed. "The owner of the botanica on Westminster Street didn't know anything about its origin, just that she thinks it's pretty."

So that's what he was doing at the botanica.

"What made you go in there to look for it?" I asked.

"The scroll work on the hilt is entwined snakes. It looked like it could be Satanic, so I figured I'd check it out with a botanica."

I sighed and dropped my head closer to the table to get a better look at the knife. Of course, he saw snakes and thought Satanic. But symbolically, snakes mean knowledge and they are not demonic at all. But they are affiliated with witchcraft.

"May I look at it more closely?" I asked.

When he nodded, I lifted my hands, holding my cuffed wrists out. "It'll be easier for me to look at it without these."

Max reluctantly removed the handcuffs. I rubbed my wrists, which had a lovely rash from the metal, and he pushed the knife towards me. It felt strange in my hands. I looked closely at the scrollwork and saw that it was different from mine. The snakeheads on my knife were missing.

"Was the knife you found at the crime scene the same knife that was used on me in the bar?" I asked. Marcello's knife was definitely not this tin replica. The drag on my neck felt substantial. A tin piece couldn't do that.

"We don't know. The only blood match was to the victims..."

"But he could have cleaned it." I guess I finished his thought, because he nodded.

I dropped the knife on the table. "What do you want from me, Max?"

"I think you know more than you are letting on. I think that the attack in the bar was not a random attack," he said, crossing his arms. His eyes bore into me. "And I think that these serial killings are connected somehow to what happened to you."

"You have quite an imagination, Agent." I pushed the knife across the table to him. "But I'm afraid there isn't much I can help you with. So are you going to release me or what?"

I stood up, and Max jumped to his feet as well. He grabbed my arm and yanked me out of my chair, across the table towards him, my forearm on his chest.

"Watch it," I cautioned. I could feel his muscular chest under his shirt, his heart beating just under my wrist. My face was close to his neck, and I could see his carotid artery pulsing. My fangs began to slip into place. I closed my eyes and took a breath, trying to center myself so I didn't lose control.

Shaking my head, I pushed myself back in my seat. "Am I free to go now?"

"I'll take you home," he said.

"I don't know if that's such a good idea." I shrunk back in my chair. I didn't trust myself not to bite him.

"Nina, it's after four in the morning." He stood there, looking practical. "You need a ride."

"Babe, or Dr. O...they should be here," I stammered.

"I told them you wouldn't be released until morning." He at least had the courtesy to look sheepish.

Guess our date wasn't quite over yet.

CHAPTER 22

A hot, wet tongue slowly burrowing into my ear woke me from a very sound sleep. It was accompanied by some very heavy breathing. I sat bold upright, pulling a kitchen knife from between the mattress and headboard. But it was only an expectant-looking Dog hovering over me.

I flopped back down again and stared at the ceiling. Max and I spent the entire ride back to my place arguing. He refused to release my weapons until he saw my concealed carry permit. Of course, in Rhode Island it was illegal to carry concealed weapons, but my Department of Defense permit would trump state law. I'd be outed as DOD, but I was more concerned about my getting my stuff back. The wrist blades would be hard to replace.

By the time we got to my place, the argument was full throttle and I stormed out of the car before it came to a complete stop.

Dog jumped off the bed and sniffed around at a stack of unopened boxes in the corner. I leapt from the bed, shrieking like a loon, when she began to squat. Grasping her by the scruff of her neck, I interrupted her attempt to relieve herself in the house.

"Outside," I said sternly, yanking my coat on over my tank top and sweatpants. I stepped into my boots, sans socks, and took her outside.

I needed to get a leash for her, but if she was my familiar, I figured she wouldn't wander far. We walked along broken sidewalks on the desolate streets, passing graffiti-covered buildings and sidestepping broken bottles of booze. Dog went a bit ahead, sniffing around to locate a prime spot to pee. It was late morning, and I could see some hustle and bustle on the main street, but most of the factory buildings stood lonely. I felt like a pioneer in an urban wasteland. I half expected tumbleweeds to drift through the intersection.

The sound of a truck backing up caught my attention. It must have caught Dog's too. She tilted her head to listen and then she raced around the corner. Shit. I raced after her, feeling awkward and slow without my usual jolt of morning coffee.

I turned the corner and almost tripped over Dog. She was huddled against the building, her hair on edge, watching. I stopped and huddled with her, crime scene tape keeping me from moving much further. The truck backing up had been an on-site CSI command post. There were a lot of cops. Considering this controlled chaos was directly behind my building, my soundproofing apparently worked.

"Come on." I tapped Dog lightly on the head and turned to go back home when a flash of light caught my eye. I looked up. The roof was crawling with cops, and standing at the edge was Max, staring straight at me. He crossed his arms over his chest.

Awkward.

I turned on my heel and retraced my steps back to the apartment, while Dog continued her sniff-and-pee routine. My gait was rather stiff, since it was all I could do to not break into a sprint. It felt like it took an eternity when I finally unbolted the outside door and stepped into the warm building. Dog and I marched down the hallway. I shrugged off my coat before we were inside my apartment.

With coffee on the brain, I made a beeline for the kitchen. I hit the button on the coffee grinder, and fell into my familiar morning routine.

While I was filling up the pot at the sink, I caught another flash of light from my back windows. After pouring the water into the machine, I flipped it on and, against my better judgment, decided to give it a look. I craned my neck up and saw some figures on the roof again, but since that building was five stories high, it was hard to see clearly from my second-floor vantage point. Then Max came into view. He had binoculars pressed to his eyes, and the sunlight was bouncing off of them. Another flash hit me in the face and blinded me for a brief moment. When my eyes cleared, it looked like Max had the binoculars trained directly on me.

For a brief second I considered doing something smart-assed and naughty, like flashing him.

"Oh crap!" I smacked myself upside the head. If he was at the crime scene, it was another freaky murder. I bet Casper was around too. I had to ask Babe if she could ghost proof my home.

I peeked up at the building's roof again. Only uniformed cops were milling about now, maybe a few from the crime lab. I squinted into the sun, trying to see something translucent but not quite invisible. Either Casper wasn't there, or I just couldn't see him in sunlight.

Dog tucked herself back in for a sleep in the bed. I huffed in her general direction, and she lifted one ear and gave me the sad-eyes routine. She was sprawled in the middle of the bed, her head on the pillows. She looked comfortable. I didn't have the heart to boot her off.

I thumped my way to the kitchen and poured a cup of steaming hot goodness into my favorite mug. After adding a dollop of half and half, I inhaled the fragrant steam. As I was moving the mug up to my lips, a knock on my apartment door made me jump. Coffee spilled down my white tank top.

I was edgy for good reason. Who the hell got past the locked front doors? And Dog? Wasn't she supposed to be barking? What good was a Hell Hound if they weren't up for some basic security? She barely lifted her head when she looked at me. Her expression said, "Well, aren't you going to answer it?"

I grabbed a paper towel and blotted at my shirt on the way to the door.

"Who is it?" I yelled at the closed door.

"It's Max. Nina, let me in." He sounded like he'd mellowed over the past few hours. Now he just sounded annoyed.

I unbolted the lock and swung open the door. Max walked in,

staring me down as he brushed past me. Dog managed to raise her head and snort hello before settling back in for her mid-morning nap.

"Good guard dog," Max sniffed, removing his coat.

I took him in for a moment. His purple silk tie was askew. His beautifully patterned dress shirt, a deeper purple than the tie, was a little rumpled, and the back had come untucked, hiding what was a near-perfect ass in a dark pair of jeans. He looked exactly like I expected him to look in his work clothes -- like a little kid playing dress up.

Sounds of him searching through my cabinets pulled me back to reality.

"Can I help you?" I slapped my hand against the maple wood of the cabinet he was peering into and slammed the door shut. He jumped back.

He held up his hands. "I thought I would help myself to some coffee."

"It seems that you forgot your manners, Agent Deveroux." I yanked open another cabinet and grabbed a mug, handing it to him. "There is half and half in the fridge, and sugar over there," I said, pointing in the direction of the sugar bowl on the table.

"Thanks," he responded gruffly, pouring out the brew, and then crossing to the fridge for the cream. I sat slowly down at the long wooden kitchen table, the Grimoires still sitting on one of my couches caught my eye. I fought back the urge to hide them. I wasn't going to lie to him anymore. But I wasn't going to point them out either.

"What can I do for you, Agent?" I sipped my coffee and did my best impression of nonchalant. Except my hands were shaking.

"There were more murders last night," Max said. He pointed towards my back windows.

"Of course. Crime scene tape plus you equals murder," I said. "I assume my alibi for last night will hold up? Cookie?" I opened the lid of the cookie jar sitting center table and plucked out a chocolate chip. I then pushed the jar slightly towards Max. He shook his head. I shrugged and put the lid back on the jar.

Max just sipped his coffee, his eyes glued on me. I met his gaze and refused to let it go.

"So are you just being friendly? Telling me there's a killer on the loose and to remember to lock my doors?" I bit into the cookie. Clearly the cookie worked magic on Dog, because she roused herself from the bed to sit at my feet, waiting for crumbs to drop. Or for me to cave in and give her a chunk.

"Picked up a dog?" Max pointed in Dog's direction. Drool puddled on the floor beneath her. She really wanted a piece of cookie. "She's a mean-looking thing. She's big, even for a Rottweiler."

I nodded and took a chip-free corner of the cookie and gave it to Dog, who damn near took my fingers off in her excitement.

"My weapons are a great deterrent as well," I scoffed. "When I have them."

It pissed me off that my weapons were rotting in some evidence room at the police station. "So what can I do for you?" I stood stiffly and crossed the kitchen to get another cup of coffee.

"I want to talk about last night."

I cringed. "Max, I really didn't want to talk about last night unless it's about the return of my stuff." I drained the remainder of the pot into my mug and shut the machine off.

"There are parts of last night that I don't really remember." He squinted, as if concentrating hard on his spotty memories of last night. "But I do remember some strange shit going on at the restaurant. I remember Alfonso giving me something bitter and foul-tasting to drink. Most of the night was like a dream, and I was waking in and out."

Eying him, I eased back into my seat, my anger starting to bubble to the surface. He didn't know half of the freaky shit that went down last night.

"And what do you think I can do about this?" I asked too forcefully. I wanted to know what he thought before I just balls-out told him my story.

"I think you owe me the truth." He wouldn't meet my eyes. "No matter how crazy I think it sounds."

I took a breath, weighing my options, when a knock at the door interrupted us. The sound of keys rattled in the locks, and then Babe's voice pierced through the apartment. "Nina? You decent?"

Babe and Dr. O made their way through my apartment's foyer and to the living room. They stopped when they saw Max and me at the table.

"Oh good," Dr. O said. He smiled and pulled off his coat. He placed it on the back of the chair and sat down next to Max, across from me. "You're up."

Babe tossed her coat on the couch and made her way to the kitchen.

"What are you guys doing here?" I stammered, not sure what was going on.

Babe pulled the coffee carafe out of the machine and looked disappointed.

"I'll make a fresh pot," she said. She smiled, humming softly while she measured out coffee and water.

"Babe had a feeling you may need us this morning," Dr. O said, beaming at Max. "So here we are."

"We were discussing what happened last night," I deadpanned.

"Oh good! Don't let us stop you." Dr. O rubbed his hands enthusiastically. "How far along have we gotten?"

"Not very," I said glumly. I got up and went to the fridge, yanked the door open and stared into it. I wish they had brought donuts. I pulled out eggs.

"I was telling Nina that I was open to hearing her version of last night's...events." Max eyed the still-brewing coffee. "No matter how weird I may think it is."

"You think you can keep an open mind, then?" Dr. O practically jumped up and down in his seat with excitement.

Babe laughed. "Forgive him. We don't get to tell many regular people."

"WHAT?" I roared, nearly dropping the eggs. Dog perked up at that, but probably because it involved eggs almost landing on the floor.

"Your aunt and I discussed it this morning," Dr. O said, nodding at Babe. "We think it's best if the FBI worked with us on this."

Babe took the eggs from me. "Go sit down, sweetie. I'll fix you an omelet."

Stunned, I went back to the table and dropped into my seat. "Shouldn't we wait and do this with Frankie?"

"I don't think so," Babe said as she busied herself with the omelet-making. "We can bring him up to speed tonight. More coffee, anyone, before I put the eggs on the fire?"

All hands at the table went up, and she brought over a mug for Dr. O and replenished my and Max's empty cups.

Max wore a poker face.

I sighed. I had a feeling they were going to make me do the honors.

"I guess when you're FBI you see a lot of strange stuff, right?" I started, staring into my mug. I was about to drop a bomb on him, and I couldn't look.

Max nodded in agreement.

"Have you ever seen anything that you just can't explain? Crimes that go unsolved?" My stomach tightened.

Max nodded again, still with the poker face on. But he didn't take his eyes off me. It was kind of unnerving.

"Keep going, Nina, you're doing GREAT," Babe said by way of moral support. I heard the eggs sizzle as they hit the pan.

"Okay," Max said, breaking his stone-faced silence. "Like these murders. They aren't gang-related but I can't explain what else they could be, so gang sounds good."

I nodded, but he stopped me. "If last night hadn't happened to me, I would never believe it. But I need you to tell me first, whose side are you on?"

Dr. O pulled out his government-issued badge and flashed it. "We're on the same side, Max."

Max's eyes went wide as he took it. "Department of Defense? Blood Ops? I don't know what that is."

"Not many people do, my boy." Dr. O took his badge back and slipped it back into his pocket. "There aren't many of us. Nina, Frankie, myself, less than a hundred back at the base..."

"You, too?" Max looked at me, eyes wide.

I shrugged and nodded.

"Not me!" Babe shook her head emphatically at the eggs cooking in the pan. "I just sort of help out from time to time. Kind of like a consultant."

"Department of Defense," Max was shaking his head, still processing it.

"So my concealed carry is legit. *Now* can I get my shit back?" I fished my own badge out of the bag hanging on my chair and pushed it over to him.

Max just nodded. "I'll process the paperwork this afternoon."

"Good." I felt slightly smug and somewhat satisfied before continuing. "Before we go any further, you need to understand that you cannot tell anyone about this. It would put all of us in extreme danger. So not your best friend, not your partner. Definitely no one in any government agency. And if you do, we will emphatically deny it all and a sudden psych discharge will appear for you. We outrank you and can make it happen. Got it?"

Max looked over to Dr. O, who was nodding slowly. Max cleared his throat, his eyes slightly wide, "So what kind of program is Blood Ops?"

"Most of those unsolved crimes are taken care of by us," I explain. Notice that I didn't say "solved." You couldn't exactly call what we did solving.

Babe dropped a plate of eggs in front of me, and I dug in with

171

gusto.

"But no perp has ever appeared in court, to my knowledge, for any of my cold cases," Max said. He looked peeved.

I shook my head, my mouth full of fluffy, cheesy omelet goodness.

Dr. O took over for a moment. "These are cases not solvable for mortals."

Max choked on his coffee. "Mortals?" he coughed out.

"You need to hear us out, Max," Babe chided him as she placed a plate of eggs in front of him and then Dr. O.

He nodded and pushed the omelet around his plate. "I'm listening."

"Babe's omelets rock," I smiled at my aunt. "You should try it."

Babe's caramel complexion turned slightly pink and she grinned.

"We don't arrest them, really," I said with my mouth half-full. It was tough explaining what it was, exactly, that we did to perps. Killing them wasn't exactly accurate. Or legal. "It's more like we send them home?" I looked at Dr. O.

He just laughed at that one. "Max, let's stop running in crop circles here. We deal with the unexplained, the supernatural."

"The supernatural?" Max snorted. "Ghosts? Vampires? Leprechauns?"

"Leprechauns," I pointed my fork at him, "aren't real."

"The wee folk? Yes, they are, Nina," Dr. O said, then he plopped a bit of egg onto his tongue.

"Well, I've never seen one," I said matter of factly.

"They don't call us in for the wee people," Dr. O explained through chews of his omelet. "The wayward leprechauns mostly stick to financial crimes. That's a whole other department."

172

"They only call in Blood Ops when the humans are getting killed," Babe added. She finally sat down next to Dr. O with her own mug of steaming coffee.

Dr. O shook his head. "Though with the greed we've seen from them recently, we may get called in soon enough. The government isn't very happy with them at the moment."

I am not easily surprised, but leprechauns were a shocker. Lifting my jaw off the table, I looked at Max. "Well, then, yes, ghosts, zombies, even currency-manipulating leprechauns. And other. Things."

"So how does one bring in a ghost, or a vampire?" He looked almost amused, but more like he was laughing at us, not with us.

"One doesn't," I snarled. "We kill them."

Max's face went pale then. My heart skipped when I sensed his fear and my fangs began to push at my gums. I fought down the instinct to attack, an instinct that was getting frustratingly harder to keep a lid on these days. I placed my hand over my mouth. Babe raised her eyebrows.

"Excuse me," I whispered, jumping up with my unnatural quickness. Dog leapt up beside me, the hair on her back on edge. I rushed to the bathroom and slammed the door.

Turning the faucet, I splashed cold water onto my face. Face dripping, I caught my reflection in the mirror -- eyes bloodshot, skin pasty. I bared my teeth; my fangs were visibly extended. Hoping they would retract in a minute or so, I sat on the edge of the tub and steadied my breath.

A knock at the door startled me, and I almost fell into the tub. "Nina, you okay?" Dr. O called quietly through the door.

I unlatched the door and pulled it open an inch. "I don't know."

"May I?" he gestured to come in. I swung the door open wider and resumed my seat at the edge of the tub. He closed the door and sat on the closed toilet seat.

"The vampire urges are getting stronger?" His kind green eyes met mine, and I nodded.

He sighed, looking tired. "We didn't think this would happen. Clearly, we were wrong. Once the witch part of you was triggered, it caused the vampire gene to go haywire."

"So these two...genetic mutations...can't exist together in the same body?" I pulled at my hair impatiently.

"We don't know, I am sorry," he shook his head. "You're the first of your kind -- that we know about anyway. No one knows what will happen."

"My parents really messed this up." I shook my head.

Dr. O's mouth relaxed into a small smile. "They didn't know. Your mom was just tickled to be pregnant. They didn't think about the...consequences."

I closed my eyes. "That's just great. Now what do I do?"

"Wait and see? Continue to fight the urges?" Dr. O shrugged. "I don't really know."

At least he was honest. I sighed and leaned my back against the cold tile. I missed Darcy. I wanted to curl up on the coach, eat ice cream, and cry about how unfair it was that our lives were so fucked up. You know, something you can only do with your best girl friend. I hoped she'd get through her banshee business soon, so she could fly out here.

"We just wait and see," Dr. O repeated, not meeting my eyes. I knew exactly what he meant. If I turned and couldn't be controlled, I'd be dealt with.

It could take centuries to learn to control the blood lust. Back when Frankie and my dad were figuring out how to live with vampirism, there were only superstitious villagers and a few overzealous priests. While it was easier for vamps to hide in plain sight now, it was also more deadly with Blood Ops running around. We weren't human and not as easy to slaughter.

Frankie was one of just a handful of vampires that were part of Blood Ops. And there was a good reason for that. Even the centuries-old vamps had a hard time pulling themselves together. While blood lust could be controlled, apparently the press of power that immortality promised was hard to overcome. That rush of power nailed the coffin,

174

so to speak, on their humanity.

I pushed myself up off the edge of the tub and opened the bathroom door. Turning back, I caught Dr. O's eyes. "We'll figure this one out, Nina," he said. "That I promise." He reached for me and gave my hand a quick squeeze. I smiled faintly. I needed to keep my shit together. I could do this.

When we got back to the table, Babe was dragging Max on a nostalgia trip through Catemaco. He was listening politely, but looked spectacularly uncomfortable. In fact, he looked almost green.

"You told him about Tito Gonzo, didn't you?" I slipped back into my seat and thought about the few stories Babe shared about the weird family in Mexico. Tito Gonzo was a medicine man, and stories I once assumed to be just superstitious tall-tales about animal sacrifices and other bloody rituals were clearly part of my family's ancient, witchy ways.

Babe simply smiled, and reached out and patted Max on the hand. "Don't worry, honey. We don't do a lot of blood sacrifice around here."

Max's green hue turned pale.

"You *told* him?"

"Well, you weren't going to do it," she snapped back at me.

"Great," I groaned. "Did you tell him the other thing?"

"What other thing?" Max now looked positively alarmed.

"The vampire thing?" Babe tossed out nonchalantly. She slapped her hand over her mouth.

"Vampire thing?" Max now stood.

I jumped up, too quickly, and he began backing away from the table.

Max's fear blanketed the room, and once again my fangs pushed through my gums, forcing their way out. The shock of pain ripping through my gums made me gasp, and I flashed my fangs right at Max, who went white as a sheet and pulled out his gun.

175

"Max, no!" Dr. O cried out and Babe leaped up from the table.

I closed my eyes, and turned my back to him, trying to remember the deep breathing techniques I learned from a yoga magazine I flipped through at the hair salon. He wouldn't shoot me in the back. Would he?

All the commotion put Dog on edge. She stalked out from under the table where she was snoozing and eyed Max. The black fur on her back stood on end, and a low growl vibrated her entire body.

This was not going well.

"Dog," I cautioned her in a low voice without turning around. "Come to me."

Obediently, she sat at my feet, the growl now low in her throat. She was still eying Max like she wanted to eat him.

My fangs retracted as I gathered myself and turned back to him.

"Put your gun away," I cautioned. "That won't do much good here anyway, and will probably get you killed." I gave Dog's head a scratch for good measure.

Max grudgingly holstered the gun, but kept his hand on the butt. "You're a witch *and* a vampire?"

"Half witch, half vampire," I clarified. "But not a true, honest-to-God, dead vampire. That's Frankie."

He looked positively freaked by this point.

"You are all nuts." He pushed past me and strode to the door. "Stay out of my investigation."

"Yeah, about that..." I stopped him cold. "You said yourself that those murders weren't the work of gangs."

"Then who?" he turned to me again, his eyes blazing with anger.

"You aren't going to like my answer." I crossed my arms and waited.

"Stay out of my investigation," he repeated and stalked out, slamming the door hard enough to make me jump.

"That went well," Babe pursed her lips and started clearing the plates off the table. I flopped on the couch and closed my eyes. Damn it. We were all in way over our heads.

CHAPTER 23

Final exams were over, so Babe's on the Sunnyside was packed. The neighborhood regulars like Alfonso squeezed between the frat boys from Brown University slamming fuzzy nipples, giggling every time they ordered a new one. The Goth girls from RISD ordered Bloody Marys and looked appropriately depressed. The music was loud, the crowd was rowdy, and I had to subtly slip into vamp speed to keep the customers in booze. Babe was behind the bar with me, and still we could barely keep up.

I pushed another whiskey at Alfonso, who took it with a nod. "Sorry about last night, Kid. My age is finally catching up to me."

"Don't worry about it," I shouted over the noise. "We came out alive. How old are you anyway?"

He laughed and drank the whiskey down, and pointed to the other end of the bar.

A bunch of the frat boys were causing a commotion, grabbing at two women who were pretty much keeping to themselves.

"Not in my bar!" I stalked over to the offenders. "Back off!" I yelled at the four boys.

One of them looked at me with piercing green eyes, smirked, and kept right on bugging the women, who were then physically pushing the guys away, rather unsuccessfully.

I jumped onto the bar and yanked yellow eyes by the top of his hair. "I told you to back off!" I pulled him up so that his toes barely touched the floor and shoved him back into his friends. They caught up, levered him back upright, and he lunged for my feet. I jumped up and he hugged air. Sidestepping him, I jumped down off the bar into the crowd. I wish I could say I stood eye to eye with him, but damn it he was tall. I was staring directly at his chest.

So, intimidation wasn't going to be easy. He sneered at me, and drew back his right fist, aiming for my jaw. I ducked and he hit air again. But before I could get up, his friend tackled me from behind. He slammed his body into my lower back first, then he pushed my face into the bar. I pushed my hands in front of me, so they could absorb most of the blow, then donkey-kicked him right in the balls.

"You bitch!" He doubled over in pain.

"And who are you talking about, Mate?" I heard a voice intone.

I winced. Frankie. I was not going to live this down.

Frankie picked the guy up by the scruff of his neck and literally threw him out the door. "Right, then. Who's next?" Frankie smiled at Mr. Green Eyes standing on the other side of bar door's threshold, and he flashed lots of fang.

Mr. Green Eyes' friend edged around Frankie's towering frame and quickly slipped out the door. The bar erupted in a round of applause, and then everyone went back to their regularly scheduled drinking.

"Thanks," I said, sitting on the bar and swinging my legs over to jump to the other side.

"Oh, my pleasure," Frankie said. He grinned at me as his fangs retracted.

I rolled my eyes at him. "Bourbon?"

"Please," he responded, surveying the room.

I poured him a double shot of Old Granddad, hoping that the irony of the bourbon I chose was not lost. "I had it under control, you know."

"I know you did, Love, but I enjoy helping. Makes me feel useful." He winked at me.

I began filling pitchers with Narragansett beer, which I sent sliding down the bar to Babe. She placed them in front of the Religious Studies grad students that Alfonso loved arguing with. Since it looked like Al bought this round, the argument must be a doozy.

I was about to head down that way to eavesdrop when the door swung open, the cold air cleared a few heads. The noise of the bar immediately died down, leaving Alfonso's string of curses hanging in the air. Ami Bertrand stood in the doorway, flanked on one side by Tavio and the other by Max.

When Babe caught sight of who had arrived, she joined Alfonso in a cascade of impressive curses, some completely new to my ears.

Like the Red Sea parting, the crowd made room for the three men. Bertrand looked impeccable in a winter-white wool coat and a black Borselino with a red band. He smiled and shook hands as he walked through the crowd. The students crowded around were enamored.

When he got near the bar, a pretty brunette stepped in his path. She was gushing about the shelter he financed for Downcity's homeless population. He had rehabbed an abandoned building adjacent to the Biltmore into a housing facility for the homeless. The co-ed prattled on about the self esteem-building, forward thinking that went into the idea.

"Tavio, give this lovely young lady your card." Bertrand's voice was like silk. "You should intern for me this summer. City Hall could use a young woman with such compassion."

She giggled and ... was that a swoon? He was old enough to be her grandfather!

I heard Babe snort behind me. "The election isn't for three more days. He's not in the Mayor's office yet."

With a turn, Bertrand dismissed the co-ed and faced me and a fuming Babe.

"Babette," he said with a cold smile. "Feisty, as ever."

"Shut up, Ami," she scowled.

"Babette," Tavio was sharp. "Be polite."

"I don't take orders from you, cabrón." She lingered a bit on the Spanish insult, which literally translated to goat. I heard Cookie Puss hiss from under the bar, where she was twirling around Babe's ankles.

Tavio stepped towards Babe, his lip raised in a snarl. I jumped when I saw the white fang peeking just under his raised lip. Frankie noticed it too, and he moved closer to Babe.

Bertrand laughed and touched Tavio's arm to hold him back. "She's right, my friend. The last time we saw her, you were an old goat."

Bertrand smiled at me. "Lovely to see you again, Nina."

The hairs on my neck stood on end. This guy gave me the creeps.

My vampire ears picked up the sound of Alfonso muttering in a weird language that sounded something like Latin but not quite. Tavio was staring at him.

"What can we do for you, Mr. Bertrand?" My voice was polite but measured, as I tried to ignore Al's chanting.

"I paid a visit to Mr. Deveroux today, to see how the investigation was going." He looked around warily. "Did you have Last Call yet?"

Babe raised her eyebrows. It was barely midnight. We wouldn't do last call for another hour.

"Call it," Bertrand didn't let go of Babe's eyes. "Now. We need to talk."

Babe scowled but she rang the last-call bell. The crowd groaned and a few complaints were hollered.

"Blame me, my friends!" Bertrand called out. His voice rose above the din. "Important election business tonight, and I wanted to get out of the office. Last round is on me, for everyone."

An appreciative roar came over the bar, and Babe and I methodically began to refill pitchers and pour out liquor. I went to refresh Al's drink but he put his hand over his glass. "I take no gifts from that hombre maldito."

Our patrons drained their glasses and the place started to clear out. Bertrand stood by the door, still flanked by Tavio and Max, saying good night to every single person as they left. Everyone adored him. Except for us.

When the last customer was out the door, Bertrand turned the dead bolt and he, Tavio and Max sat down at the bar. Bertrand smiled at me again. "I'd love a drink, Nina."

"I got it," Babe said. She reached for one of her unlabeled cobalt bottles on the top shelf.

"As much as I love your moonshine, Babe, I would like Nina to pour me a grappa." He smiled at Babe, but there was no humor in his black eyes.

Babe harrumphed but nodded at me to go ahead. I grabbed the grappa, wiping the dust off the bottle, and poured it out into a shot glass. I heard Tavio sniff, disapproving of my glassware choice. Babe shot him daggers with her eyes.

Bertrand smiled at me once more. "Thank you, Nina."

Then he just stared. It was the kind of stare that sent shivers up my spine. I raised my eyebrows.

"Forgive me for staring, Nina," he said, finally looking away. "But you look so much like your mother."

Tavio nodded in agreement. "So much."

Before I could stop myself, I gasped. Babe gripped my arm.

"You knew my mother?" I placed my hands on the bar to steady myself. I felt Frankie move in closer.

"Of course I knew your mother!" Tavio's accent was thick. "You know nothing about your family?"

"My family? My family was murdered," I spat out and turned on my heel, grabbed the tequila and headed to Alfonso. I poured both of us a shot.

Al raised his glass, winked and smiled. "To your new family." He downed the shot and looked at Tavio through watery eyes. "Ego lingua, ego spiritum, ego lingua, ego spiritum."

Tavio gripped his throat and began to cough and sputter. He looked up, his face contorted. He opened his mouth and an engorged purple tongue flopped out.

Frankie grabbed his throat as well, but was smart enough to move swiftly away, crossing the bar in less than a second. He stood behind Al, out of reach from whatever spell Al was throwing.

"Enough, witch!" Bertrand's eyes were black slits, and his voice reverberated, rattling the bottles on the shelves that ran up the walls behind the bar. Several glasses fell, breaking into shards when they crashed at my feet.

Alfonso looked at Tavio grimly. "Silentio Lamia." And then he released whatever hold he had on the man. Tavio's tongue rolled back into his mouth, shrinking to normal size as it retracted.

"That was powerful, witch," Bertrand said with a smirk. "I hope you can teach that to Nina. It's more effective than your usual parlor tricks."

Alfonso gripped the bottle of tequila I left in front of him and poured out a double shot. Looking defeated, he slammed that back. Tavio eyed him warily.

"Your friends are protective of you," Tavio said, refocusing his attention on me. "Your father would be proud."

It was my turn to yell, but it didn't have quite the same impact as Bertrand's booming voice. "Why don't you explain, Mr. Tavio? How you know my parents?"

A collective hiss went up between Babe and Alfonso. I silenced them both with a raise of my hand.

"Your father was my brother," Tavio beamed triumphantly. "You are my niece, who I have not seen since you were a baby."

"That's it! This is stopping right now," Babe said. Then she reached under the bar and pulled out a gallon jug of water. It was our stash of Holy Water, which she was getting ready to dump on Tavio.

"Wait," I said. I grabbed hold of the jug, splashing a bit on my hand. It met my skin with a soft sizzle, and steam rose up from where the water landed. "I didn't think anyone from my father's side survived."

"They didn't," Babe looked fiercely between me, Tavio and Bertrand. "He's an abomination, even worse than the vampire he is."

Max, who had been sitting quietly at a table against the wall, got up suddenly. "He's a vampire, too?" He looked incredulous, and slightly defeated.

"Yeah, you can't get much more abominable than that," I crossed my arms and leaned against the wood, my eyes darting between Max, Tavio, Bertrand and Babe. Frankie, who was now behind me, let out a low whistle.

I know Babe didn't mean to call me or Frankie abominations, but the word still stung. It was true. We were crimes against nature, which was why witches hated vampires. Or part of the reason, anyway. But dammit, Frankie and I did so much good with our curse. I hated having to justify our worth.

Tavio smiled, Cheshire Cat-like. "Watch it, Babette. Nina has our temper."

"You know nothing about my niece," her voice cracked.

"*Our* niece," he corrected her. "You ran off with her before our side could claim her."

"What the frig is this, the goddamn 15th century? Nobody has any claim on me!" I slammed my fists down on the bar, and the wood cracked. "SHIT! Sorry, Babe."

"No worries, honey," Babe's eyes were focused on Tavio. "We'll fix it."

Tavio just laughed. "Yes, see! Just like my brother."

"Who are you?" I turned my wrath toward him. The vamp kicked in, and I was across the bar before anyone could blink. I faced off with him squarely.

Bertrand sipped his grappa, his face like stone. "We are your friends. And friends help each other."

"Help each other what?" I eyed him warily. I wasn't sure I liked where he was going.

"This city seems to have a pest problem," he continued, his voice like ice. "This witch killer is screwing up my campaign and I want him dealt with."

Max stood up suddenly. "Wait -- witch killer? You know who is committing these murders, Bertrand?"

"Of course I do, human," Bertrand said defensively. He looked at Max, his eyes completely coal black, the whites gone.

Max smartly took a step back. Then he not so smartly reached for his gun.

Bertrand looked at him lazily. "Put that away before you hurt yourself."

But Max got off a shot before Bertrand finished his sentence. It hit Bertrand square in the chest, but nothing happened except for a circular scorch mark marring his luscious white coat.

Bertrand looked down at the charred hole in his coat. He scratched at it, the black gunpowder smearing slightly.

"This was my favorite coat," he said, flicking his wrist and waving his hand at the gun. Max yelped and dropped it. His hand was burned where it gripped the weapon. Bertrand turned it molten.

"Now let's get down to business," Bertrand said, turning back to me, smiling, his eyes still black voids.

I stood very still. I knew exactly what he was. And it had me unnerved. "I don't deal with demons," I said through gritted teeth.

"I think this time it is in your best interest," he replied.

"So why don't you take care of Marcello?" I spat at him. "Not demon enough to take him?"

Bertrand twisted his face in disgust. "He is in the protection of witches. They have him cloaked with some spell, and I can't penetrate it without...coming out of the closet, so to speak."

"And what do you think we can do, if a demon can't take care of its own pests?" Frankie paced back and forth, like a cat stalking prey.

Tavio faced him. "Then we will give Marcello what he is after."

"Which is...?" I was getting really fed up with their hedging.

Bertrand pointed a long, elegant finger at me.

"You," he said.

Babe gasped and clutched the bar. Al reached over the bar, clutched both of her arms and steadied her.

"He's been after you for 30 years, Nina," Tavio said. He looked at Babe and sighed. "Why do you think your parent's died, child? Protecting you."

"You expect me to believe that after 30 long-ass years, this vamp suddenly comes out of hiding gunning for me? I've been walking around for decades, no problem."

"The spell broke." Babe's face drained of color. Tavio nodded.

"What are you talking about?" I whipped around and faced Babe.

"A spell your mother put on you, to keep you hidden from the vampires like Marcello," Babe said. She lowered her head and shook it slowly.

"And she should put a spell on you against witches too," Tavio grunted. "It was the witches Marcello is working with who broke the spell. Too bad she was too short-sighted to see that witches are abominations too."

"She married a vampire," Babe raised her voice.

"That woman still carried the prejudice with her," Tavio spat back.

"Well it was a vampire that killed them," she countered. "So maybe she was right."

"Okay, can we debate my family's bigotry some other time?" I jumped in. They were missing the larger point. "Why would Marcello want me dead?"

"He didn't," Bertrand said. He poured more grappa into his now-empty glass. "One of my associates wants you dead. Marcello was in it for the bounty. And then you survived."

"That's just fabulous," I muttered. "So now it's personal?"

"It appears so," Bertrand said with a shrug. "My associate wasn't too happy with Marcello's failure, so it's been a difficult few decades for him. He's very – how can I put it? – *motivated* to finish what he started."

"Well, there will be more Marcellos if there's a bounty on my head and everyone knows where I am." I said. I looked at Bertrand, who smiled.

His coal-black eyes held mine. "Not if I protect you."

"And what's in it for you?" This was certainly not out of the kindness of his heart.

"Ah, yes, what is in it for me? Right now, I unofficially run this city. I want it to be official next Tuesday."

"Bullshit," I countered. "You've been buying up votes for weeks. You'll win regardless."

"I have my reasons for wanting certainty on this matter. Let's just leave it at that." He smiled, and the wrinkles around his eyes became more pronounced, making his black eyes slightly more human.

CHAPTER 24

I blew out of Babe's with such force that I almost took the door off the hinges.

I rounded on Frankie, who was at my heels. "The protection of *demons*? Oh that's rich!"

The door pushed open and Max stepped out. I leapt on him, fists flying, but Frankie pulled me back.

"Whoa!" Max helped up his hands. "Truce. I didn't know they were...you know..."

"Demons, Max! They are demons! Or Bertrand is a demon." I looked at Frankie. "Is Tavio a demon?"

Frankie shrugged. "Not technically, but he's worked with them for a long time. Over the centuries he's probably picked up a few demonic...Ticks."

"Like day-walking?" Vampires plus sunlight equals disaster. Tavio could walk in the sunlight. Only a demon could make that happen.

"Yes, like day-walking," Frankie nodded. "That's what indebted him to the demon in the first place."

"That's just great," I gritted my teeth. "And you didn't tell me because?"

"There's a lot I didn't know, Nina. And of what little that I did, like Babe said, we thought you were covered. Literally."

"Does it really matter?" Max interjected. "Shouldn't we focus on staking that vampire? Isn't that how you kill them?"

"I wish it were that easy, Rookie," Frankie said with a grin. "This guy has some sort of witchy protection, and that's something we cannot take lightly."

"Well, Babe and Nina are witches," he countered.

"Babe is a witch," I said. "She can spell. I just talk to dead people and throw shit with my mind."

"Don't underestimate your witch powers, Nina," Frankie said, raising an eyebrow. "Your mom was the finest witch I ever saw. Babe is a very close second. And you've got that witch ghost possessing you. He could probably teach you a thing or two, you know, make himself useful while he's rattling around in your brain. Even if he doesn't know much, between him and Babe, you'll be stirring spells in no time."

An ethereal snort caught my ear. I turned my back on Max and Frankie. Casper sort of faded in and out of view in the streetlight. Then he dove straight at me. By force of habit, I lifted my arms up as protection. A hell of a lot of good that did me. I shuddered as the cold plasma oozed into my body.

"Tell that *pendejo* that I can stir more spells that would blow his elderly assed mind!" His accented voice echoed inside my brain.

"How long have you been here?" I hissed. I hated when he did that. I wish we could communicate out of my body.

"Who is she talking to?" I heard Max query Frankie.

"Who do you think?" Frankie responded.

Max turned to me. "Nina, who are you talking to?"

I doubled over, pressing at my temples, and shushed him.

"I heard the whole thing," Casper said as his ghostly grin animated my face. "We're going vampire hunting."

"You are not going vampire hunting!" I said. I paced up and down the sidewalk in front of the bar. I could faintly hear Babe and Tavio raising their voices at each other on the other side of the wall. I wanted to eavesdrop but Casper was being too damn noisy in my head with his objections. Ghosts are not quiet entities.

"Casper, please!" I raised my hand at him, which probably looked ridiculous since he had no corporeal form. "You are...you are...transparent. You cannot hold a stake!"

"But..." I could feel his agitation rising.

"Stop, let me finish," I warned him. "I am useless when you are inside of my body. I can't think straight. And even if we can kill a protected vampire, I don't know what those witches are capable of. Do you?"

Casper sulked like the teenager he was when he was murdered, but I could sense him nodding. It broke my heart that he died so young.

Cold plasma oozed out of me once again. I inhaled deeply. I was getting better at holding and releasing the possession. That was something. But regulating the vampire blood sugar post-possession was still a problem. I tried not to eye Max like a prime rib eye. Some relationship we had.

I leveled my slightly vamped-out stare at Frankie. "So can we trust Bertrand?"

"We have no choice, Love." He ran his hand through the tangles of his jet-black hair. He didn't like this either. But like he said, what choice did we have?

"Demons? You are willing to trust a demon?" Max was still looking in the general direction of Casper, like he was expecting a body to form out of the air.

"The enemy of my enemy, and all that," Frankie shrugged.

"You asshole," Max starred at Frankie, incredulously. "You actually think we can play ball with one of those things?"

"No, I don't," Frankie said. His fangs flashed and his eyes flared. "But I will trust a demon if it can save Nina's life."

"Yeah, about that." I looked at Frankie. "How do we even know he can save my ass? I don't see him willing to get the drop on some witched-out vampire."

"No, that wouldn't be expedient," Bertrand said suddenly. He was on the sidewalk with us. A snapping sound, like a branch snapping off a tree, preceded his appearance. "But I can give you the tools to kill him."

"We do your dirty work?" Max glared at him.

"No," Bertrand countered smoothly. "Nina does the dirty work."

"No deal," Frankie said as he stepped in between me and Bertrand.

"She's the only one," Bertrand said. Interestingly, he took a step away from Frankie. Vampires have a hell of a time besting demons, but Frankie made Bertrand uncomfortable. "Nina and her ghost."

"I have to be possessed to kill Marcello?" I shuddered.

"Only a knowledgeable witch can do it, and since you have been a witch for about 48 hours, you'll need the ghost of a witch to help." He adjusted his coat and glanced around. He clearly felt Casper's presence.

The cold ooze washed over me quickly, a "Booyah!" echoed in my skull, and then Casper popped out again. I smacked my hand against my forehead. Goddamn teenagers.

Bertrand motioned elegantly at my feet. "And you need the blade in your boot."

Frankie and Max looked at my feet. I reached down and pulled the knife out of my hidden boot sheath. "How did you know?"

He smiled slightly. "We have a history."

"Really?" I flipped it around in my hand, finding comfort in its weight.

"Use it like a stake," Bertrand instructed.

He reached for the knife. I pulled it closer to me.

Bertrand continued, "A direct hit to the heart. Then remove the head and burn the heart. But only use that knife. Now that he's under a witch's protection, this is the only weapon that can kill him."

"Why?" I was being as surly as Casper but I didn't care.

He looked surprised at my ignorance. "Because it kills witches."

"That makes no sense," I countered. "It's a witch's blade. It shouldn't kill a witch."

"We made some alterations." A wide smile spread across his handsome face. "Oh dear. You don't know."

I held the knife, ready to pounce. "Know what?"

"That was the knife that was supposed to kill your mother." Bertrand was so happy that he was positively glowing.

Frankie made an angry lunge at the demon. Bertrand motioned for the dagger with a flick of his wrist, and it leapt out of my hand and into his. Then he grabbed me and pulled me to him. I could smell his cologne. At such close proximity, it barely hid the stink of demon fire and death.

A gunshot rang out and a bullet narrowly missed my head. It lodged into Bertrand's temple. Max, in shooting stance, had his Glock held steady, eyes trained on Bertrand.

"You fool!" Frankie spat, his eyes darkening, never moving from Bertrand's gaze. "Let's go over this one more time. You can't shoot a demon."

A trickle of near-black blood slipped down Bertrand's face. Then he laughed and lifted the knife to my jugular. I was getting tired of being in this position.

"Frankie, Max," Bertrand 's velvet voice washed over all of us. "I am not the enemy here. I suggest you focus on the one who is."

"He has a point, guys," I squirmed under the weight of Bertrand's arm across my chest. "Bertrand's not today's problem."

"So we're just supposed to trust the devil?" Max kept his finger on the trigger.

Bertrand laughed again. "There is no devil. Only demons."

"Same thing," Max's grip tightened on the gun.

"They aren't the same," Frankie said. He still hadn't moved. His stillness was unnerving. "The devil is an angel cast down from your heaven. He was created by your God. Demons are their own creation."

"We answer to no one," Bertrand explained further. "Which makes us infinitely more dangerous."

Max slowly dropped the gun and holstered it under his coat. His face was ashen. I had no idea how much more he could take. The fact that he hadn't broken yet was a testament to his mental strength. Not many people could handle the truth about all the boogie men that were out there. Poor Max was getting a course in Supernatural 101 in just a few hours.

Bertrand released me, but held onto the dagger, cradling it like a precious artifact.

"Hand it over," I scowled at him.

"I remember when I created this with your father," he said. He continued to stare at it, enthralled. "He couldn't even touch it at first. I had to rework the spell. Such a dirty, witchy job." He didn't bother concealing his distaste. "But it was never truly a witch killer until we made it so." He smiled again, his eyes lost in a memory. "Just two of them, to start. So the witches would finally feel a vampire's wrath."

Bertrand slipped the knife back into my hand, and it was my turn to stare at it.

"So why is he killing other witches? Why not just me?" I asked. Assuming Casper was right, all the victims of supernatural activity in Providence – at least lately – were witches. If it was me that Marcello wanted, why leave a trail of bodies along the way?

"Because the more witches he kills with the blade, the more power is drawn to the blade," Bertrand said with finality. He puffed with pride. "He's making himself invincible. It was a brilliant idea. Wish I could take the credit for it, but it was your father's stroke of genius."

I glared at him and at the blade in my hand. My dad created a weapon that not only killed witches, but drew out their power. That explained why this particular weapon was the weapon of choice. A run-of-the-mill kitchen knife could kill a witch but only a witch's blade could channel a witch's power. And some sort of demon spell allowed the blade to capture it.

"A pity," Bertrand sighed. "Your father was very powerful--the most powerful of his kind. And it was all wasted on a pretty little witch."

And with a snap of the fingers, he was gone.

As if sensing his boss's departure, Tavio exited the bar. He touched my arm, and I bared my fangs at him.

CHAPTER 25

After Bertrand's bombshell, I had to cut and run. The omissions and half-truths that came from Babe, Dr. O and even Frankie felt like a betrayal. And while I know they were trying to protect me, I was still pretty pissed at the lot of them.

Sipping a chilled glass of white wine, I soaked in my bubble-filled tub until I pruned. Dog lounged on the floor outside of the tub. Once in a while she would huff in response to my out-loud ramblings about my craptastic life.

With my wine glass drained and my body sufficiently wrinkled, it was time to get out. I stood, water sliding down my body. My hand stopped short of grabbing my towel. I heard the apartment door open and close.

Dog pricked up her ears and growled, low and guttural. Damn it to hell. Could this night get any shittier?

I had nothing but a towel to keep me covered and certainly no weapons. I hoped Dog would be all I needed, but with vampire assassins after me, and demons calling an uncomfortable truce, I doubted it was a neighborhood thug doing a quick home invasion.

I wrapped the towel around me and, still dripping, gripped the door knob. Dog leaned against me, the hair on her back was on end.

"On three?" I whispered and looked down at her for approval. Her soulful brown eyes gave me her okay. "One. Two. Three..."

I don't know what I expected us to do, but Dog and I both rushed out of the bathroom like our asses were on fire. Dog clearly had a better plan. She lunged on the figure that was standing over my iPod speaker dock. He sprawled out on the floor, while Dog stood triumphantly on his back, her left front paw pressing into the back of his neck.

I ran to my bedroom and grabbed a gun out of the armoire. I stood dripping on my hardwood with the Desert Eagle pointed to the back of the intruder's head. I pulled back the slide, and the gun made a satisfying click.

"Don't shoot, Nina," a familiar but muffled voice called out from his face-plant in the floorboards.

"Max?" I released the slide and hooked the safety. I motioned Dog off. I grabbed Max by the back of his shirt and hauled him to his feet. "Are you trying to get yourself killed?"

He shrugged. "Sorry, I knocked. When you didn't answer, I picked the lock. I thought something happened. To you."

"I was in the tub." I carefully put the pistol back in the holster I dropped on the bed.

"Yes I see." He looked my towel-clad form up and down.

"Well, what do you want?" I pulled the bottle of wine out of the fridge. My glass was still in the bathroom. I considered swigging direct from the bottle, but then decided to just grab a fresh glass.

"I wanted to return those," he motioned to the table where my weapons that he confiscated were piled up. "Sounds like you'll need them.

"Thanks," I poked gently around the pile, making sure everything was there. Then I filled up my glass. "You want some?"

He nodded and I grabbed a second glass and filled it. "I think we both could use a drink. Lots of surprises the past 24 hours." He paused and glanced around my loft. "Is Frankie around?"

"Frankie?" I looked out the window, and saw the reddish pink light of the sunrise peaking out from behind the crumbling brick factory buildings across the street. I sighed and gave my eyes a rub. Great. I hadn't been to bed yet. "Nope. He's probably underground by now."

I shifted awkwardly from foot to foot while Max shrugged out of his coat. I had to admit he looked fantastic in just a simple t-shirt and a pair of loose jeans that were belted around his narrow hips. The shirt was just tight enough that I could see the outline of his abdominal muscles.

Max caught me watching him and smiled. My face suddenly flushed with embarrassment. I was fabulously underdressed, but there wasn't much privacy in an open loft, and Max was getting comfy on the couch.

"I don't really know what to make of all this," he said. He leaned forward, his elbows on his knees, the glass of wine in his hand. "It's like a nightmare, really. Witches? Demons? Vampires?"

"What can I say, Max? It's my family." My laugh was devoid of humor. Cold and distant, just like I felt. I turned my back and headed over to my armoire, pulling out an oversized Dead Kennedys concert t-shirt and a pair of sweats.

"So now what?" I paused for a moment. Did he mean what do we do about the vampire serial killer? Or did he mean us?

I yanked the t-shirt over my head and shimmied it down over my towel. After pulling the towel off from under the shirt, I hopped on one foot and then the other to put on the sweats. It was awkward and weird, but it was this or stand around in a towel. A few days ago, I would have been totally good with that option.

"I go on a witch hunt and stake a vampire," I said. Kicking some ass sounded good right about now. I wanted to stick a stake in Marcello. Badly.

Max laughed. Did he think I was joking?

"I'm sorry, Nina." He smiled gently, trying to ease the tension. "I've been…"

"An asshole?" I offered.

He laughed again, this one full-on and infectious. I smiled in spite of myself.

He motioned for me to sit next to him. I gulped down more wine. With the help of liquid courage, I curled into a corner of the sofa. Dog hopped up onto the couch, stretching out between us. I scratched her behind the ears.

"I just… Well… I'm a cop. We tend to see things in black and white. Good guys and bad guys." He swirled his wine. We both stared at the whirlpool in his glass, feeling spectacularly awkward.

"Yeah, well, we exist in the shades of grey," I broke the silence. "Like Frankie. He is one bad-ass vampire, and he's killed a lot of innocent people. But, you know, that was before he learned control. Now, he's one of the good guys. And I am definitely glad he's on my side."

"And Bertrand…" His face went dark.

"How can we work with a demon?" I finished for him. "I'm not at all happy with this partnership but we don't have much of a choice. A demon is only in it for the good of the demon. I'll work with him but I don't trust him."

Max sipped at his wine. He looked thoughtful, like he was actually considering what I said. "Guess I have to learn to live in the grey."

"It's more colorful than you think." I smiled at my stupid joke, hoping to lighten the mood a little bit.

"You think?" He shook his head, smiling. "Vampires, demons and witches running around New England with modern technology and stakes. It's like the bastard version of Grimm's fairy tales."

"Did I mention my best friend is a banshee?" I bit my lip, holding a grin back.

"No, I don't think you did." He chuckled.

A droplet of water shook loose from my hair, trickled down the side of my neck across the healing puncture wounds and the newly formed pink scar where Marcello tried to slit my throat. Max leaned over Dog, and gently traced the water's path with his finger.

Dog growled, but scooted off the couch. Traitor.

My heart raced, and my breath to caught in my chest. He paused at the crook of my neck before pressing his lips gently down and following the scar across my neck with his mouth. I closed my eyes and a small moan escaped my lips.

I pulled back from him. "What are you doing?"

He caught me behind the neck and stopped me. "What I should have done weeks ago." Gently, he pressed his lips on mine. His tongue flicked out firmly, sliding my lips open and gently, tentatively exploring my mouth.

I pulled away again, "But..."

My protests were smothered by his mouth, now pressing against my lips more urgently. His hand slid from the back of my neck down to my arm, leaving the feeling of sparks against my skin in its wake.

"Max," I dropped my head down to his neck, and he moaned in pleasure as I pressed my lips into the dip just behind his ear. "Should we do this?"

"I don't know." He pulled my head back and pressed his lips on mine again, this time with even more urgency.

He gathered me in his arms, lifted me up, and carried me to the bed. Gently, he placed me onto the soft mattress and his body dropped beside me.

I pulled his shirt over his head. Pushing him onto his back, I ran my tongue down his defined chest. I paused right above his groin. I reached down and felt his excitement swelling against the fabric of his jeans. I unzipped them and slowly freed him. He began breathing faster, and I moved my mouth to the tip. I slowly took him into my mouth, tasting him, while my hands moved up, feeling the lines of his muscular abs.

Max moaned, his fingers stroking the back of my hair. I could feel wetness seeping between my legs.

"Yes?" Max questioned as he pulled at my shirt.

"Yes," I whispered. He pulled me towards him, removing the shirt over my head. He kissed me deeply. I shook with pleasure as his hands ran over my breasts, waist and then hips.

"You are so beautiful," he said as he slid his body down between my legs. His mouth explored my breasts, my stomach, my thighs.

Warm waves flowed over me. I couldn't catch my breath.

I parted my legs and his warm tongue touched me lightly, teasingly. I arched my back with pleasure. His tongue was languid as he probed deeper into me.

I was so close to rapture. Both our bodies were glistening with sweat.

He slipped a finger in, moving it deeper, searching for the spot that would bring me to ecstasy. I sucked in when he found it. He massaged me deeply, his mouth still sucking and flicking.

I couldn't hold it in anymore, and I exploded in pleasure. My back arched at the release. Wetness spilled out of me, and Max pulled himself on top of my body. He pulled back my hair and kissed my neck.

A raw, carnal moan escaped my lips and my fangs sprung through my gums. Opening my mouth, I scraped my fangs along his neck, the desire to bite intense. In a split second, my lust turned from sex to blood.

I leapt out of the bed and caught my eyes in the mirror. They were glowing an almost-neon green in the dark. The intensity of my orgasm turned me vampy.

I walked quickly to the kitchen. Gripping the counter, I breathed deep, trying to keep my vamp-out contained. I opened the fridge and pretended to look for something.

I had never lost it at orgasm before. It only happened when I was angry. And I had learned how to control them, more or less. But to have it happen right then? That was pretty unnerving. What if I bit him...? I didn't want to think about it.

My fangs receded almost as quickly as they turned. I poured a glass of cold water and took it to the bed.

Max was still where I left him, watching me curiously. I held out the water. He took a long drink and placed the glass on the bedside table. He pulled me to him, his muscles tense against mine. He cupped my ass with one hand, and pulled my head down with the other to kiss me long and hard. I felt him grow turgid again, and I ached to feel him inside me.

"Condoms?" I pulled away from him.

"No, you?" His hopeful smile made me burst into a fit of laughter.

I shook my head, disappointed but relieved. I was losing control of my own internal beast, and I was not sure why. Until I figured out what was kept pushing me to the edge, I had to keep my feelings in check.

"I guess we'll just have to improvise," Max lowered his head to my breasts, and I shuddered again. So much for keeping my lust under control.

CHAPTER 26

I had the heebie-jeebies.

Babe eased the Fiat into a spot across the street from the downtown botanica that I had trailed Max to. In the shadows of the tall buildings, with the cold gray December morning light, the place was forbidding. But even on a bright summer day, the freaky clutter in the dusty front window -- filled with animal skulls, chicken feet, headdresses and other voodoo-like paraphernalia -- would give the best slayer chills.

Babe nonchalantly reapplied her lipstick. "Hey, if you are going to get hexed, may as well look good for it," she insisted.

I, on the other hand, still had sleep crust in my eyes and a serious case of bed head. I would have been in my PJs except I went to sleep without them. So a pair of baggy jeans, a tank top and a hoodie was my fashion statement. Of course, my silver cross was around my neck and a small 9-millimeter revolver was stuffed in the back of my pants. I wasn't going anywhere without some sort of weapon.

Babe's 9 AM call was not welcome. It had been a late night to begin with, then Max's unexpected visit, and our, um, unexpected make-up session. I had just fallen asleep when my cell phone started chirping. And Babe was around the corner, so it was a mad dash to get out of the loft. I hadn't even had any coffee.

"Can't we get coffee first?" I pleaded with my aunt, whose puckered lips were getting a final coat of fire engine red color that looked sensational on her. "They aren't even open yet."

As if on cue, a short, round, middle-aged woman lifted the security gate. As it rattled up, her unkempt black-and-gray hair fell from the loose knot that kept it on top of her head. She hastily repositioned it, looking up and down the street while stabbing a few bobby pins back in it to keep her hair held. Then she turned and walked back into the building, the heavily painted black front door slamming behind her.

I leaned back in my seat and groaned. Babe patted my leg maternally. "I'll take you for coffee after."

"What if she tries to kill us? I don't know how effective I'll be in a fight without coffee." I pleaded.

Babe gave me a look and opened the car door. "It looked like I could take her. Let's get this over with, alright?"

She was across the street before my butt even lifted out of the car seat. I sighed and followed her. There was no arguing with Babe. When she had a plan, you couldn't diverge from it. Even for coffee. Yeah, she was pretty inflexible.

The door to the botanica jingled when it opened, and the pungent combination of mold and Frankincense assaulted my nose.

"Hi, I'm Eva!" a cheery, nasal voice called out, and the rotund woman came barreling down a narrow path that cut between all the clutter of the shop. "What can I help you with today? Looking for a little luck in love?"

She held up a hideous pink candle of a man and a woman facing each other, genitals touching. The sight of it made Babe howl with laughter. "The Face-to-Face Lovers candle," she giggled. "I haven't seen that since I was a teenager!"

Eva's eyes were as wide as saucers. "Were you brought up in The Craft?"

"The Craft?" Babe looked puzzled for a minute. "Oh yes, The Craft, of course." She collapsed into another fit of giggles and mouthed "fake" at me.

"But you don't need this, do ya, honey?" Eva held up the X-rated candle and winked at me. "I bet you're lucky in love."

I felt my face grow hot and I turned, pretending to examine a group of Orisha statues in the far corner.

"Well come in, come in!" Eva motioned us towards the back of the store. "I have my cards set out if either of you lovely ladies would like a reading!"

Babe and I shuffled after her, zig-zagging around overflowing tables haphazardly placed. I could see a card table set up by the cash register, a deck of tarot cards dramatically overturned around several lit candles. This place was one fire code violation away from shutting down.

"I'd love one!" Babe gushed. "How much?"

Babe turned to me and winked. She was clearly enjoying conning the con artist.

"Fifty dollars." Eva beamed.

"Oh, dear, that's quite a bit of a financial commitment." Babe's movements towards the table slowed.

Seeing Babe's waning enthusiasm, Eva went all in. "I sense some tragedy you are trying to come to terms with, and the cards will show you how to overcome this hardship. They will show you direction, and guide you to peace."

"I don't know..." Babe fingered a bar of African Black Soap.

"And prosperity!" Eva hastily added. "And since I think this is important to your inner peace, I will drop my usual rate to 30 dollars."

"Oh why not," Babe said, slipping into the chair with a smile. "For 30 bucks? I could use some...guidance." She erupted into more giggles. God, she was going to blow it. Undercover work wasn't her strong suit.

Eva interpreted Babe's laughing as a fit of nerves. She sat down across from Babe and patted her lightly on the hand. With a cat-that-swallowed-the-canary grin, Eva picked up the Tarot deck and began shuffling. Babe gave me a quick nod and eyebrow raise. With

Eva otherwise engaged, it was time for me to take a good look around.

I poked my through the cluttered counter by the register. It was the usual cheesy crap found in Wiccan shops and botanicas -- love potions, jinx-removing spell kits, a pretty hilarious Big Money candle. There was a jewelry case underneath, a few Orisha bracelets, and some Saint medallions were carelessly tossed inside.

Turning back towards the entrance, I shuffled to the left to examine another glass case against the far wall, where a glint of silver caught my eye. I tripped over a stack of cast-iron cauldrons, swearing under my breath at the pain shooting up my shin.

I gingerly inched my way to the case. It was locked. The top shelf was filled with glass vial necklaces, and the sign beside them advertised them as "fairy dust." The contents looked like glitter. I snickered. Good for the club kids. The middle shelf was overstuffed with all manner of crystals -- crystal balls, crystals cut into hearts, fluorite and amethyst worry stones, crystals cut into pyramids. I caught sight of some nice looking rune sets among the mess.

Squatting down, I had to crane my neck a bit to look into the bottom shelf of the glass case. Jackpot! Tossed haphazardly among other athames were several replicas of my blade. I slipped my knife out of my boot, and compared the embellished hilts. They were a close match. Mine was well-worn and iron-forged. These were shiny-new, and definitely not even sterling silver. Not with a $14.95 price tag.

I sprung up when I heard Babe yelp. With a lot less care, I stumbled back through the clutter, kicking several cauldron stacks out of the way to get to her. She was standing, her eyes wide, staring at Eva who was convulsing in her seat. Instinct took over, and I went to grab her. Babe's arm shot out, stopping me.

"Let her go," Babe shook her head. "She's having a psychic vision, and pulling her out of it could have consequences."

"Psychic vision? I thought she was a fraud."

Eva slid down to the floor, her open eyes covered with some sort of white film. Yeah, she looked freaky.

"She thought she was a fraud too." Babe shook her head slowly. "But there's a witch in there. The seizures are a sign of a novice. She doesn't know how to handle the visions. She probably just thinks she's epileptic."

The convulsing slowed and then stopped, and Babe knelt on the floor beside her. She shook Eva's shoulder lightly, "Eva? Eva? You still with us, honey?"

Eva's filmy eyes cleared and she sat up. "Oh God. Did I have a seizure?"

Babe nodded. "What did you see, Eva?"

"What do you mean?" Eva looked at Babe in confusion.

"You had a vision," Babe said. Her voice was soothing, but her eyes were intense. "What did you see?"

"What are you talking about? I had another epileptic seizure." Eva looked spooked. "I need my medication, that's all."

Unsteadily, she used the chair to get off the floor. Straightening, she looked at me, and gasped. "You!"

I eyed her warily. I didn't quite trust Babe's judgment on this woman. I shifted my messenger bag, pulling it, and my wallet, closer to my body. "Yes?"

"I saw you!" Eva looked down, her voice was almost a whisper.

"Saw me what?" I shifted my weight back and forth. She was making me nervous.

"You...you were dead," Eva said slowly. A tear slipped down her cheek.

"That's just great!" I slammed my fist down hard on the counter by the cash register. The force of the impact caused the glass to crack. My fangs pushed through so quickly that I barely registered the usual pain. Eva stepped away from me, her eyes wide.

I advanced towards Eva, my nostrils picking up the scent of her fear. I could hear Babe in the background, but couldn't make out what she was saying. I was hyper-focused, stalking my prey. She was just inches from me, her racing pulse visibly pounding under the turtleneck sweater. I reached to grab her when a familiar cold ooze dropped straight into my body.

"What the hell are you doing?" Casper's voice echoed in my head. "Abstare lamia."

His voice ricocheted through my brain, and my skull wanted to split in two. My witch half waged war with my vampire nature, trying to bring it back into check. Dropping to my knees, I forced myself to take steady, calming breaths until I felt my fangs retract. The pain in my head eased slightly, but Casper was still cursing up a storm. I winced with pain at every expletive.

That was close. The internal war that waged between my formerly dormant witch genetics and my vampire genetics was making me completely unstable. The witch gene let ghosts drop into my body for a chat. And apparently the witch gene meant I could create all sorts of meteorological phenomena by sheer will. That I couldn't control this stuff was really no surprise. I had been a witch for like 72 hours.

But I had never lost control of my vampire instincts before. Calling this troubling was an understatement. Eva somehow pushed the right vampire buttons that sent me direct to fangville. If Casper hadn't popped into my body and yanked me out of my trance, Eva would have been dead or bound to me. Since I was turning into a rampaging hybrid, dead was more likely.

"What do you want from me?" Eva was full-on wailing now. She had moved behind the cash register and was pounding blindly on the keys.

I shook my head. Now that Casper had settled down, the throbbing was reduced to a dull ache. "Eva, we aren't going to hurt you." I grimaced as I said it. I wasn't entirely sure I could make that promise.

"That's what the other one said." She laughed bitterly and pulled at the collar of her sweater. Her neck, exposed for the first time, was covered with puncture wounds. "Where they hell did you people come from? Some weirdo cult?"

"Oh shit," I blurted. Babe stared at me, wide-eyed.

Eva finally got the register open. Grabbing a wad of cash, she thrust it at Babe. She was keeping a good six-foot distance from me.

"Who did that to you?" Babe held up her hand, declining the return of the money.

"As if you don't know." Eva choked back a sob.

I shifted from foot to foot, uncomfortable in my own skin. "Skinny, lanky guy? Stringy black hair?"

Eva glared at me silently but nodded her head. Babe swore under her breath and did the sign of the cross.

"What did he want?" I pressed, hoping Eva would keep talking. I didn't know how much longer she would be willing to spill it. Rather than kill her, Marcello let her live and bound her to him. And there had to be a reason. He was piling up witch bodies. Why would he leave one, even one with only novice powers, alive?

"I... I...." As Eva looked back and forth between me and Babe, confusion worked its way into her expression.

"Dammit!" Babe barked. "Eva, listen to me. Do you have any benzoin?"

Eva shook her head, staring right through Babe without really seeing her.

"Okay, what about rosemary? All good witches have rosemary, right Eva?" Babe smiled encouragingly at Eva, like she was a child.

This brought a smile to Eva's face, and she pointed behind me. I turned and saw a shelf full of dried herbs against the wall by the knife case. Stumbling once again around stacked cauldrons, I tripped my way to the dusty shelf. The herbs were bagged but the bags were an unorganized jumble. All the herbs looked the same to me. Hell, I didn't even know what rosemary looked like.

Casper pushed himself into my consciousness with such force that I grabbed the shelf to keep myself from falling over.

"Ow!" A splinter from the wood pushed into my finger. "Don't do that!"

"Sorry." He didn't sound sorry to me. "Rosemary's there."

Sighing, I let him guide my hand toward one of the bags. He nodded, which made my head flop around, sending a sharp pain through it. I tossed the bag of rosemary across the store to Babe. She snatched it out of the air and ripped it open.

208

"Okay, Eva, take a breath," Babe commanded. She practically shoved Eva's nose into the bag. "I need you to focus now. This is important. Can he day-walk?"

Oh God I hoped not. Eva's sudden confusion meant that he had definitely bound her to him. Marcello scared the crap out of her, and she did not want to protect him. But Marcello's binding gave her no choice. Her free will was clearly battling against the binding, one of the cruelest things a vampire could do to a human. I would rather be dead than bound.

Eva gave her head a shake, as if to clear it. "Day-walk?"

"Do you see him when the sun is out?" I asked gently. I tried to keep my voice like Babe's -- firm but kind, but it was laced with tension. Thankfully Casper had receded to the back of my mind again, so there was only a dull ache.

"No," she said, sounding surprised. "No, I never have seen him at daylight." She seemed to relax a little at this notion.

"Either way, we got to get her out of here," Babe said urgently. "The rosemary will only clear up her confusion, but not for long. She's still bound to Marcello. I'll have to cloak her." Babe waved her hands around. "And all this is mostly tourist crap. I can't use any of it."

Eva was too scared to process the insult.

"Alright, what do we do?" I wasn't so sure that Eva would go anywhere with me, much less in a confined space like a car. I could tell from Babe's expression, she was thinking the same thing.

"Did you find the knife?" Babe asked me as she kept her eyes on Eva.

"Yeah," I said, motioning to the glass case. "There are like ten in there."

"Those knives? Those are his. I ordered them for him," Eva looked scared.

Babe shushed me with a look. "We need the knives, Eva."

"But he'll kill me if I give them to you," she whispered.

I kicked the bottom of the display case with the steel toe of my boot. "Not if I steal them." The shattering of glass drowned out Eva's shrieking. I pulled knives out by the handful, shoving them into my messenger bag.

Babe reached her hand to Eva. "Eva, you have to come with us now. We can keep you safe. I promise."

"How?" Eva sobbed. "He knows. He always knows."

"I'm a witch, too, Eva," Babe soothed. "We can keep you hidden."

That swayed Eva to our side. Or maybe it was the incantation Babe was humming under her breath.

"OK let's go," Eva said through sniffles. She stepped out from behind the counter. Babe took her hand, and we hauled ass out of the store, pausing only long enough to yank down the security gate. We piled into the Fiat and Babe peeled out of the parking spot and raced down the deserted street.

With the botanica in the rearview mirror, I opened my bag to take a better look at the knives. Just like I thought, they were silver-plated, not sterling. That explained the cheap price tag. Since the silver content was so low, they had no impact on the vampire in me. But running my hand over them, they just felt wrong. Casper, who had been lurking in the back of my head, gently came forward, fully into my mind. Wincing at the discomfort, I let him control my hand, moving it along the ornamental hilt, then up the blade, finally hovering over the lot.

"We think there is a spell on the knives," I blurted out, slapping my hand against my mouth. It was Casper that actually said it, not me. Great. I felt like a puppet.

But even Casper possessing me didn't stop my excitement. We'd have to have a discussion about that possession stuff later, not then. I wanted to enjoy this moment. We had just stolen Marcello's weapons cache, along with the witch he channeled power through.

CHAPTER 27

The sun had barely disappeared beyond the horizon when Frankie crashed through my apartment door. I was trying to yoga-off the stress and adrenaline of the day. He barged in while I was on my fifteenth asana, shouting my name over the Gregorian chants. What can I say? I like to mix and match my spirituality.

I moved into the downward dog yoga position and stared between my legs at an upside-down Frankie. Dog sauntered over and plopped herself on my yoga mat, right underneath me. She laid down, face near mine, and licked my nose.

"Lovely," Frankie raised his eyebrows and gave me a fangy smile.

I jumped my feet to my hands, not an easy feat with Dog still under me, and slowly rolled up. I stared out the window, feeling each vertebra slip into place. The sky was streaked with vibrant swirls of pink, red and orange.

I grabbed the remote and turned the chants down. "You're up early, Frankie."

"How'd it go?" he settled himself down on one of my couches while I headed to the fridge.

"Better than I imagined." I popped open a can of Narragansett

Beer. Yoga over.

Frankie cocked an eyebrow at me.

"He was using Eva," I explained. "Eva, the woman who owns the botanica? Anyway, he was using her as a magical conduit of some sort, not sure what yet. But I managed to grab about two dozen knives that have some sort of hex on them. Dr. O has them now. He's unraveling the curse. Babe is doing some sort of witchy thing to Eva, to hide her from Marcello. He bound her to him."

For a fleeting moment, Frankie looked worried, but then his expression turned to curiosity. "He didn't kill her?"

I shook my head. "Babe said she's a witch, but Eva doesn't even know it. Honestly, we thought she was a fraud when we walked in. But Babe said she gives accurate readings and is a diviner, whatever that means." I shrugged. It was getting embarrassing how little I knew about witches and witchcraft. Especially now that I knew I was part witch.

"She wouldn't be the best witch to siphon power from," Frankie mused sensibly.

"Well Casper was a pretty powerful witch for an 18-year-old kid. But he retained his power even in ghost form, so Marcello definitely didn't siphon his power. Maybe Bertrand's playing us for fools." I twisted my hair in frustration.

"Maybe because his spirit never crossed over?" Frankie offered.

"Okay, assuming Bertrand's being straight, why keep Eva alive at all? Why not siphon her too? Why the binding?"

Dog got up from the yoga mat and nuzzled my hand. Time to feed her. I busied myself getting her food together.

Frankie shrugged. "Some of us want eyes and ears during daylight. Some just like the idea of a human to do our bidding. Some, believe it or not, are in love."

I snorted at that suggestion, pulling a can of dog food from the cabinet to mix with Dog's bowl of dry.

"Honestly, Nina, you are the most unromantic woman I have ever met," Frankie chided me.

"Oh please," I rolled my eyes, spooning the wet slop into her bowl.

"If you were human, and I bound you to me, you would not be immortal, but you would remain young and vital for decades beyond a normal human life," Frankie said as his eyes darkened. "Can you imagine loving someone so much that you didn't want them to experience something as horrific as turning into a monster? But knowing that they are human, and their time with you would be too fleeting? What would you do?"

"I don't know. I don't think about this shit," I said and put the bowl on the floor. "You're just from another era."

Dog shoved her nose in and went at it with gusto.

A pounding on the door interrupted our argument. My heart rate accelerated. Frankie and I looked at each other. Dog continued inhaling her food.

"Want me to get it?" Frankie asked. I held up my hand in the universal "wait a second" gesture. I bolted to my armoire and pulled out my Beretta. I checked the chamber and then nodded at Frankie. We went to the door.

At the sound of the safety releasing, Frankie pushed the door open. Max froze when he saw us, his eyes wide. I wasn't sure if it was Frankie's fangs or my Beretta Bobcat causing his unease.

"How many guns do you have, woman?" Max still didn't move from the doorway.

I sighed and dropped the gun, clicking the safety back into place. Frankie stepped back, letting Max pass, his fangs still in view. He was like a goddamn peacock with those things.

Max went straight to the fridge and pulled out a beer. "I just came from Bertrand's," he began.

"Well, don't leave us in suspense," Frankie said, repositioning himself on the couch.

"Tavio told me to give this to you," Max said as he handed Frankie some sort of medallion. "Said to invoke it if the witches got the best of you. I have no idea what that even means."

Invoke it? That meant it needed blood to work. I snatched the medallion from Max's hand. The nerves in my hand immediately were set on edge, like a million tiny electric surges.

"Frankie, it's freaking demon magic." I fumbled the gold disk. "You can't use that."

"What if I have no choice?" Frankie held out his hand, and I handed it off reluctantly.

"You can't dance with a demon," I warned.

"Not even the mambo?" he chirped. He slid the trinket into his jacket pocket.

"I wish you wouldn't be so casual about that," I said, not bothering to hide my exasperation.

He shrugged, examining the piece.

"I think we need Bertrand's help," Max said, lacing his fingers through mine.

"Not you too," I pulled my hand away from him. "You don't deal with demons."

"I am not sure we have a choice." Max looked stunned. Was it because I pushed him away or because I was anti-Bertrand? If it was the former, his ego was the size of Mount Everest. If it was the latter, he was an idiot.

"I hate to agree with the human, but...." Frankie glanced up at us.

"Come on, Frankie. You know better than this."

"I want you out of this, Nina," Max said firmly. "With Bertrand's help, I think we can take Marcello out without you. There's a price on your head, and his incentive is strong. It's better if you hang back."

My rage hit a boiling point. I didn't even try to hide my fangs

214

when they forced their way out.

"Did you just tell me to hang back?" I said in a low growl that was echoed by Dog.

"Yes, I did," Max said, not backing down. "It's personal for you, and there's a good chance you'll do something stupid."

That made Frankie snort. We both looked at him. Frankie held up his hands in mock surrender. "This is all on you, Max. Nina can handle herself."

"It's better if it's personal, trust me," I squatted to the floor and scratched behind Dog's ears.

Max looked away, uncomfortable. "We can discuss this later. Privately."

Frankie's eyes flicked between Max and me. He looked suspicious.

"Max, there is nothing to discuss later. If anyone should stay behind, it's you. *Human*," I spat out.

"Not quite," Max said so quietly that I almost missed it. Frankie's vampire hearing picked it up too. We both stared at him, mouths gaping.

I stood slowly, cautiously. "What. Did. You. Do?"

"I called in a favor," he hesitated just enough.

"Bertrand?" I dropped back to the floor, and leaned my head against the cabinet. I wanted to knock Frankie and Max's heads together. Trusting Bertrand was beyond stupid. They were getting themselves way too deep in demon muck to come out the other side.

"So what super power do you have?" Frankie scoffed. Did he think Max was bluffing?

"It's nothing too awesome," Max sounded a bit slighted. "But I have a medallion too. It changes night to day, so I can burn him out."

"Oh perfect," I said, my sarcasm dripping out. "In the meantime, you also burn up Frankie. Nice power to ask for."

215

"I didn't ask for it," Max fumed. "I went in to ask for help, and I walked out with this."

"See why you can't deal with them?" I shook my head at both of them. "You asked for help, you get crap. Do you owe him anything in return?"

Max shook his head.

"Good, because this is a stupid reason to owe him a favor." I bristled at the thought of owing any sort of allegiance to Ami Bertrand.

The air in the apartment shifted, and I looked up to see Casper hovering around Max. I thought I saw an odd look on his translucent face. I motioned for him to come over.

He floated in front of me. I braced myself, and nodded. He oozed into me, and my hands hit the floor while I took the pain of his entering my body.

Frankie looked at me curiously. "Guess Casper is here?"

I nodded.

"Bertrand gave him something -- not just ability to call the day," Casper's voice echoed in my head privately. He obviously wanted only me to be able to hear him.

I nodded for him to continue.

"Don't know what," Casper went on. "But something's off with him. Watch your back."

"Does he know?" I asked Casper. For a split second, I considered how insane I must look, having what appeared to be a one-sided conversation.

"No," Casper popped out quickly, and disappeared into the air.

"What was that about?" Max crossed his arms.

"I'm not sure yet." I stood and stalked to the bedroom. I flopped down on the bed, nursing the migraine Casper left in his wake.

"You read through the Grimoires yet, Nina?" Frankie called over to me.

"Nope," I pulled a pillow over my eyes. The cool fabric felt good against my throbbing head.

"Don't you think you should give them a look over?" Frankie pressed.

"Nope," I repeated.

I heard Frankie's feet thudding towards me, and the bed shifted under his weight as he sat down on the edge. "You're going to need to learn to be a witch, Nina," he said softly. "Whether you like it or not, it's part of you. It's in your DNA."

"Thanks, Dr. Phil. What do you know about family? You ate yours."

I felt Frankie stiffen, and I immediately felt awful. I shot upright. "Shit. Sorry Frankie. I didn't mean it."

He stood and turned his back to me. "Don't worry about it. Speaking of, I have to feed. I'll check in later."

And with that, he walked away. I jumped at the bang the door made when it slammed shut.

"Feed?" Max asked. I forgot he was still there. "He's going to kill someone? Shouldn't we do something?"

I sighed and rolled onto my stomach, propping my head up with my hands. "Frankie doesn't kill when he feeds, Max."

"He eats squirrels or something?" Max looked relieved.

"No, it's human blood," I admitted. I deliberately didn't elaborate so that I could see his reaction, and it didn't disappoint. He went pale, and absently moved his hand to cover his neck.

"Vampires don't need to kill to feed," I deadpanned. "It's just the newbies and the psychos that kill during bloodletting. Frankie's plenty old enough to know how to do it right. And he's not a psycho. I don't think."

Max looked incredulous. "But who would give him blood?"

"Frankie has no problem finding willing donors. Trust me." I hated going to clubs with him for this very reason. While I skulked about awkwardly in a corner, Frankie was overloaded with attention, both male and female. "You just have to know where to look. There's a whole subculture of 'vampires,'" I said, using air quotes. "There are people who see vampirism as a sort of spiritual thing -- like a religion -- and they practice with other consenting adults. Frankie just happens to be real." Of course his paramours don't know that, and I wasn't about to tell Max that little detail.

"I am surprised you don't know about them," I went on. "They are considered a cult, sometimes a gang. Every once in a while a group goes off the rails and murders someone. That always makes the news." I rolled over on my back and stared at the ceiling.

I could sense Max shifting uncomfortably. Was it the conversation? Or was it because the last time we were alone in my apartment we did some wonderfully naughty things? Maybe he was feeling regretful. Was he worried that if he dumped me I would suck him dry and leave him for dead?

I sat up and looked at Max. "We need to talk."

"About?" He looked everywhere except at me.

"About last night. About what happened between us." I motioned for him to join me on the bed. "I promise I won't bite." I smiled. He didn't. Guess he didn't find it that funny. But he did come over and sit stiffly on the edge of the bed.

Crossing my legs underneath me, I leaned against the pillows at my back. "It's cool if you want to forget what happened between us. I won't go all vampy or witchy on you. We can just forget it happened if that what's you want. Okay?"

"You could not be further off base," Max protested, but his eyes told a different story.

I held up my hand. "Stop it, okay. Let's just get through the next 24 hours without you or Frankie turning me into Bertrand's bitch. We can't afford distractions."

He nodded curtly. My cell phone buzzed, breaking the uncomfortable silence between us. I let out a breath I didn't realize I was holding and looked at it. A text from Babe. She and Dr. O were on their way over. We were hitting Marcello the next night. Apparently, my apartment was becoming the War Room.

I looked at Max's pinched face and put my hand on his shoulder. "We go in less than 24 hours. Get ready because this is going to be like nothing you've seen before."

CHAPTER 28

Babe, Dr. O and Max sat around my kitchen table as the smell of fresh brewing coffee wafted through the loft. In a low voice, Babe (apparently the only person alive who could figure out Etrusian) was translating a Grimoire to Max, who was dutifully writing down every word. Dr. O mixed an herbal concoction, chanting quietly in some ancient Druidic tongue. Since I was more a doer than an incantor, I sharpened my blades. Dog was sprawled out on my bed snoring.

Frankie had returned a few hours earlier, his cheeks flushed from feeding. He immediately retreated to a makeshift workshop he installed in his basement chamber. Near 4 AM, he gave a brief knock before letting himself into my apartment. He dropped an enormous crossbow in the center of the table, followed by a handful of wooden crossbow bolts.

The weapon was extraordinary. It was a simple crossbow, but somehow in its design and construction, the bow became a work of art. I examined the carved details closer. Streamlined and of a light weight that belied its size, the bow felt slightly warm and alive in my hand.

Dr. O stood over my shoulder, admiring the craftsmanship. "It's gorgeous."

"How did you do this?" I marveled.

Frankie grinned with pride. "Pretty good, right?"

I handed the bow to Dr. O so I could get a closer look at the bolts. "Runes?" I squinted and pulled them closer.

Dr. O took a bolt with his other hand and, closing his eyes, spun it between his thumb and forefinger. "Blackthorn tree, yes?"

Frankie beamed. "Witches aren't the only ones who can work a bit of magic!"

I took the crossbow back from Dr. O and looked through its site. It was calibrated perfectly.

"This is awesome, Frankie," I marveled. "You are a master craftsman."

His pale skin blushed a faint pink. "I know you'll take good care of them. They've been made to take care of you."

I gave him a hug. "Thanks, Frankie."

"Don't mention it." He squeezed me quickly before letting go. "Right, so now what?"

"We go after Marcello," I fiddled with the crossbow, shifting it awkwardly around my body. It was super cool, but I had no idea how to carry it.

"Do you have a plan?" Frankie quipped.

"Find him and kill him, Genius," I shot back. Frankie's sarcasm was grating, so he deserved to have some snark tossed right back at him.

"And how do you propose we find him? We're the ones watching the bodies pile up, remember?" Frankie crossed his arms, his long, lean frame lounging against the counter.

"We have his witch," I said with a grin. Eva was holed up at Babe's, with Alfonso keeping an eye on her. When Babe left, Al was wearing a blue streak because Eva misread his Tarot cards. Babe was pretty certain Al would school her on proper Tarot technique while we were away.

"No, you don't," Babe piped up, her voice stern. "Not for that. I promised her I'd cloak her and I did. But I won't risk exposing her. You are not going to use her for bait."

221

"Come on, Babe," I moaned. "It'll just be for like a minute."

Babe shook her head. "Forget it."

"It's the most direct way to flush him out," Max offered.

"Eva has no idea how to control her powers. Hell, she doesn't even know she has powers. There's no way she can protect herself." Babe pursed her lips, then continued. "By now, Marcello definitely knows she's been cloaked and it doesn't take a rocket scientist to figure out who's hiding her. If we expose her now, he'll kill her. So forget it. Come up with a Plan B."

Plan B? Really? I knew she was right, but Eva was our only link to Marcello. I didn't want to see her dead either, but she was our best way in. Frankie was right in that we were always one step behind Marcello, getting there just in time to clean up the bodies. Hell, sometimes even the cops were getting there first.

"I think I know how to find him," Frankie said with a pensive expression. "Or lure him out, anyway."

Dr. O raised his eyebrows. "Go on."

"I have to take Nina home," Frankie said quietly.

"Home? I am home." Great. Now Frankie was making no sense.

"No, Nina," Dr. O smiled gently. "He means home, where you lived with your parents, before--"

"Before they died?" I finished his sentence. "And that brings him out...how?"

"He killed them there," Frankie explained. "Not in the house, but the barn.

"Barn?" I lived in the country?

"Yes, your mother and I had a connection to the land there," Babe offered. "It was Native land."

"But we're not native here. We're native to Mexico."

Babe just shrugged. "Somewhere in our bloodline, we have a

connection to this place. No idea why. One day, maybe we'll learn. Until then, I just go with it."

"Do all witches share this blind faith thing you have going on?" I just didn't buy this "connection to the land" business, not to mention it was the fastest way to end up dead. If I followed these ugga bugga feelings blindly, I'd be twice dead, true dead. Freaking witches.

I turned to Frankie. "So where is this place?"

"Chepachet," he responded. "It's a lovely old farmhouse."

"And how do we get access to this lovely old farmhouse?" Why was I suddenly the only practical one?

"You have the key." Frankie grinned slightly.

"What do you mean? I OWN it?" When this was over, I was sitting down with Babe and Dr. O and finding out exactly what I had inherited.

Babe shrugged and nodded. "There was no point in telling you until the time made sense. Now, it makes sense."

"I am getting tired of this witchy stuff," I grumbled.

"We get pretty sick of vampires sometimes, too," she raised her eyebrows at me. "You'll adapt."

I ignored that.

Max piped up, "So we go there. Then what? How do we know he'll show up?"

"I'll take care of it," Frankie stood. "We leave at 10:30 tonight."

"And what are you going to do?" I really hoped he wasn't going to do anything stupid.

"Making sure Marcello shows," he grinned, showing some fang. "I'll track him on the vampire network."

"Frankie, that is the biggest load of bullshit you have ever given me," I said, rolling my eyes. Seriously. Vampire network? Did he think I was an idiot?

"When you die, you'll understand," he quipped. He was so obnoxious.

"Just make sure he shows," Dr. O chimed in, probably to stop our bickering.

"Nina, would you go see the good Father tomorrow afternoon and get the weapons sorted? I'll drop a note in the box before sun-up, to let him know you'll swing by," Frankie rubbed my head, ruffling my hair. See? Obnoxious.

CHAPTER 29

Holy Ghost Catholic Church was almost at the crest of the hill that led into the Federal Hill, the old Italian section of Providence. It is sandwiched between two derelict neighborhoods. Where Federal Hill was once a fashionable enclave for Italians to live in Rhode Island, it was now just a shell of a Little Italy. Behind the façade of red, white and green flags, it was a rough-and-tumble neighborhood for new immigrants, mainly from South America.

I sprinted two at a time up the endless stairs leading to the front entrance. I caught my breath at the top, then pushed open the front door. Only when I wasn't struck down by lightening did I exhale.

An elderly priest looked up from the altar.

"Nina," Father Dougherty genuflected at the altar before rushing down the center aisle. He was a sprite old man.

He hugged me tight and kissed me on top of the head.

I smiled up at him. "Good to see you, Padre."

My mom and Babe were raised at the knee of Father Dougherty, who came to Holy Ghost as a young cleric direct from Ireland. I wasn't religious, but I still inherited my mother's strong personal bond with Father Dougherty. The Catholic thing was just a slight inconvenience. That said, I appreciated the ritual of a Catholic mass.

And Father Dougherty, he got it. In fact, he was the one that introduced my parents to Dr. O. He sheltered both of my parents on several occasions from various supernatural freaks, as well as some human ones, that were after them at one time or another. And he was the one that imbued my weapons with their demon-and-vampire-blasting power.

Dr. O and Father Dougherty were old friends -- how old I wasn't quite sure, but I always suspected that the good Catholic was a Druid in hiding.

Father Dougherty steered me towards the confessional box. I panicked for a second. Confession was the last thing I wanted right then.

"Padre, I am not here for confession..." I stammered.

"I know," he whispered, pushing gently on my back. "But get in there so we can talk privately."

He slipped into his doorway. I sighed and entered my side of the confessional, shutting the door tightly behind me. Claustrophobia creeped at me. You have no idea how relieved I was to find out vampires don't really sleep in coffins, because I don't do well in confined spaces. Turns out, as long as the room was sealed off from sunlight, no coffins are required.

Father Dougherty slid open the partition between us. "Sorry, Nina, but we can't risk being overheard. You have the blades, correct?"

"Yes, of course," I was confused. The blades were the reason I was here. "Can't we just go into the little room...?"

"We need to talk," he jumped in. "Nina, have you heard about the murders happening around the city?"

"Yeah, the gang killings. So?" The tiny enclosure was making me anxious and more impatient than usual.

"So you know, those people that died were members of this church. They were not gang-bangers. They were decent men and women -- with families." Father Dougherty was angry, protective of his congregation.

"We know they aren't gang killings, Father." I sighed deeply. "We are chasing down the right people."

"It's not just that!" Father Dougherty snapped. "Sorry, Nina...I know you and Frankie and Loch are on top of it but...the congregation. Well, some of them are superstitious. They are whispering about vampires."

I couldn't see him from behind the confessional screen, but I imagined the wrinkles on his face more pronounced from worry.

"They are right," I said, keeping my voice calm and measured. "We are after a vampire. The one that killed my parents."

Father Dougherty sucked in his breath. "They are pulling closer and closer to you, Nina. To us."

"Who? Marcello?" I didn't like the sound of this.

"We need to get you ready." Ignoring my question, he slid open the door to the confessional. The rustle of his robes let me know he'd exited. I stumbled out of my little box.

Father Dougherty moved at a brisk pace to a small room behind the altar. He threw off the cloth covering an old wooden table that was carved with intricate symbols and motioned that he was ready. I unwrapped my leather carrier and pulled out my wrist knives, my dad's knife and the crossbow bolts. I dropped them on the altar.

Father Dougherty picked up one of the bolts admiringly. "These are new."

"Yeah, Frankie made them last night. The crossbow is pretty impressive too." I fingered the bolts.

He pulled a bolt closer to examine its detail. "Did you know Frankie drew these ruins in blood? His blood?"

I shook my head. "No. Does that mean something?"

"That sort of bloodletting is an ancient practice. It imbues the weapon with a lot of power. The vampire blood makes it even more powerful. It's an impressive bit of magic that Frankie must have picked up somewhere over the centuries, before the falling out with the witches."

Father Dougherty began chanting in an ancient language that sounded an awful lot like the language in the Grimoire. Happy that Babe wasn't the only one to know the arcane language, I made a mental note to bring it with me next time.

His chanting became louder and faster, and he poured Holy Water on the weapons from a large silver pitcher, also covered with rune-like symbols. The water washed over the cache and I could have sworn they were struck by lightning for a split second. I blinked and looked at them again, but the ritual was over, and they simply looked like weapons sitting in a puddle.

Father Dougherty picked them up and carefully wiped each of them down before handing them to me. Hot against my fingers, I slipped them quickly into the leather pouch. They were practically vibrating.

"Be careful, Nina," Father Dougherty said to me grimly. "I know what you are facing, and it's formidable. He almost made it into the church some years ago." His eyes filled with tears.

The way the story goes, Father Dougherty tried to save them all those years ago. But my father, being full-blooded vampire, could not cross the threshold of the church. He left my mom, along with Babe and me, at the church. But Mom slipped out to fight by her husband's side. That decision left me an orphan.

I touched his hand, "Not your fault, Padre. Mom was stubborn and willful and there was no way she was going to sit back while Dad was in trouble."

The priest smiled at me grimly. "You inherited your mother's willfulness."

"Of course I have," I said with a grin. "But it's combined with my father's ability to kick ass."

A young altar boy walking past the chamber stopped short. He looked horrified at my words. Father Dougherty threw his hands up, as if Heaven would intervene. But I caught him suppressing a chuckle.

I bowed my head at the offended boy and made my way back towards the pews. "Lo siento, por favor."

We walked up the center aisle towards the doorway together.

"Are you sure these weapons will do it?" he whispered.

"I don't know," I replied quietly, as we passed a group of elderly Mexican women praying quietly in Spanish. "They are the best Frankie's ever made."

"Good," he said, seeming a little more at ease. "I have something extra for you."

He slipped something into my hand.

I smiled at the two smooth glass vials attached to leather chords. "Holy Water?"

He shook his head. "Gregorian water."

I looked at him blankly.

"Dr. O didn't give you any religious education beyond the basics, did he?" His voice was thick with annoyance.

"Afraid not, Padre. But he also blew off Witchcraft 101." There was a bit of a professional rivalry between the Dr. O and Father Dougherty, and I wanted to diffuse any perceived slight. "So, please, can you explain?"

"Gregorian water is stronger than Holy Water. It's a mix of Holy Water, wine, ashes.... We use it to consecrate the ground before we build a church, we use it to bless the altar," he explained. "Sprinkle it around you, and evil cannot touch you. The ground will be consecrated as if it were a church. It won't last long without a priest's blessing, but it should buy you enough time to get out of trouble."

I nodded, slightly overwhelmed. It was a brilliant gift. Gregorian water wasn't exactly something I could pick up at the local religious store.

"I used it on your blades too," Father Dougherty continued. "And the Holy Water in it is from Lourdes. I am not taking any chances."

He stopped suddenly by the Holy Water vessel that sat at the church entrance, dipped his fingers in and blessed me.

"En el nombre del Padre y del Hijo y del Espíritu Santo, Amén," he intoned. I found myself chanting along with him, to his delight.

I hugged him tightly. "Gracias, Padre."

He kissed the top of my head. "Of course, Nina. God be with you, my child."

I sprinted down the steps of the church and into the overcast afternoon. I wasn't so sure it was God that I needed. In fact, I suspected it might be a demon that I needed. I had one more errand to run before the sun set.

CHAPTER 30

I stood outside the Biltmore's revolving doors, staring up at the dilapidated building. Was I out of my mind?

I suspected Ami Bertrand was holed up at the hotel. What other creep-a-zoid would have the gall to call himself the Mayor when he hadn't won the election yet.

I fiddled with the vials of Gregorian water looped around my neck by leather straps. I was going in unarmed, my weapons safely locked away at home. I didn't like the way he held my dad's knife the last time I saw him, like it pained him to give it back to me. I didn't want to chance him stealing them. Especially my spectacular crossbow. That was one of a kind and, thanks to Frankie's blood, a unique and powerful weapon. It was certain to grab his attention.

But I didn't want to go in completely unarmed, so the Gregorian water was my only protection.

Not that my weapons would do me much good anyway. There was no way to kill a demon. Well, no way that we knew. Exorcism only made them temporarily go away. And we had ways to make their lives miserable. But to permanently disappear? Nope.

Luckily, there weren't many demons hanging around in the open. They were mostly the schemers of the underworld, preferring to stay hidden in plain sight while unleashing their misery through their conduits. Although impossible to prove, there were often demon tentacles attached to rogue vampires or rabid wares. Like any good politician, they excelled in keeping their hands clean.

So while Bertrand was definitely well suited to run for political office, it was highly unusual that he was doing so publicly.

Breathing deeply, I pushed at the revolving door and spun into the lobby. I pushed my way past a sweaty, balding man in a stained dress shirt. Drunk, he stumbled into me, and then grabbed my arm to hold himself up. He reeked of cheap gin. I shoved him off a little too hard. He went airborne, landing in a heap at the bottom of the steps.

"Hey! Lady!" A skinny guy working reception stretched over the desk, as if that was going to stop me.

Ignoring his call, I nudged the drunk guy out of my way with my foot and bounded up the stairs, looking for the bellboy ghost. Suicide bride was doing her usual tumble down the staircase. Right behind her, the young man appeared.

"Please let the mayor know I am here to see him." Dutifully, the ghost turned and motioned that I should follow him up the stairs. I wished real people were that agreeable with me. I just hoped he remembered that I couldn't walk on or through walls.

He ushered me down a long, mirrored hallway. At the very end, he swung open ornate wooden double doors. I passed him while he stood, hand out for a tip.

"Er," I reached into my pockets and came up empty. What do you give a dead bellboy anyway? "I'll getcha next time?"

"Very good," he snarled and slammed the door. It was almost like he was alive.

I was in a small anteroom, with another set of wooden double doors in front of me. For a split second, I considered turning back. But we had to have a chat. I gripped the handles and pushed.

I swept into a luxurious modern office. The dark cherry wood of the sleek furnishings was complimented by muted sandy beige and light moss green fabrics, giving the space an almost Zen feel. Ami was sprawled on a comfortable-looking sofa, his shoes kicked off, and files all around him. Tavio was in a chair in front of Bertrand's large desk, nursing a Scotch and reading the Daily Racing Form.

"Gentleman," I said tartly, hoping I didn't look too wide-eyed impressed at the beautiful room.

Bertrand stood, removing his glasses and extending his arm to me. "Nina, what a lovely surprise."

I stepped back before he could touch me. My hand instinctively reached behind me for my gun, which wasn't there. Tavio took note, and with his vampire swiftness, he was beside me before my next breath.

"I have to pat you down," he said. He sounded almost apologetic. "We can't be too careful these days."

I nodded and he ran his hands quickly around my body, checking for weapons. He drew back quickly when he neared the vials of water around my neck.

"Those?" He pointed, keeping an arm length between his finger and my neck. I couldn't tell if he was unwilling or unable to get closer. I suspected the latter. He would have removed them if he could.

"They stay," I said firmly. "I am not stupid enough to show up here completely naked. As it were," I added when I saw Bertrand's raised eyebrows.

"It's perfectly understandable," Bertrand smiled, his teeth perfectly straight and white. He motioned to an overstuffed armchair close to the coach. "Please, sit. Can we get you a drink? Coffee? Tea? Blood?"

The offer of blood threw me off balance, and I hesitated just long enough for him to notice. He smiled wider. "Joking, my dear. Now what can we do for you?"

"I have questions about the knife and I'm betting you can answer them," I blurted out. To hell with the polite formalities.

"Really?" He seemed amused. "I told you all I know."

I fingered the vials and looked at him. "I don't think so."

"What is it worth to you?" he asked smoothly, closing up a few files sitting on the cushions beside him.

"This is not a negotiation," I bristled, reaffirming that I was not willing to do a deal. "You are getting Marcello dealt with. There's your value. And if you want to see me come out of this the victor, I suggest you tell me what you know."

He leaned back, stretching his arms over the couch, Cheshire cat smile on his face. "You have five minutes. I have a campaign to run."

"How is he using multiple knives? How many of them are there?"

Bertrand raised an eyebrow. "Your father's was supposed to be the only one. I wonder if he made more without my knowledge."

"How did you spell it?" I pressed.

"You, witch novice, wouldn't understand." He steepled his hands, staring at me intently with his black eyes.

"Try me," I returned his gaze. I felt my fangs shift and push through my gums. I let them show.

"Nina, your father betrayed me. I shared my information only because you are the only one who can put an end to these murders. If I thought killing you myself would put an end to it, I would. So if you think I am going to offer anything more without proper payment, you are deeply mistaken. Now, if are you done preening, I am a very busy man," he said with finality. He looked at me expectantly, grinning like a bored professor during office hours with a stubborn student.

"Yes we are done," I seethed. I stood quickly, but Tavio was by my side before I had risen to my full height.

"I'll see you out," he said. Then he gently took my arm and escorted me into the anteroom.

"He won't tell you this, but your father wasn't the only one to betray him," Tavio whispered once the door was closed behind us.

"Then who?" I glared.

"Another demon. There was a second knife that had an incomplete spell. He stole it." Tavio slipped a stone in my hand.

"What's this?" I fingered it carefully. I felt carvings etched in it.

234

"Keep it close," he said. "It slows the blades effects. I see it already started."

"What are you talking about?

"The witch blade released the dormant gene, it tainted your blood," Tavio said, flashing his fangs. "The stone stops the poison when you hold it. You will be vampire once again."

"I won't take this," I pushed it back at him. I did not want to owe the demons any favors.

"No, no, take. Please." He held up his hands and backed away." Your DNA is at war. You will die. Bertrand needs you, Nina. I can't let that happen."

"Demons require no assistance to get their vile work done," I scoffed.

"Maybe hell needs an angel," Tavio grinned slightly. "Or, at least, a beautiful woman." Was he trying a charm offensive? That enraged me even more.

"I want nothing from you or your boss." And with that, I turned on my heel. Dropping the stone at Tavio's feet, I stormed into the Biltmore's hallway. I was more comfortable dodging poltergeists than having this conversation with my demon-tainted vampire uncle.

I was who I was, dormant gene or not. I would not sacrifice my witch side to my vampire side, or vice versa. I'd figure out a way to find a balance. I refused to be a casualty of their pointless war.

CHAPTER 31

Of course the night we decided to hit Marcello was the night the nor'easter blew in. The country highway leading into the rural enclave of Chepachet was pitch black on a good night. With the heavy snowfall and whipping winds, it was treacherously foreboding. Frankie and I drove through it in a nervous silence, broken only by Dog's aggressive panting from the backseat.

I fidgeted around, and Casper was lying dormant inside my body, waiting to be called into action. I once again checked my weapons. I knew they were all accounted for, but it took my mind off of what we were walking into and the dull ache that Casper's possession left in my head.

Frankie reached over and squeezed my hand. "You okay?" He took his eyes off the road for a split second. "We're almost there." He turned off the dark highway and onto an old farm road. Shoving Max's Suburban into four-wheel drive, we plowed through snow that was already piled two-feet thick on the road.

"Where the hell did they go?" I muttered, looking behind us. Babe, Max and Dr. O were following behind us, but since Babe's little Fiat was crap in this weather, they couldn't keep up with us.

"They'll be along soon," Frankie said feebly. "We're here."

He made a sharp right turn, and, directly in front of us was a farmhouse. It was white. It was huge. It was old. Our headlights bounced off of grime-covered, leaded glass windows. The partial frame of an old barn, burned down by the fire that claimed both of my parents, loomed large behind the house.

Frankie killed the engine and we both climbed out of the car. Dog hopped down from the warm comfort of her seat into a snow bank. We all trudged to the porch. Frankie unlocked the front door and we stumbled in. Our footsteps echoed in the empty house, and Dog's nails tap-tap-tapped along the damaged wood floors. The air was thick with dust. Dog growled, her hair standing on end. I was happy I wasn't the only one creeped out by this place.

"Right, so here we are," Frankie looked warily around. He hadn't been here since the night my parents were killed. His trepidation betrayed his usual cool detachment. Shit. This was not the time for Frankie to get spooked.

I punched him lightly in the arm. "Yes, here we are. Now focus, please."

"Right." He shook his head, clearing the cobwebs from his mind. "Look. There is a stream running directly under this house -- it's visible in the basement. Once we get down there, I won't be able to cross it."

"Why not?" I questioned. There was an old superstition that vampires couldn't cross water, but that wasn't actually true.

"I don't know," Frankie said. His patience was wearing thin and he looked ready to explode. "But I can't cross it, and your dad couldn't cross it. But your mom had no problem with it. So clearly it has something to do with vampires."

A stream a vampire couldn't cross. Odd definitely but, I didn't have time to second-guess Frankie.

"So if you run into problems, get your ass downstairs and cross that stream," Frankie continued, pacing back and forth, his boots cutting through the dust on the floor. "You aren't a true vampire, so you should be able to cross it. He shouldn't be able to catch you once you get to the other side. From there, take him down with the crossbow. That should weaken him enough so you can get in with the knife and finish him off."

I nodded. No point in questioning why vampires couldn't cross the stream. I could see that Frankie wasn't in the mood to tell me. I decided to chalk it up to one of the great mysteries of the world and leave it at that.

"What if I use the Gregorian water?" I fiddled with the vials that I looped around my neck with a leather cord.

Frankie looked at the two vials thoughtfully. "I'd prefer to see those remain around your neck. They could deflect a bite."

"What if the witches show up?" I asked, staring out the window. With the blanket of snow over the wooded area in the back, the farmhouse was picturesque. But sadness weighed heavily on this place. I could sense restless spirits in the graveyard out back.

"Leave the witches to me," Frank said vaguely. In the dark, his eyes were orbs of brilliant blue light looking right at me. "You alright, Nina? You don't seem yourself."

"Neither do you," I pointed out.

He acknowledged that with a short nod.

I looked out the back window, where I sensed the graveyard. "A lot of ghosts out there."

I watched Frankie's aristocratic profile in the dim light by the window. He had followed my gaze to toward the old cemetery. Neither of us could see it, but I could feel it. "Your mum put some sort of spell on the graveyard to hold them in. As long as they aren't released, they shouldn't overwhelm you."

"And I'm here if they try." Casper moved forward in my mind with a quick tightening at my temples, before receding back again. I winced a little at the pain.

"What the hell happened to our backup?" I muttered under my breath.

"I think we are on our own, Love." Frankie's vamp kicked in suddenly, and I felt a whisper of wind before he appeared at my side in less than a blink. My skin prickled. Dog's fur stood on edge. She let out a low growl.

"They're coming," Casper whispered, darting back into the recesses of my mind before the pain hit me full force. I gave him a small groan of acknowledgment.

"It's time," I said as I squeezed Frankie's hand then dropped it when the door blew off the hinges. A gust of freezing air and snow whooshed into the room. Marcello, holding a witch blade, stood at the threshold, flanked by the two women he met at Babe's the night he attacked. Marcello's laughter reverberated off the walls. My body let out an involuntary shiver, which did not escape his notice. With that split-second chill, he caught my fear and held fast to it.

I released the blade on my left arm. The familiar sound of the metal sliding down the sheath calmed my nerves a bit. Out of the corner of my eye, I saw Frankie double-fisting two silver-tipped stakes. He was in full vamp mode. Fangs out, his eyes were a vibrant blue. He twirled the stakes effortlessly in each hand.

"Francesco," Marcello bowed his head slightly at Frankie. "I don't wish to kill you."

"No worries. You won't," Frankie snarled.

Marcello grinned and plunged the blade into the chest of one of the women. She shrieked, a mix of pain and surprise. The knife burned white hot, containing the magic that it extracted from her. Marcello twisted the knife, then exchanged the blade for his own hand, pulling out the heart. It was still beating when he sunk his fangs into it and let out a triumphant roar. The witch woman slumped to the ground. Her companion sank down beside her, holding the lifeless body. In the dark, I could barely make out two puncture wounds on her neck. Marcello had bound them. That explained why they were so docile while being attacked.

Frankie and I were too stunned to move right away, which was a dangerous mistake. Marcello flicked his wrist towards us. Frankie's head jerked away and, when it snapped back into place, he had streaks of blood running down his cheek. Four claw marks sliced through his porcelain skin.

"Hand over the girl, and this all ends," Marcello said ominously. He pulled his hand towards his body.

Frankie gasped and clutched his heart. He dropped to his knees, his eyes wide with a trail of blood trickling from his nose and mouth.

"Frankie!" I grabbed his jacket and tried hauling him away from Marcello. Casper forced himself to the front of my mind. I screamed when the sudden pain ripped into my head.

"Not much time," he huffed. "He pulled a lot of power out of the witch. Let me take over. Or your friend will die."

I gulped back tears and nodded. I pulled the blade back up into the sheath to give my hands the freedom for Casper to weave his spell. Casper's Spanish poured from my mouth. Frankie dropped to the ground and lay still. Casper pulled me away from Frankie, whispering, "He's alright. Needs a minute."

With our focus now on Marcello, Casper shifted into a Latin chant. But pulling Frankie out of Marcello's spell had left him too weak, and I was a poor conduit for his advanced witch powers anyway. I had a feeling we would have to do this the old fashioned way: with fists and weapons.

"Hang back!" I yelled at Casper. I could feel him weakening, and it was painful as hell. Casper slipped back quickly, and the pain in my head diminished so I could focus again.

"Finally, just the two of us," Marcello said as he crossed the threshold and reached out to me. My body involuntarily jerked towards him.

Panic, mixed with a good dose of anger, surged through me. I scowled and forced my body to stand its ground. Offing me was not going to be that easy. Screw that.

Determined, I willed my undisciplined magic. The wind began to pick up and swirl around me. I whipped around and faced off with him. Eyes narrowed, I reached my hand out and pulled at the air. Marcello was yanked forward with enough force that he hit the wall on the other side of the room, sliding down to the floor.

Not moving from his position, Marcello arced his hand over the air, chanting unintelligible words under his breath. My throat suddenly constricted and I gasped for air. Casper moved forward again, and with a quick yelp, my lungs opened up again. Before I could steady my breath, I reached for my holstered Magnum, and sent off a round in Marcello's direction. A silver bullet tore a hole into his stomach, but he laughed sinisterly while his skin knitted back together. Damn vampires.

Frankie stirred a little in the corner, but Marcello was too focused on me to notice. Whatever power he stole from the dead witch was running low, and he came after me with his fangs bared.

Charging toward me at full force, he didn't notice -- or maybe he didn't care -- that Dog was still at my side. She leapt up, blocking Marcello. After a fearsome bark, she sank her teeth into his shoulder.

Reeling from the attack, Marcello still lunged forward, grabbing for me. But Dog pushed her teeth in further. With a bloodcurdling scream, Marcello gave Dog a brutal shove and she was tossed across the room like a stuffed animal instead of a 125-pound Hell Hound.

Marcello grabbed the lapels of my jacket and threw me, headfirst, into the window behind me. A blast of snow blew into the house, and sounds of shattered glass ripped at my ears. I felt the unmistakable feeling of thick, wet blood at the back of my head a split-second before its coppery scent hit my nose. Marcello caught the smell too. He leered at me and licked his lips. Gross.

He charged me, but this time it was my turn to grab his lapels. I pulled him to the floor. Straddling him, I pushed the flat of my hand into his nose, giving myself a moment to enjoy the sound of it breaking. He pushed me off, and I scrambled to my feet before his vampire speed could catch up.

Frankie was shaking off the magic blow. As he was getting to his feet, the forgotten witch snatched up one of his stakes. With an ear-piercing scream, she staked him from behind.

"No!" I shrieked, lunging after Frankie as he staggered forward.

"Run, Nina!" he screamed. He gripped my arms, blood smearing down my jacket. "Basement. NOW."

Frankie shoved me towards the cellar door, pushing me so hard that I nearly burst the hinges off the door as I fell through. I tumbled down the stairs into the cellar. The crossbow painfully cut into my back at each tumble, until I finally landed face down on the cold stone floor.

Marcello was right behind me. The door slammed shut, and I

could hear Dog scratching at the door, whining.

I was still orienting myself after the tumble down the stairs when Marcello grabbed my hair and yanked my head back. As he moved in to bite me, I pulled the stopper out of one of the Gregorian water vials. He was ready to rip at my neck when I spilled the water out. It rushed down my neck and ran into his lips. I heard the sizzle of seared skin, followed by the scent of charred meat. Marcello released me, crying out in agony.

I spun into a roundhouse kick and made contact with his head, sending him momentarily reeling. But it was short-lived. Pissed off and determined, he came at me with a football tackle that took the wind out of me and knocked me off my feet. I swept my legs under him, and he came down beside me. I scrambled to my knees and brought my elbow down to his solar plexus. He rose up, grabbed me around the neck, and pulled me down on top of him. I rolled into a backward somersault, trying to get my neck out of his grip. I roared as I ripped my head out of his grasp. But he caught my hair again, and he slammed his other fist into my cheek. Dammit! I was so cutting my hair off.

The force of my head snapping back made him release my hair. I turned and swung, landing a punch directly on his ear, probably shattering his eardrum. I followed with a series of five uppercuts that pushed him back towards the stairs.

While Marcello shook off the punches, I ran across the basement, towards the sound of running water, hoping it was the stream that ran under the house. My foot splashed through a small puddle. It was so dark in the basement, I couldn't tell if I was safely across the running water or just caught a foot full of leaky basement. I turned and faced off with Marcello. I was just out of his reach, and he couldn't come any closer. I took another step back, breathing heavy.

"It's not over, bitch!" His white fangs glinted in what little light there was in the dank cement cellar.

I grabbed behind me, trying to pull the crossbow over my shoulder. It was stuck on something. I yanked at it harder, and the sound of splintering wood made me slump. The blow to my back damaged the crossbow. It was a poorly held together pile of toothpicks.

Releasing my left knife from the sheath, the razor-sharp blade dropped out of my sleeve and rested just over my hand. I ducked down and cupped a handful of the stream water with my right hand. It burned my skin when I touched it. Frankie was right. Something was up with this water. I would have to ask Father Dougherty how this was possible.

With a primal scream, I sent an arc of water at Marcello. The smell of burning flesh hit my nose again, and Marcello screamed in pain.

I lunged at him with the blade. Missing my mark, it landed just under his heart and lodged in his ribcage with a snap that let me know I had cracked at least one of his ribs. He howled and grabbed my throat and tossed me back over the stream. I landed hard on my back, and the pressure of the fall pushed splinters from the broken crossbow into my flesh.

I groaned. Frankie had done some sort of blood magic to the crossbow, and shards embedded in my back were weakening me. I looked at Marcello, who had my weapon still lodged in his ribcage. The second witch was next to him. He handed her the witch blade.

"Kill her," he commanded with a grin. His teeth were still coated in the blood of the other witch whose heart he'd eaten.

Crap. She could cross the water. I struggled to get back on my feet, but his binding power over the witch made her swift. Still on the floor, I pulled my dad's knife out of my boot. As she came down on me with her blade, I pulled her arm towards me. Since she was expecting me to push away, not pull, I used her split-second confusion to my advantage and shifted my position. I yelped as her knife plunged into my shoulder. But with momentum still on my side, I pulled her down onto my knife, a direct hit to the heart. She cried out. I could feel her power draw into the blade. Her beautiful face aged half a century as she expelled her last breath. A skeleton with sparse hair and rotted flesh slumped on top of me. I reached in and pulled out her heart. I threw it angrily at Marcello.

The power I drew into the blade surged through me, killing the ill effects of Frankie's crossbow. Pushing the witch off me, I scrambled to my feet.

Marcello's eyes were red with anger. I had killed his last witch and pulled her power to me. He picked up her heart and bit into it, blood dripped down his chin. He began chanting in that weird language. Wind picked up around me, and he pulled at me again. I was dragged across the stream, my legs burning as they skimmed across the water. I hovered directly over the stream. No matter how hard I tried, I was unable to move my body. Then suddenly Marcello released me and I dropped straight into the water. It felt like my entire body was engulfed in flames.

I pulled myself out and laid on the floor, my body singed. But I was on the wrong side of the water. Marcello picked me up by the scruff of my neck and threw me further away from the stream. I pulled myself to my knees and the room was spinning. Marcello staggered across the room after me, and Latin flowed out of his mouth with more urgency the closer he got. My skin began to blister. A blister broke out on my right palm, and the open wound hit the iron hilt of the blade that I still groped. A white-hot burning sensation exploded through my arm, killing my nerve endings. I dropped the knife, and it landed with a heavy clang on the hard, cement floor.

Marcello held me by my throat against the wall. A stake was in his right hand, his left hand gripped around my throat, pulling at me until my feet were off the ground. He drew his head to me and whispered in my ear, "You were worth the wait."

I screamed and he rammed a stake into my heart.

My body went cold. He released my neck and I slumped down to the floor. My breathing was shallow. Casper was pushing forward again, trying to use his magic to piece me back together again. But like Humpty Dumpty, I was beyond repair.

Marcello stood over me, his twisted laughter echoing off the cold, hard walls. Marcello reached behind him and pulled a long blade out of a sheath that ran down his back. He swung a samurai sword over his head. It wasn't the way I wanted to go out, but at least I was going down fighting. I resolved not to close my eyes when he decapitated me. I just hoped I didn't scream.

I did a double take. A hulking shadow came up behind Marcelo. I blinked and looked again. It was the shadow of a man, but twice the size of a normal-sized person. A huge hand caught the side of Marcello's head, and he went sailing across the room, the sword clattered on the cold stone floor. I heard the satisfying thud of Marcello's body hitting the wall.

At close to eight feet tall, the giant stooped over to keep from hitting his head on the ceiling. Taking him in slowly, I saw that he was built like a pro-wrestler, but twice the size, enormous muscles popping out everywhere. His eyes blazed red and his face was twisted with rage.

With the speed of a puma, Marcello leaped on top of the giant. I watched him sink his teeth into the strange thing's neck, and the giant roared in anger. His huge hands whipped around, and he sent Marcello sailing again. This time, he stomped after him.

I couldn't find enough strength to lift my head and see what was happening, but I could hear the crunch of bones and shrieks of pain as the fighting continued. Though they were mismatched in size, Marcello's age meant that he was stronger than other supernatural beings. Add in the witch stuff, and he was damn near unstoppable. So he and the Giant were formidable opponents. A huge crack and a thud of a body hitting the ground pulled me back to attention. I opened my eyes and stared in horror as Marcello, bloodied and bruised but already healing, came at me with a renewed vigor.

Marcello's maniacal laugh cut off with a sudden grunt. My father's iron blade pushed through his chest and came out the other side. I looked at his face -- a mix of confusion and euphoria. In one swift move, the sword was swiped from his hand and struck at his neck. Marcello's head was lobbed off with such force that it flew out of view. It landed with a splash in the stream.

Frankie's tear-streaked face came into focus. He dropped to the floor beside me. I reached a bloody hand up and touched his cheek, replacing his tears with a trail of blood. He grabbed my hand and shook his head. "Please forgive me," he whispered. His fangs pushed through, and his eyes turned a deeper cerulean blue than ever. He kissed my fingers, dropped his face to my neck, and his fangs slipped slowly, gently, into my neck.

I moaned, the mix of pain and euphoria faint as my heart slowed. Frankie pulled at my blood with more and more intensity. Casper slipped out of my body, leaving me limp in Frankie's lap.

"I'm so sorry, Nina. I have to bind you to me to save you," he whispered. "I'm so sorry. But you can't die."

Without lifting his mouth from my neck, he carefully pulled the stake out of my chest, then held his hand over the wound, pressing

245

gently when my blood spurted in time to my slowly beating heart. His warm tears mixed with the blood dripping down my chest. I reached my hands around his neck. He pulled me closer to him.

Faint voices were yelling, and swift footsteps descended the stairs, stopping suddenly at the sight of us. Babe screamed.

"What in the name of Morrag!" Dr. O called out, and it sounded like someone took a tumble the rest of the way down the worn steps.

Pulling against Frankie, I tried to lift my head to see what was happening. But a massive force pushed Frankie away from me, almost taking a chunk of my neck with him.

"Nina! Run!" Frankie pushed at the giant, but with a swift swipe of his hand, Frankie was tossed into the wall.

A pair of enormous hands made their way towards me, and I squirmed away from them. The beast had a body of a human, but so much larger. It was muscled up like a Venice Beach bodybuilder on super-steroids, his thighs the size of tree trunks. Veins bulged out of his biceps, which had to be over two feet in diameter. His face was twisted in rage.

I pulled at the vial of Gregorian water around my neck, and yanked it open. I threw it blindly in front of me. Inexplicably, I hit my mark. The beast let out a roar that was part animal, part human. It dropped to the floor and its body began to shudder and convulse. When the violent spasms finally slowed down, I realized that the thing was changing, becoming more human than animal. It was Max, lying naked and shaking on the floor.

"What the hell?" I whispered. I could hear Babe and Dr. O moving across the dark basement. I tried pulling myself towards their voices but collapsed in a heap. I could go no further.

I felt a pair of strong hands pull me. Frankie drew me to him. Falling limply into his arms, I took a deep, shuddering breath and let the dark take over.

CHAPTER 32

It was 33 degrees Fahrenheit so we were the only fools on the beach. Well, Darcy and I were slightly less foolish than Frankie and Max.

Darcy had finally stopped her wailing and made it to Rhode Island from Nevada just in time to see me discharged from the hospital. And it was perfect timing too. She had to use her banshee charm on my doctor for an early discharge. He was witnessing way too many "miracles" at my recovery. She convinced him that it was simply his amazing healing abilities. I think she even lined up a date with him for after the New Year.

We were doing a beach run, bundled up in the finest winter running clothes available at the overpriced running store. Max and Frankie were actually in the ocean. The vampire was learning to surf.

It was a cold but brilliant day. The sun was high and vibrant, one of those winter afternoons when the sun is almost blinding.

We plopped ourselves down in the sand and watched the two guys in their wet suits climbing back onto the surfboards. Frankie gave me what I call The Bat Signal, our "go for it" sign. I closed my eyes and, taking a breath, conjured the waves. When I opened them, the water was churning, and the waves were larger. Max, already standing on the board, coached Frankie through his next steps. Frankie looked elated as he lifted his body up from the board. A wave crashed over him, tossing him into the water. His head bobbed up to the surface, and his black shaggy hair didn't hide his megawatt grin. It made the shooting pain in my head that came with using my witch magic almost worth it.

"He's so happy!" Darcy smiled.

"He hasn't seen sunlight in over 700 years. I'd be happy too," I said with a giggle.

"Yeah, I guess that'd put a smile on anybody's face," she said as she uncapped a thermos and poured out a steaming cup of hot, rum-spiked cider into the tiny cup. After a sip, she passed it over to me.

It warmed me to my toes. "Every vamp fantasizes about day-walking, but to get it from demon taint? He's gotta be wondering what the catch is."

Frankie had broken the medallion my dear old uncle gave him after the witch attack at the farmhouse. The residual effect of the demon magic was that he could be in sunlight again. But Bertrand's help didn't come without consequences. We just didn't know when he would come calling to get the favor repaid. And we didn't know how long the day-walking would last. He could fry in the sunlight any minute. Between Max and Frankie, I wished demon magic came with an instruction manual.

Darcy pushed a lock of her lavender-streaked, white-blond hair away from her face. "Maybe he'll deal with that tomorrow?"

I wish he was dealing with it at all. Instead, every day was like Christmas. I was worried that he was enjoying it too much. Max learned about those consequences the night I almost died. Bertrand made him a monster just like us. I watched this muscles work to stand on the board, his wet dirty blond curls flopping into his face. A beautiful monster, for certain, but a monster all the same.

"Maybe if Bertrand wins the election, he'll consider the favor called in?" Darcy tried.

I shook my head. "I doubt it. Today's the election and he's got the thing won. He knows it."

Bertrand had been all over the news crowing about how he was responsible for calling in the FBI agent who took down the most dangerous serial killer in New England since the Boston Strangler. He had the whole thing in the bag. I'd have to call him Mayor Demon now.

"It's good to have you here, Darcy." I dropped my head on her shoulder and she planted a sisterly kiss on my head. "How was it?"

"Different this time," she said with a shrug. "It took a lot longer to get back to myself than it usually does. I need to talk to Dr. O, but I think I may need to call someone to death soon. I don't think I can wail anymore without the cry being sated."

Darcy was the first banshee that Dr. O had ever worked with, so she was kind of a guinea pig. He didn't know how much of her banshee nature could be suppressed. He didn't want her to have to kill, but she may not be able to help it. Unlike vampires who could get human blood without killing their supplier, a banshee visit always ended in death.

"He'll figure something out," I said, trying to comfort her. I handed her the cup back. "He always does."

I looked down the length of the beach, where Babe and Dr. O were talking a walk and squinted. "Darcy, does it look like they are holding hands?"

"Sure does," she giggled

"Oh God no!" my hands flew up to cover my eyes. I heard Darcy squeal, "Don't open your eyes yet! You don't want to see them kiss."

"At least my aunt's getting lucky?" I was happy for her, really, but still. I shuddered at the thought. "Wonder how long that's been going on."

Darcy shrugged. "Probably longer than we want to admit. Speaking of which, what's up with you and Max?"

"Don't know. I am not sure if he's going back to the West Coast. Life as he knew it is pretty much over."

"Right," Darcy said quietly. She watched Frankie and Max, who were now back on their boards. "Glad they were able to forgive each other."

"Well, Max had no idea that Bertrand turned him into a Berserker, so it's not really his fault." I sighed. I told both Max and Frankie not to trust Bertrand. I still needed to rub that into Max's face at some point, but I would save it for later. He wasn't exactly handling the whole Berserker thing well. Of course, how does someone handle turning into the Incredible Hulk when riled up? I couldn't blame him. But even if Max wanted to go back west, Dr. O would probably nix it until he was sure Max knew how to control himself in the transformation. He had a lot to learn about all of us before we could unleash him on the world. Sure, he thought Frankie was killing me, but Frankie was saving my life.

"Berserker, wow," Darcy said, taking a sip from the Thermos mug. "Makes me grateful for being a banshee."

"I don't know. He's ass-kicking HUGE. I think it's pretty badass."

She ran a hand through her hair. "There's got to be a downside."

We all knew too well about downsides.

"Well," I said, "throwing himself into battle in a frenzied rage can reduce his lifespan dramatically." This was a major downside. If he didn't learn to control the raging, he was more of a threat than an asset.

Darcy stared out at the guys, still paddling their boards, waiting for the Big One. Since we were the east coast, I would probably have to conjure it up for them. "He loves you, you know that, right?"

I choked on air. "Max? Darcy, please. He can barely look at me after what happened."

"Not Max," she sighed impatiently. "Frankie."

"Frankie?" I squished up my face. "Come on, I've known him forever, since I was just a kid. He loves me, but he doesn't *loooove* me."

"Don't think so." Her voice was slightly smug.

"He just feels badly about the binding-me-to-him thing," I insisted, though I couldn't meet Darcy's eyes. To be honest, I wasn't so sure that he felt all that bad about it.

"Yes, he does." She crossed her arms and gave me a look. "But he wants you to love him for him, not because you are bound to him."

"You're wrong," I said flatly. Then I stared down the shoreline, watching the waves crashing along the rocks.

Darcy scoffed. "Am I? I am a damn banshee, Nina. About love and death, I am never, *ever* wrong."

I couldn't argue with that point. I stared at Frankie, who was up on the board again. With his jet-black hair and pale skin, he looked completely out of place on a surfboard. He looked over at me and his grin widened.

I shoved my hands into my jacket pockets. "I need this like I need another stake in the heart."

Darcy stared at me, expectantly. "So what are you going to do about it?"

"Exactly what any other woman would do. Ignore it." I scrambled to my feet and gave Darcy a hand. I hauled her up and we linked arms. The crashing waves followed us as we walked and talked the length of the beach. A group of teen boys were clustered at the end of the beach, smoking a joint and watching Max surf and Frankie make a fool of himself. They reminded me of Casper.

I hadn't seen or heard from him since he disappeared from the farmhouse. I had no idea if he finally moved on from this realm or if he was haunting someone else. I kind of missed his smart-ass running commentary in my head. I didn't miss the migraines he gave me. I still got them whenever I used my witch powers, but they weren't nearly as intense as when he was possessing me.

"Nina, check it out." Darcy's voice pulled me away from my thoughts of my ghostly friend. I followed her gaze down the beach. A familiar-looking man in an Army uniform was goose-stepping through the sand towards us. His expression was set to hard, like most military lifers.

"Crap," I muttered. Generally, the Department of Defense left us alone. Once in a while they would show up on our military base and demand a tour or a fight demonstration. I think it was more out of a "look-at-the-freaks" curiosity than making sure we were tax money well spent. But since only a handful of humans knew that we existed, the visits were seldom. For him to show up at a beach in Rhode Island in the middle of December meant he was serious. And that he had to show up on a beach in Rhode Island in the middle of December to find us pissed him off more.

By then, Dr. O was so far down the shoreline that he and Babe looked like two moving dots along the horizon. Frankie was in the surf. That left me and Darcy to deal with whatever the U.S. government wanted to throw at us. Yay.

"Nina Martinez?" the guy barked from about 15 feet away. I seriously hoped he did not expect me to salute. We might have been under the umbrella of the DOD, but I wasn't military and I wasn't about to salute Major Hardass.

"Yes," I nodded, closing the distance between us.

"Ms. Martinez, you have a difficult team to find," he growled.

"And you are?" I stared at his uniform. His stripes said Major and his nameplate said "Smith." I wasn't convinced I was dealing with the real thing. I stretched my right arm behind me and felt my tiny Beretta tucked into the small of my back.

He stopped a few feet away. "Major Adam Smith."

"Major Smith, are you aware of the chain of command in our unit?" I kept my hand near the gun.

"We have been trying to reach Dr. O'Malley for several days now." He looked toward me warily. "He is not returning calls."

"Perhaps he is on holiday," I offered with a small smile, professional but cold.

Smith snorted. "We have reason to believe there is an unregistered Berserker in the area."

"I'm sorry, did you say Berserker?" I feigned surprise and spared a glance at Darcy. While her face was a complete blank, all the color drained from it, leaving her almost glowing white.

The DOD liked the creatures to be "registered" but for obvious reasons not every creature complied. The government believed that registering meant that you were friend, not foe. But even the

252

friendlies avoided that list. There was serious mistrust. A list made it way too easy for the government to round us all up and take us out if it ever became necessary. And since we technically did not exist, there was no way to pursue a civil rights violation if our rights weren't respected.

"With all due respect, sir," I continued cautiously. "A Berserker hasn't been seen for thousands of years. Our research shows they disappeared with the Norsemen around the 11th Century. We're talking no sightings since before the middle ages."

I smiled nervously as Major Hardass evaluated the two of us. Who could have outed Max? I was sure we were the only ones that knew.

"Tell O'Malley that we want to talk to him," Major Smith barked at me.

My smile turned to a sneer. I wasn't true military so he could take his orders and shove them up his ass.

Smith turned on his heel and goose-stepped away.

"Dr. O's avoiding the Department of Defense?" Darcy whispered incredulously. I shook off the thought. I could think of a thousand reasons why anyone would want to avoid the DOD. But while Dr. O wasn't exactly a by-the-book guy, he would never just blow them off. Not without a good reason, anyway.

We needed to figure out the "good reason" -- and soon. I suspected it had to do with Max becoming a supernatural creature that was, for all purposes, extinct.

I looked at Frankie and Max still bobbing around in the icy surf. If Max couldn't learn to control the Berserker in him, we'd all be screwed.

About the author

An award-winning playwright, Karen Greco has spent close to twenty years in New York City, working in publicity and marketing for the entertainment industry. A life-long obsession with exorcists and Dracula drew her to urban fantasy, where she can decapitate characters with impunity. HELL'S BELLE is her first novel.

Made in the USA
Lexington, KY
16 October 2013